Order Of The Dragon

Question of Time

By
Pauric Brennan

Order this book online at www.trafford.com/07-1247
or email orders@trafford.com

Most Trafford titles are also available at major online book retailers.

Note for Librarians: A cataloguing record for this book is available from Library
and Archives Canada at www.collectionscanada.ca/amicus/index-e.html

Printed in Victoria, BC, Canada.

ISBN: 978-1-4251-3311-5

www.trafford.com

North America & international
toll-free: 1 888 232 4444 (USA & Canada)
phone: 250 383 6864 ♦ fax: 250 383 6804
email: info@trafford.com

The United Kingdom & Europe
phone: +44 (0)1865 722 113 ♦ local rate: 0845 230 9601
facsimile: +44 (0)1865 722 868 ♦ email: info.uk@trafford.com

10 9 8 7 6 5 4 3

Order of the Dragon is dedicated to
Mam and Dad.

The Thank You Bit...

While writing the trilogy several people have given me their support and to those I extend a very warm and special thank you. To Amanda for putting up with me while I created and acted out the story. To my family for reading it and pointing out the way. To Peter for his blind eye. Mark who spent time reading it and to everyone who gave me support and inspiration, thank you.

Arrival at Midnight

The shadowless sun shone down on the Surbia wasteland, desolate and uninviting to everyone who came near. Very few people had settled in these wastelands and of those who had tried, few remained. It was a breeding ground in olden days for the large populations of dragons that had once roamed free on the face of the earth. It was hot, featureless and barren, the perfect conditions for the rearing of young dragons, away from the developed cities and towns. A small village still existed in the arid wasteland of Surbia, its survivors staying only to mine the large deposits of diamonds.

Bill arrived in the early morning, avoiding the stifling heat of the midday sun. He had received a message from the village elder two days before his arrival, informing him of a dragon's nest in the area. Bill had left with three of his best trappers as soon as the message had reached him in Dylan Drive. Dragons were supposed to be confined to the stables of the members of the Order of the Dragon. Perhaps this one belonged to the Order?

Bill stood a safe distance from the mound watching for signs of the occupant's presence. His black hair danced on the warm winds that blew across the plains of Surbia. His long brown coat concealed the sword his uncle's friend had given him centuries before. Bill was twelve when he received the sword. He had only aged five years in appearance in his four hundred years as a Keeper and still had the youthful looks of a young boy. His years had been eventful since he had taken on his role as The Keeper of Secrets. He had seen the great wars of Mercsburg and the great sea battle at Berfeld.

Moving closer, Bill gave the signal for his trappers to take to the air and prepare to capture the mother and possibly its young baby. If the mother had delivered a young dragon then the capture would be made all the more difficult, females had been known to destroy whole cities to protect their off-spring. Bill watched as the gyro-copters of his trapper gnomes took to the air. A blast from a horn caused Bill to turn away from the dragon's nest, leaving him open to an attack from the dragon if she were in the nest.

Bill focused in on a cloud of dust moving towards them, the con-tinuous horn blast coming from the plume of dust. A banner flick-ered in the breeze, its red and gold colours reflecting the sun's rays as it kicked and struggled to free itself from the black pole to which it was attached. Bill recognised the colours and the rider who sat at the front of the column of dragons. The colours belonged to the Prince of Swaylian, the only other person permitted to keep drag-ons in his stables. Bill covered his mouth and waited for the dry dust to settle again before he greeted the young man.

"Prince Vladimir, your dragon I presume?" A smile spread across Bill's face as he pointed towards the dragon nest. The Prince dropped down from his own dragon and drew his sword.

"Is this how you talk to all your friends, Brickton?" His sword's point was resting on Bill's chest. Bill weighed up his opponent and decided he was the better.

"Only those who can't hold their sword." Bill kicked the Prince's hand causing the sword to fly high into the air. As Vladimir watched the sword, Bill grabbed his hand and pulled him forward towards his own body and then with a burst of energy, changed direction as their bodies met causing the Prince to loose his balance and fall. "And those who can't stand on their own two feet!" Bill smiled down at Vladimir, who had a disgruntled look on his face. Bill held out a hand to assist the young man back to his feet.

Brushing himself down, the Prince turned to Bill. "Who called a boy here to do a mans' job?" A smile crossed his lips.

"The dragon is mine, one of the more... lively ones. Come I shall tell you how she got away from my stables." Vladimir placed his arm around Bill's shoulders and guided him towards his tent. The Prince's tent was being set up next to Bill's, dwarfing it in size. As Bill entered the tent his eyes were drawn to a rug in the centre of the main chamber. Its vibrant colour jumped from the floor. In the centre of the rug was the great warrior Ali Al Shallack, a member of the Order of the Dragon. Shallack had gone missing in the Mercsburg Mountains shortly after Bill had become a Keeper and member of the Order. Shallack's disappearance had mystified the Order and many members had searched in vain for him. The rug depicted Shallack's great victory over the Black Dragon Kraylin.

The Prince signalled to Bill to take a seat. As Bill sat four servants began laying food and drink in front of them. Listening to the story of the dragon's escape and how Vladimir had been searching for two months for his prize dragon, Bill couldn't help feeling suspicious about the details of the Prince's story but in the end he put it down to being a Keeper for too long.

"Bill, you will sleep in my tent tonight and tomorrow I'll take Cynthia home with me and make sure she does not wander so far again." Prince Vladimir stood and bid Bill a good night's sleep and disappeared from the main chamber leaving him in the hands of his servants. Bill sat in silence, watching as his golden mug magically filled itself. The silence was only momentary as a familiar voice filled the room.

"Brickton you old dragon wart, how are you?" Bill looked up from his mug to see the crooked nose of Ivor Jones. Ivor was one of Vladimir's oldest and most trustworthy servants. Bill knew of no man better in the heat of battle, be it with or without weapons.

Standing up, Bill held out his arms to greet his friend. Bill retired shortly after his conversation with Ivor. As he was shown to another room, the second biggest in the tented palace, Bill reflected on his conversation with the Prince. The room was filled with patterned rugs and tapestries from strange and distant lands. Lying down on some of the cushions and rugs, Bill waited for sleep to over power him.

The camp lay still in the blackness of the Surbian night, its occupants unaware of a solitary shadow moving between the tents. Even Vladimir's guards had drifted into a deep sleep and were unaware of the shadow's presence. Silently, it slipped under the cloth walls of the tent and moved across the main chamber. The shadow's hand was closed around a small blue bottle filled with a poisonous liquid. Slowly pulling back the curtains that separated the chamber from the rest of the tent, the shadow saw his prize. Bill lay still in his dreams, unaware of the shadow looming over him.

Back at Dylan Drive the sun was rising and the members of The Gnome Intelligence, Information, Retrieval, Research, Reconnaissance, Security, Protection, Surveillance, Spying and Being Sneaky Unit or G.I.U. for short were returning for duty. At six o'clock on this particular morning, a chorus of cheerful singing could be heard coming from the rear of number ten. The black dog, that lay at the front door of the house leaped to attention and ran to the gate leading to the rear, ears up and sniffing. He soon found the source of the singing.

"I'll sit fishin'
And I'll sit drinkin'
I'll sit wita scowl
And pretend to be fowl
Why?
Cause we're gnomes

8

Why?
Cause we're Garden Gnomes
Hooray for whom?
For Garden Gnomes
That's who, Garden Gnomes

The black dog sat watching, his red eyes smouldering like burning coals in a blacksmiths forge. At the end of the garden sat three gnomes, laughing and singing, that was till they saw the black dog staring down at them.

"Eh up Nugent." The tallest of the three stood up. Tall for a gnome is not very tall, say a bit taller than a cat. On his head sat a red pointed hat with a small golden bell on top. "Did we wake ya big fella? It's only gone half past five my dear fellow or have you come to sing with us?" His pearly white teeth shone in the morning sun as he smiled at the dog known as Nugent. He had pulled out a small time piece from the pocket of his purple waistcoat so he was sure it wasn't any later in the morning. Nugent continued to stare at the gnome, drool hanging down from his mouth.

"Hello! Anyone at home or are you just going to stand there looking at me like I'm breakfast or are you going to say something, eh?" The gnome turned to his companions shrugging his shoulders as he did so; Nugent wagged his tail and walked away towards his mat. "Strange individual at times isn't he?" The gnome picked up a tankard and drank heartily from it.

"That he is but most nights he'd talk the legs off old farmer Brennan's mule." A gnome leaned forward to take up a tankard of ale, his banjo sitting on his lap that he had been playing before they saw Nugent. He too was wearing a pointed hat; it was green in colour and matched his trousers. Now it is common knowledge for anyone who is familiar with the goings on of city garden gnomes and more so with their dress sense, that they love to wear bright colours. These colors can be, at the very best of times hideous to big people and would never been worn in public. But for gnomes the brighter the better, colours like luminous green, or sunburst orange are among their favourites. Not to mention blinding daffodil yellow, but this is only worn on special occasions, such as the Gnome New Year or Liberation Day. The latter being the day they were freed from Goblin oppression in 1536, a most special day in the gnome year.

"Guess he was having a pleasant dream or something like that." He had emptied the tankard and began to fill it again. "What time are we on watch at, Sebastian?" The third picked his head up off the ground and opened one eye.

"Seven or so, why? You got plans for today!" He chuckled as his head disappeared behind his belly. A great lump of a gnome lay on the grass beside an empty tankard of ale; his waistcoat was a bright nauseous blue and didn't go at all with his trouser, which was a pale pink with yellow daisies on it.

"Seven or so yea around then no sooner no later not that I'd be late or anything like that." Rambling Sebastian was a gnome who constantly muttered under his breath even when the big folk were nearby. "Think he'd know; he got the roster like everyone else; think he'd read instead of eating it." Sebastian looked up wondering where the tankard was.

"What ya do with it Mickey, the tankard before you ask?" Sebastian looked around for his tankard in the hope it had been refilled for him. "Ah here lads could you not fill it for me, the things a gnome has to do to get some ale. Wasn't bad enough that ye took all of my money last night playing cards and then ye let the Leprechauns take it from ye!" Sebastian knew that Mickey wouldn't be pleased about this but it was a good way to get back at him for not filling his tankard.

"Now you know as well as I do Sebastian that those Leprechauns are tricky little blighters at the very best of times, I don't need to remind you of the 1896 incident between them and the Fairies." Mickey smirked at his companions. "Now it was a clever trick to play on them but messing with Fairies isn't a good idea." The bell on Mickey's hat tinkled as he laughed.

"Aye it was a good one but who reckoned Fairies were that stupid. At least the Leprechauns should have sold Lichburg Castle to one of them big folk then they would have gotten away with it. It was a good thing that the Keeper of Secrets was on hand to get the gold back." The tallest gnome raised himself off the ground and stretched. "Yep, old Sven here remembers that. Nearly led to war that one did but good old Bill Brickton, Keeper of Secrets was there to keep the peace." Sven sat back down on the grass and took a drink from his tankard. "What time is it now?" He took his watch from his pocket and looked at it. "Where has that Sorden got to?" Sven looked around. "Its breakfast time and he's not here yet. What is that young gnome doing?" At that moment a small gnome came crashing over the garden fence. "Where have you been Sorden?" Sven wasn't at all happy and waited for Sorden to answer.

Sorden was a young gnome dressed in blushing red from his socks to his hat, even his bell was a glowing red. "Well I was with Melinda." He brushed himself down and picked some leaves from his beard. "She's the one who lives four gardens up from 'ere but her dad saw me and well from the last glimpse I saw of him, he wasn't too happy looking." Sorden pulled on a white apron and took off his red hat replacing it with a tall white one. "How many for breakfast?" He looked to Sven for an answer. He wasn't going to say anymore about what had really happened with Melinda as Sven looked mad enough and might not see the funny side of it.

"Well there's fifty gone to that conference over in Glen Eosin and another twenty are with Bill in Surbia tackling that dragon. So all in all I think there's still one hundred give or take fifty." Sven shrugged his shoulders. "Cook for hundred and fifty and we can use some for lunch if anything is left over." Sorden nodded and shortly afterwards the sizzling of three hundred sausages could be heard.

"So what's that conference all about? I heard that..." Sven cut

Sorden's line of questions off before he had time to start.

"If you were meant to know then you would be at the conference so until you're asked to go to one, don't be listening to gossip." Sven emptied out his tankard on the grass and raised himself to his feet and tossed some rashers to Sorden. "Might do a few extra rashers today would you Sorden?"

"Aye nay problem, pass us a tankard would you?" Taking his tankard Sorden threw on an extra fifty rashers.

The street outside Number Ten Dylan Drive was now full of activity; a newspaper boy flung his delivery over the fence and into the massive jaws of Nugent. The gnomes took up their positions all around the house and watched for anything unusual. The day moved along slowly as days tend to do when you're sitting around. Nugent made his hourly patrols and every now and again would pick up a gnome who needed to stretch their legs out of view of peeping neighbours and nosey passers-by. Lunchtime came and passed with some gnomes looking plumper than usual.

Sebastian could be heard every now and again sayings things like 'the trouser on yer man' and 'the hat on that woman looks like a skinned turkey its not Christmas is it?' The other gnomes would chuckle at Sebastian who spent the whole day laughing at the big folk and complaining about their clothes. As the day passed by and as the sun began to retire to the other side of the world, the gnomes steadily disappeared from the front of Number Ten Dylan Drive. Once the moon had taken up its spot over Wobblington and the last of the gnomes had retired to the house, Sven called them all into the sitting room to organize the night time watch.

"Now as you may or may not know, I received word that the Keeper of Secrets will return tonight. Apparently some of our brethren from Swaylian claimed the dragon and have taken it back with them." Sven looked around to make sure everyone was there.

"Right, night watch will be doubled tonight. Ashwen, Yuen, Tiddles and Nugent, will you take the front of the house? At the rear, will Paddy, Mickey, and George take that?" This brought a swirl of whispers from the room. Was Sven expecting trouble on the Keeper's return? What did he know that the rest of them didn't?

"Quiet down now, quiet. OK then, our party shall be arriving at midnight. They'll approach from the river and shall send out the usual signal on approach. Is everyone clear on what the response is?" Everyone nodded and Sven continued. "Right then. Before rumours start, we're not expecting trouble, but times are tense at the moment and you all know what's happening at the conference in Eosin, and if you don't, then you don't need to know or at least not just yet. Right then. Those who have duties to tend to please do so, the rest of you please remember that there's a three o'clock return tonight and not the usual turn up for breakfast. Sorden, a word." Sorden followed Sven to the kitchen.

"The Keeper has requested that you have some food ready for his party's return later and we'll need breakfast at five in the morning." Sven nodded to Sorden who returned his nod and set about the task.

Paddy sat at the bank of the river watching for the signal of the Keeper's return. At one minute to midnight, Paddy saw the red flare burst into the sky not far down the river. Turning, Paddy ran up the rear lawn tripping the switch on the cannon to shoot the all-clear signal flare into the night sky, and into the house where Sven was smoking his pipe.

"Bill is back; the flare just went up." The Keeper of Secrets and his party had returned on the stroke of midnight, as the moon shone brightly down on their arrival. The water flowed quietly as the gnomes moored the boats and cast a spell to hide them from prying eyes.

"Has the party from the conference returned yet?" Bill had barely set foot on the pier at the rear of Number Ten. "Once they return,

13

I need to talk to Tilterman. Some disturbing news has reached me and if it's correct, then Tilterman will have heard it!" Bill sat down just as a voice of a very excited gnome could be heard outside. Sven hurried to escort Tilterman to Bill.

The young gnome wore a brown jerkin over a dark blue high-necked jumper and black trousers. His beard was midnight black with streaks of white through it. He had a small black skullcap instead of the usual pointed one of traditional gnome dress.

"Tilterman old friend, good to have you..." Before Sven could greet him, Tilterman interrupted him.

"Are they back? Has the Keeper returned? I must talk to him right away." Tilterman was usually very calm but tonight his face held a grave look upon it. "I must speak to him about the conference." Tilterman met Sven halfway up the garden path that led from the boats. "Sven, is he back?" Tilterman urged Sven to bring him to Bill.

"Tilterman this way, he has just returned. He's looking for you; he wants to see you right away. What happened at the conference?" Sven searched Tilterman's face for any clue as to what was going on.

"I can't say till I speak to Bill." Tilterman fell quiet and said nothing more nor did Sven ask any more. "Bill I am glad you're back, a rumour has started!" Before Tilterman could utter another word Bill interrupted him.

"I must stop you there. Sven, can you gather the gang in the room for a briefing? I'll fill you in afterwards and can you tell Sorden to prepare food for those who have just returned." Sven nodded and left Tilterman and Bill alone while he gathered the gnomes together.

Some hours later, Sven was called back to the room, only Bill remained. "Sven, I have a very important task for you. I need you to bring this letter to the Council of the Seven Elders. I received word that the Book of Demons is going to be stolen. You must hurry!

Morgab is saddled and waiting for you. Once you have this delivered, wait for a reply." Handing the letter to Sven, Bill lay his hand on his shoulder. "May the speed of the Elders guide you safely on your journey." Bill turned to walk away but Sven had a question.

"Where do I find the Seven Elders?" Sven had only heard stories of the Seven Elders and of how they had brought peace during the dark times.

"They are expecting you and Morgab knows were to find them. Now away with you and return with the four winds as your speed." After Bill left the room, Sven turned to pick up his crossbow and sword. Morgab, a griffon, was on the back lawn, wings spread and on his hind legs; standing six feet tall and wings twice that, and eyes set on fire by the dawn sun. He let out a joyful roar as Sven sat into the saddle on his back.

"Away Morgab and waste no thought on me. Fly high and hard, mighty friend." With this Morgab soared towards the few clouds that sailed across the sky. Sven had set out on an errand of which no one knew the true importance. "Morgab, how far is our destination?" Sven spoke to himself as they soared across the morning sky. The land lay still beneath them, sparkling in the early dew. Sven hadn't noticed that not far behind him were two more creatures flying high and trailing him and Morgab...

The Seven Elders

The sun had risen to its noon position in the sky and the land was fully awake under Sven and Morgab as they flew towards the island of Watu. Not far in the distance, Sven could see a long slender shimmering lake, with a large green and brown dappled wood to one side.

"Morgab, once we reach that lake we'll set down for lunch." Upon these words, Morgab started to descend. "Look for somewhere sheltered my friend." Morgab landed in a small cove near the edge of the wood. "Some fish would be good for lunch what do you think?" Morgab flew out across the lake and it didn't take long for him to convince some fish that they had lost the will to live and would be much better off on their dinner plates. When he returned, Sven had a fire lit and the spit was prepared for the food. "Nice catch and some for tomorrow as well."

As Sven spoke these words, he drew his sword closer to him; Morgab too had become aware that they were being watched from the trees.

"Looks as if we have company Morgab." Sven sat down by the fire and put one of the fish on the spit and placed it over the flame, Morgab was ripping the tail from his catch and was enjoying his small feast. The lake was still except for the occasional fish leaping out of the water sending ripples across the surface to be swallowed up by the shore. The trees stood tall and still in the glaring sun.

"Still there my friends, hiding among the trees. Why not show yourselves?" Sven smiled and turned to face the trees. "Come join me and enjoy the fish we took from the lake." He placed some fish on a leaf and left it to one side of the fire hoping to tempt the unseen persons among the trees. Sven slipped his sword into his hand and waited for a response.

"I see you've not lost your touch gnome, but you are out numbered at least two to one." A voice came from a little inside the tree line just out of sight. "Even with your friend I assure you, you are no match for us. Lay down your weapons and let us enter in peace." Sven nodded to Morgab to back up and he dropped his sword to the ground letting the hilt rest upon his foot. A tall person clad in green and holding a bow in one hand emerged from the trees and walked towards Sven.

"You look well my friend, but have you forgotten who dwells in these woods?" He pulled his hood down and revealed his face. Sven knew this was no foe but a very good friend. A wood elf, tall and handsome with long golden locks of hair. "So Sven, what has you in these parts?" Sven flicked up his sword and returned it to its scabbard.

"Drego my old friend, I've not seen you since the Council of the Seven Peaks in 1710." Sven held out his hand to greet Drego. "I'm on my way to see the Seven Elders on Watu, there's a rumour that Ehmunnra has risen again and the Keeper has sent me to check that the Book of Demons is safe." A grave look fell upon Drego's face.

"Sven old friend, I fear these rumours may be very true." Drego sat down at the fire. "About two months ago a young girl from a farm near here went missing; the locals said she wandered into the forest and was taken by the Banshee. But two days ago some of my people found the young girl and all her body fat had been taken.

There's no one in this forest that would do this or none that we are aware of. We know that fat is used in the magic of flight and only one person would do this and he's not around now." Drego looked at Sven who was now writing on a piece leaf.

"You're sure that was all was missing?" Sven looked up at Drego and asked. "The girl, where is she? I need to see her, she has to be checked for other signs that might indicate who did it, take me there now." With this Sven stood up and walked towards the woods. "Morgab stay here, I will be back shortly. Summon a messenger when I get back; I'll have to inform the Keeper of my findings." They disappeared into the darkness of the forest and out of Morgab's sight. The trees stood high closing out the sky and casting all into dappled darkness. The elves walked in front and behind Sven.

"Where was she found Drego?" Drego slowed his pace so that Sven could walk beside him.

"Not far from Terock's lair. It's a good thing he's in hibernation or we'd never have found the girl." The elves left the path they had walked along and headed deeper into the dense forest. The undergrowth was thick off the paths and as Sven struggled to walk through it, it appeared that the elves floated over the undergrowth.

After a while, they came to a clearing in the wood. A large rock formation jutted from the forest floor and rose high above the trees. Its greyness was a stark contrast to the dark green pine trees around it. It had always reminded Sven of the old legend about the Gods of Light being pointed at by Nannreb, the God of the Underworld and his warning that he would one day return to spread plague and pestilence on the world.

"This is the spot where she lay, her head pointed to the north and her feet to the south, hands spread to the west and the east. She lay within a circle made of stones with four fires at each point of her body." Sven walked around the area looking for clues.

Sven wondered if Terock was still in the cave asleep or had someone broken the spells put on it by Wang Wu? Terock was a Chimera and had dwelled in these parts for over two thousand years. He had been sent by Scaripdemus to destroy the wood elves but they had captured him. The Chimera had three heads, one of a snake, one of a goat and one of a lion and could breathe fire. When the wood elves had captured it, they summoned Wang Wu who put it into a deep sleep, and it would wake once every hundred years to drink and feed from the lake. The wood elves would follow it closely to ensure that no one was harmed by it. When this happened, its roars could be heard all over Crintia and people often said: 'there she is, the Banshee, calling the carriage to take someone off to meet their maker.'

"Has anyone checked to see if Terock is still in his cave?" Sven broke a branch from a nearby bush and lit it with words of magic, lighting up the entrance to the cave. He walked in with Drego at his side.

The air in the cave was stale and smelled of rotten flesh. Stalagmites hung from the roof of the cave, their greyness obscured by dark green cave moss. Sven noticed that some of the stalagmites had been recently gnawed upon. But to the parties' relief Terock was asleep in the cave. Beside him on the ground lay several large bones, some were half chewed, others still had rotten meat hanging on them. Near Terock's head lay the body of a half eaten cow; this seemed strange, as the meat was fresh.

"It's not rotten; this cow hasn't even started to decay!" Sven turned to Drego, his face held a questioning look. "It's been sixty years since he's eaten so this carcass should be decayed but it's not!" Drego looked around for other things that were out of the ordinary.

"And look here this ground has fresh blood upon it!" No sooner were these words out of Drego's mouth than a mighty roar erupted in the cave. Terock raised his middle head, that of the snake, it struck out hitting an unsuspecting elf on the shoulder. The lion's head grabbed the elf standing next to Sven, who just managed to dive clear as the Chimera's teeth sunk into the elf's body. Drego let a mighty shout.

"Get out, clear the cave, we must seal the entrance!" With this Sven and the elves ran towards the entrance where two Elves stood either side shooting arrows striking Terock in the shoulders, but they had little effect on the Chimera. "Quickly, seal the entrance before he gets out!"

The elves stood at the entrance shooting arrows and throwing spears at Terock as he ran for the mouth of the cave. Sven stood in the centre of the entrance and shouted.

"Lord of the Mountains and the Rocks, I call upon you to send forth your arm of strength and seal this cave for the good of elf, man and all who dwell under your mighty shadow." Sven scattered stones around the mouth of the cave and as the last stone hit the forest floor, a rumbling noise echoed in the forest. The Chimera had turned and was now thundering down upon Sven and the other elves with its goat's head, its horns catching bones and stones, rising dust off the floor of the cave as it ploughed elves out of its way. The rocks at the entrance rolled towards one another closing together, sealing the cave. A great thud echoed through the forest as bone met with rock.

"He's awake but how?" Drego looked at Sven who was gasping for breath. "How is it possible? Wang Wu is the only one who can lift him from the sleeping spells... I don't understand how this is possible? You must leave now and inform the Seven Elders and the Keeper." Sven had resumed his search of the forest floor and had paid little attention to Drego's talk. Sven walked around the spot where the girl was found.

"Is this where the girl was found? Drego come look at this!" On the ground he found a piece of burnt parchment; he could just make out the first few words, which read.

"Ascend from the depths of hell

And give the power of ..."

Sven held the paper in his hand and continued to look around. Not far from the place where he picked up the parchment he found other indications that someone had performed an incantation at this spot.

"Has anyone taken anything else from here?" Sven looked at Drego but all he did was shake his head.

"We haven't come back till now and the elves that found the girl didn't stay because they didn't want to disturb Terock." Drego looked at Sven. "Do you need to see the girl Sven or have you seen enough for you to continue on your journey?" Sven didn't answer straight away but continued to look around.

"I've seen enough, take me back to Morgab. I need to send this information to the Keeper." Sven turned and started to walk for the lake. "This is serious; everything indicates that someone tried to gain the power of flight. Lets hope it's not Ehmunnra and if someone else has gained it that they aren't as powerful as he was!" Sven quickened his pace along the forest path.

The moon was glistening on the lake; Morgab sat waiting by the fire Sven had lit earlier, beside him sat another Griffin. It was smaller than Morgab and when he saw Sven emerge from the woods he got to his feet and bowed.

"I am Ergwen of Glen Corrib. Morgab tells me you need a fast messenger to find the Keeper Brickton." Ergwen rose from his bow and stared at Sven. He was handed a piece of parchment and told to waste no time and to give it only to the Keeper.

"Before I leave, I have told Morgab that you are being followed. On my way to answer Morgab's call I saw two winged demons and their riders watching from the other side of the lake." With this Ergwen took off.

"Morgab, we leave now, for our business has become most ur-

21

gent." Sven mounted Morgab before he had risen from his fireside seat. "Drego my friend, I hope I will see you again soon but under better circumstances. For now I say be ready, it's likely that the Order will soon stand side by side."

"Your pursuers Sven, would you like us to deal with them?" Drego looked up at Sven waiting for his reply. Sven looked across the lake to where Ergwen had pointed too.

"No, if the time comes I shall deal with them. Farewell my friend, I will see you soon." Morgab rose into the night sky and disappeared into the moon. "Spare no speed my friend we still have two days journey ahead of us but the days must go by quickly." Sven clung to his reins and watched as the land passed underneath them. He had seen his pursuers take flight from their camp and rise higher than he was in the night sky. "We must watch our friends above us Morgab especially when we land for rest and food." Sven pulled his sword close to him as they flew through the night sky.

"Morgab somewhere sheltered and near water so we can eat some fish and keep a better eye on our friends back there." Sven had started to feel uneasy about his pursuers as they came closer to him as the night wore on. Morgab set down next to a river that ran between a cliff face and green pastures. "This'll do nicely. Now for food." Sven gathered up wood and placed it down in a small ring of stones. "Incintaro." And the wood burst into flames. "Ah fish, nothing like fresh fish to fill a gnome." Sven had started to eat his fish when Morgab rose up onto his hind legs and let out cry of pain.

"What is Morgab?" Just then a ball of flame hit the ground beside Sven knocking him off his feet. Sven screamed in pain, an arrow had hit him in the side ripping into his flesh. He tore his sword from its scabbard ready to defend himself.

"Morgab where are they?" Morgab was ready for the fight and rose into the air. Another ball of fire hurtled down from the top of the cliff, followed by a winged demon. Morgab rose up to meet the demon, their talons meeting in mid air, the demon forced Morgab

22

back to the ground both battling to be on top when they landed.

Sven rolled to the cover of some rocks just as a fireball hit the spot where he had stood. He pulled the arrow from his side in a scream of pain. Turning he saw Morgab and the demon struggling as they plummeted to ground. From the corner of his eye he saw a black figure emerge from behind rocks; grabbing his sword he turned to face his attacker.

"ARGGGG! Let's have all you then, come on." Sven charged down his attacker, striking hard and fast at his legs and stopping him dead in his tracks. "Who are you? Why are you following me?" Sven shouted into his face. "What are you after?" Sven's attacker's eyes shifted towards the river.

"Your friend no doubt!" Sven whispered and turned swinging his sword out to deflect a blow from a sturdy battle-axe. Rising from the ground, Sven fought off the second attacker with all of his might.

Morgab dispensed with his foe and was now fighting off an attack from a second and much larger one. Their claws ripped at each other's chests and wings as they rose high above the ground. Morgab broke off his attack and dived towards the ground to where Sven was locked in battle with the two warriors who stood twice his height. Diving as fast as he could, he sunk his claws into the larger of the warriors and with the demon in pursuit rose again to the top of the cliff where he dropped him.

He was now well out of reach of Sven and would leave him with a better chance of escape. Morgab turned back to his own fight and flew to a great height drawing the demon after him. Turning, he dropped down upon his attacker catching him in the chest with both of his claws, pushing him back to the ground. As he did so, he coughed out a ball of purple flame into the demon's open chest. The demon exploded into flames and fell back to the top of the cliff crushing his rider beneath his fiery remains.

Morgab's attention was now drawn back to Sven who was lying wounded at the end of a blade. Diving down upon Sven's attacker he saw two more demons approaching from over the river. His mission now was to save Sven and flee, for he knew that the battle would surely be lost. Knocking the warrior to the ground, Morgab put Sven onto his back and flew as hard as he could into the night sky.

"Morgab my friend, you arrived right on time. I am forever in your favour. Now onto Watu and don't stop till we arrive on the island." Morgab nodded his head so Sven knew he understood. Morgab knew that Sven was wounded worse than he would ever admit too, so it was back to the forest where they had met Drego and the wood elves and then onto Watu and the Seven Elders.

The morning sky was grey and cast dark shadows over the forest; it wasn't long before Morgab found Drego and the elves. Sven had passed out and lay pale on Morgab's back.

"What's happened?" Drego ran to meet Morgab as they landed. "Sven are you ok, can you hear me?" Drego turned to his companion. "Quickly bring Ranak-u here he has been pierced by an arrow from the bow of a Rennick warrior." Drego picked Sven up and brought him to his tree house at the top of a large oak. As he laid him on a bed of soft leaves he spoke softly. "Hang on my old friend help is on its way. Morgab are you wounded?" Morgab lifted his wing revealing a deep cut in his side. The cut was burning red and a steady flow of blood was coming from it.

"Morgab to the lake and submerge yourself in it, then come back here and I will treat it." Morgab flew back towards the lake and dived into the centre. Drego pulled a handful of red and blue plants together and crushed their seeds into a paste. He rubbed this into Morgab's wound. "It will burn for a few moments but it will destroy the poison." Drego stood back as the remedy took effect. Morgab rose up onto his hind legs and filled the forest around them in screams of pain. "It will heal in a day or two and you'll be good for another fight, now let us tend to Sven."

"It's been five days since we treated him. Ranak-u do you think we were too late?" Drego was worried that Sven had had the poison in his blood for too long. Gnomes were very tough and few were tougher than Sven but the poison that the Rennick warriors used was a mixture of herbal and magical ingredients. Rennick warriors had gained their knowledge of poisons from Ehmunnra as a reward for their bravery in battles when he walked Crintia. Their leader, Nunnurick, had sworn to regain the Book of Demons and to use it to bring back Ehmunnra and destroy the remaining Keepers. He had succeeded in killing three of the five remaining Keepers; only Bill and Wang Wu were left. "We have to inform the Keeper of Sven's condition." Movement from Sven's bed interrupted Drego's words.

"Where am I?" Sven tried to sit up but was unable to. "My head, what happened?" Sven looked to see if he was on his own. "Drego, what are you doing here? The Elders have you spoken with them, have you told them?" Sven's eyes closed and he lay quiet in his bed again.

"He's a strong one. Another day or two and he'll be on his way." Ranak-u turned and left Drego in the room with Sven. Two days passed before Sven moved again. He was much stronger in voice and could sit up in bed.

"Drego where am I?" His head was still spinning and he could only remember leaving Drego in the wood after they searched for clues as to who had taken the young girl.

"You were attacked by Rennick warriors. An arrow hit you and Morgab flew you back to me. Morgab was wounded but has made a swift recovery and awaits you in the stables." The room fell into quietness as Sven tried to recover the events surrounding his fight and escape from the Rennick warriors. Sven asked if the letter had been sent to the Seven Elders and if they had spoken to the Keeper. "The letter is still in your possession and no one has spoken to Bill. You still need two or three days rest before you can move from here though."

Sven started to get up from his bed and as he got to his feet he wobbled, Drego reached to catch him before he fell. "I'm ok, hand me my clothes, I must leave for Watu now." Sven pulled on his clothes and strapped his swords to his side. "Where is Morgab?" He walked towards the door. "I'm leaving, the Elders must get this letter, and it may already be too late." Sven held his side as he grimaced in pain. Drego saw the look of determination on Sven's face.

"I will go with you then." Drego took his sword up from the chair. "Come, we shall leave now, and we shall bring some of my best warriors with us." Drego led Sven down to where Morgab had spent the past couple of days recovering. As Sven entered the stable, Morgab acknowledged Sven's entrance with a triumphant roar. "I told you he would be ok, now we leave for Watu." Drego turned to the three warriors who stood near the stable. "Findel, Mordell and you Tarindel, grab your weapons and come with us, we leave for Watu." Without hesitation all three grabbed their swords and shields and followed Drego out of the stable for Watu.

Drego rode aloft a large brown eagle, a gold crested saddle sat on its back. The eagle soared gracefully along side Morgab; ducking and diving in a playful manner while Drego searched the afternoon sky for signs of trouble. Findel followed behind on a large red dragon. Mordell and Tarindel rode out front on two griffins, watching above and below for demons or signs of followers.

The inky night sky was rising into the evening. A plume of black smoke came into sight on the horizon. Sven sat up in his saddle and turned to Drego.

"It's from Watu, quickly Morgab fly hard." At this Morgab and the other riders began to dive towards the island. The plume of smoke was blacker than night and the feeling of dread entered into the heart of Sven as the island became visible. Fires raged on the ground and the land lay scorched. "The Elders!!" Sven turned to the others. "Drego, Findell with me. Tarindel and Mordell wait here, watch for anyone leaving the island, and follow them." At this Drego drew his sword and followed Sven. Findell flew low overhead watching for signs of movement. "We must enter the temple and speak to the Elders and then we must report back to the Keeper with their message."

Drego beckoned to Findell to fly toward the temple and scout the area. Black plumes of smoke were pouring from its windows, flames leaping from the roof. Sven walked through the doors into a great hall; its roof red with flames and collapsing in places.

"This way Drego, in that door." Drego pushed the door open and entered the room hidden behind it. Lying on the floor was a man dressed in purple robes; an arrow pierced his chest.

"It's an Elder Sven!" Drego turned to look for the other Elders and found five lying mortally wounded. "Sven, there is one missing!"

"Over here Drego, I've found the seventh, he's alive." Sven knelt down beside the Elder. "What has happened here? Who did this?" Pouring water on the Elder's lips, Sven placed his waistcoat under the old man's head. The Elder looked up at the face of his rescuer and spoke in a low, weak voice.

"It was a demon called Spectranos, he rose from beneath the temple and spat fire from his mouth." The Elder coughed and Sven gave him another drink from his flask. "You must warn the Keepers, tell them that Cundra has attacked us and has risen up the five Generals...." Violent coughing took hold of the Elder and drained the last of his breath from his body.

"He's gone." Sven covered his face and stood up. "We must send word to the Keeper and return to Dylan Drive." Sven and Drego ran from the temple as the fire took hold and dragged it to the ground. "Mordell, fly to the Keeper and inform them of what has happened here."

The sun had just begun to set when Mordell set out from the burning island. Sven watched as the silhouetted shape of the griffin disappeared over the horizon and then set out in the direction of the other temples on the island, surely there were other clues as to what had happened before they arrived.

27

First Meetings

Nugent lay sleeping on his mat while Sorden watched the entrance and the road outside Number Ten. The Keeper and the rest of the gnomes sat inside eating lunch. It had been two days since Sven had left for the Seven Elders on the island of Watu.

"Sven should reach the Elders today and we should have our answer shortly after that!" Bill was speaking to Tilterman. "If the rumours aren't true then we have nothing to worry about, but if they are, then we'll have to contact the rest of the Order of the Dragon." Bill continued to eat his lunch.

"What of the book? Do you think it's possible someone could have stolen it from the Elders?" Tilterman studied the expression on Bill's face, remembering what it was like the last time the Order fought Ehmunnra and his armies of the dead.

"No." Bill's voice sounded certain for the first time that morning. "I don't think anyone could have stolen it." Tilterman's thinking was interrupted by Bill's words. "It's not on the island with the Elders, it was given to Wang Wu, no one but me, and the Elders know where Wang Wu is. Shortly after we passed it to the Elders, a loyal servant of Ehmunnra nearly stole it off the island. He..."

"But you said no one could get onto the island?" Tilterman looked at him with a quizzical expression.

"That is what we thought but it was not the case. A thief known as Shang Te managed to get past all the spells, locks, and defenders. He had almost got off the island with the book when one of the Elders spotted him and trapped him with magic. It was then decided that the book was to be taken off the island. Wang Wu was chosen to take the book and keep it from harm." The Keeper stood staring out the window as he told Tilterman of the book.

"When Sven reaches the island, all our fears will be laid to rest and the book will be safe. The Elders will contact Wang Wu and confirm the book is safe." A look of uncertainty ran across Bill's face. "As you know, the book is the key to Ehmunnra's powers and his armies. When we fought him during the war of Styx's he had only gained half the power the book had to offer and we lost a lot of good friends, some very powerful people were destroyed." Bill sat back down at the table and took some tea.

"The Order has survived to keep the balance between good and evil. The Keepers that came before me and those that shall come after me will have that responsibility as well. It was bestowed on me when I was twelve. That was seven hundred and eighty years ago. At that time I had only my Father whom I saw once or twice a year, he was always off fighting some crusade for his King." Tilterman knew very little about Bill's past and his ears picked up at once as he started to talk about it.

"Argyle the Horrid took me under his wing and taught me everything about the role of the Keepers. When the time comes for me to step down, I will choose someone to take over as the new Keeper." Bill stood up again and walked towards a picture hanging over the fireplace. A smile came to rest on his face as he stared into the eyes of the man in the picture. His face held many scars, one eye was white, and the lid deformed.

"Argyle the Horrid, a man that saw over sixteen hundred years of history, most of it he created trying to defeat Ehmunnra." Tilterman stared into the face in the picture.

"What happened to him?" Tilterman turned to Bill. There was excitement in his voice. Bill had sat back down at the table and started to finish his tea. "Did he retire or where is he now?" Tilterman was hoping that he was alive and could meet him.

"Dead!" Bill put his cup down on the table and sat back into his chair. "I remember the first day we met. It was in a small tavern not far from where I lived in Denwick. I was working my father's farm in those days. Times were hard then but we made do with what we had." Bill started to think of that fateful day when Argyle came into his life and his first encounter at the Inn of Good Fortune.

The tavern was dark and smoke hung in the air. The only light came from a fire left burning inside the entrance. The tavern was halfway between Litchburg and the fortified city of Brandenburg, a safe haven for all races in Crintia, orcs, orgres, gnomes, centaurs, pixies, goblins, fairies, and humans. Two men sat at a table drinking from dirty tankards. The foam from their drinks sat on their upper lips, clinging to knotted hair before being swallowed up by a black and rotten tooth infested mouth. An old lady sat beside the open fire watching everyone, casting an eye of suspicion. A large cat with dirty black knots in its fur lay eating a large brown rat that had tried to sneak past.

At the counter of the tavern was a tall youth talking to the innkeeper and drinking milk. A white ring lay on his lips from the milk, his black hair hanging down in his eyes. "So Bill, will you have those rabbits for me? I'd hate to have to give your job to someone else, but I know you'll be good for them." The innkeeper smiled at him and walked down to the end of the bar. Bill finished his milk and left the inn. On his way out he bumped into a tall stranger. A hooded cloak hung to his feet hiding his face.

"Boy, tend to my horse, feed and water him. Make sure he has a good bed of straw in his stall and have him at the door by five tomorrow morning." As he passed by Bill, he flung the reins to him. "Do you understand boy?" Bill nodded as he caught them. The stranger disappeared into the tavern and Bill could hear polite yelling from inside.

"Barkeep a jug of ale and your finest room. I am tired and need rest, you'll have breakfast ready at four, and that stable boy of yours will have my horse ready at five, watered, and fed." A door slammed and all was quiet again. A tall black horse pushed Bill forward and snorted loudly.

A rush of hot air hit him on the neck as he led the horse towards the stables at the rear of the tavern. The horse unlike his master was good-natured, he ate and drank his fill and rolled in the straw in the stable. Once Bill had tended to the horse he left for his farm. He was expected to have the horse saddled and fed for five in the morning so he'd need an early night. He walked slowly back along the road that passed near his small farm, watching the birds diving and playing in the setting sun.

A squirrel was sitting at the bottom of a hazel tree gathering nuts for his winter slumber. When he saw Bill, he scurried up a nearby oak and disappeared in the branches. Bill reached his home shortly before the sun had gone down. It was cold and dark inside and the hole in the roof seemed to be growing larger every day. As Bill climbed into bed, he wondered where his father was and if he lay under the same stars tonight.

The dawn was cold and the land was wet with the morning dew. The birds were singing loudly from their trees heralding a new day. A cockerel was crowing telling the people it was time to tend to their chores as the new day was here. Bill could smell food being prepared, as he got closer to the inn. The horse he had tended to the night before was inspecting the farmyard from the door of his stable. When he saw Bill approaching, he shook his head.

Bill entered the farmyard and walked towards the well in the centre, two black rats scurried for cover as he approached. The tavern had a lonely candle burning in the window where the innkeeper was preparing breakfast for his guest. Bill dropped the bucket down into the cold well, letting the rope slip through his fingers until a single splash echoed up through the darkness. He glanced towards the horse, which was watching him with great interest.

"And how is our guest today? I hope your stable was comfortable and warm last nice night? Your breakfast will be ready shortly." As Bill looked across the yard to the stable he smiled and turned his attention back to the bucket.

"The stable, young Bill was very nice and if I could have some hay with my oats this morning I would be most grateful and how are you young master?" A shrill voice spoke from somewhere across the yard.

"Not bad thank you and..." Before Bill finished his sentence he looked up from the well to see who had spoken to him, but to his surprise, no one stood nearby.

"That's it Bill you've lost your marbles, talking to yourself, now is it?" He continued to fill the bucket. When he had it filled he took it to the horse and left it down inside the door.

"What's your name I wonder? You're a fine horse." As he brushed him down, Bill could hear the stranger thank the innkeeper and asked the whereabouts of Eric the One Legged.

Shortly afterwards the stranger emerged from the tavern, Bill could see his face now. It was capped by long knotted hair, dirty and black. It hung down to his shoulders and had entangled itself in his brown leather tunic's buttons. His face was weathered and beaten looking and much older than it should. One eye was white as snow and lay dead in its socket; the other eye had a scar running down its upper lid ending midway down his cheek. Part of his upper lip looked as if it had been cut off; Bill wondered how such scars could find their way onto a man's face.

"A present boy." Bill's stare was interrupted by a thunderous voice. "A present boy from a warrior in the east, a nasty piece of work but not as bad as his master." Argyle looked down at Bill. "Where's your bags boy, your belongings?" Bill didn't understand what he meant. "Your father boy didn't he tell you that I'd come for you when you were old enough to leave?" Argyle's horse shook his head and nayed in a disapproving manner.

"Now, now Hermes, it's not the boy's fault." Argyle turned back to Bill. "You have to come with me and learn the ways of our kind; it is what your mother wanted. So off with you and get your things. I will follow shortly, go on, and hurry boy." Argyle turned and mounted Hermes.

"What are you waiting for boy? Hurry we've not got all century. I will explain all but later. Now hurry." Bill's mouth hung open; he wasn't leaving his farm with a man he didn't know or with just someone who claimed to know his father. Bill stood watching the stranger ride out of the gate and wondered if he really did know his father.

Bill walked back towards his house. His stomach was now inquiring as to the whereabouts of his own breakfast. Bill wondered why his father hadn't told him about Argyle, why no one had ever spoken about him. It had been a long time since his father had been home from his crusades in the east and Bill couldn't question him about this man called Argyle.

His breakfast was only half eaten when the sound of hooves came from the farmyard. As Bill rose to see who it was, his front door came crashing in on top of the table. Two silhouetted figures stood just inside Bill's front door. He couldn't see their faces but from their entrance, he really didn't want to and the thought of running for the nearest exit crossed his mind.

"Where is he, boy?" A smaller figure stepped from behind the front two; he stood where Bill couldn't see his face. "Where's my friend Argyle, I want to see Argyle where is he?" The man stepped forward looking at Bill from head to toe. "Come boy don't be afraid, tell Uncle Scaripdemus where Argyle is." A long red cape hung over the man's shoulder and peeping from underneath, Bill could see the top of a golden sword. Its handle had a dog's head carved into it and the body of a serpent coiled around it. His gloves had large talon like fingers with dark red stains on the ends. Bill feared it was blood. Bill stared at the men standing at the door and then turned to Scaripdemus.

"Well it's like this." His palms started to grow sweaty. "I'm the only one in this house and if you care to look please do so." Bill's voice trembled, he returned to his chair and picked it up and sat back down. If he could remain calm, maybe Argyle would return and save him.

"You'd see it's only me here." Bill drank from his mug and glanced around the room.

"So he hasn't come back then? Well we can wait." Scaripdemus spoke in a cold voice; he turned to the men at the door and sent them outside to wait. "So you're a brave lad then trying to trick me." A smile spread across his face as he sat down opposite Bill.

"I've lived a long time boy so I won't be easily confused or tricked." His hand came crashing down on Bill's mug, crushing it. "Where is Argyle?" Scaripdemus stood up from the table and threw it across the room. "Has he gone to look for Eric the One Legged?" Bill nodded and pointed back to the tavern.

"Past the tavern near the lake that's where you'll find him. He left for there at dawn today so he should be there still." Bill's voice was trembling as he spoke.

"If you're telling tales boy I'll be back for your tongue." Turning in a flurry of red cape Scaripdemus left Bill sitting alone in the room. The sound of their horses soon faded into the distance and Bill slowly walked to the door to see if they had all left.

Outside sitting on Bill's cart was a guard, dressed in sheepskins and holding a bow. A large black leathery creature lay beside him, his fangs dripping with the blood of Bills best cow. The guard had pulled the hind leg off and was eating it. Bill slowly pulled the door open and suddenly the creature sprang towards him. He managed to close the door just as the creature reached him.

"Stay inside boy or you'll be desert for Cuddles." The guard shrugged his shoulders with laughter as he shouted at Bill.

"Have to find a way out without arousing that guy's attention." Bill thought out loud to himself as he looked around the room for his escape. The window in the rear had another cart up against it and he couldn't get out past that without knocking it.

"I'll have to get out through the hole, that's it, the hole in the roof!" Bill looked up over his head and there it was his escape to freedom or at least to the roof. He lifted his chair onto the table and then lifted himself onto the chair, slowly poking his head through the straw.

Down below he could just make out the top of the guard's head; he was still eating the cow's leg, occasionally stopping to pick some meat from between his yellow teeth. Bill pulled himself onto the roof and crawled over the ridge to the back of the house. Looking around the yard he made sure his path was clear before dropping down to the ground. He was almost there, he just had to make it to the cover of trees at the rear of his farm, and he could run for Eric the One Legged's place.

Crawling under the cart he checked the farmyard once more before dashing for the trees. Diving behind the first tree that crossed his path, he turned to see if anyone was following him. Slowly he backed into the trees watching the yard. Surely the guard would check on him when he had been quiet for so long? Bill turned and ran deeper into the trees directing his path for Eric the One Legged.

It wasn't long before Bill reached the edge of Eric's farm and there in the centre of the farmyard stood Hermes chewing hay. Bill ran up the yard shouting at the top of his voice.

"Argyle come quickly, someone is looking for you and." Gasping for breath, Bill started to shout even louder than before. "He

35

wrecked my house, said if I didn't tell him where Eric lived or if I lied to him he'd come back for my tongue." Bill ran out of breath collapsing to the ground just as Argyle and Eric came out of the house. "He said he was a friend of yours and wished to see you. I think it was Scaripdemus he called himself and he has guards with big black creatures I've never seen before."

Bill looked up at Argyle and Eric. This was the first time he had seen Eric up close. His skin hung loosely on his bones, pale and white. His eyes were protruding from their sockets like those of a fly. His scraggy hair hung in thin patches from his scalp. He had a scar running through his upper lip showing yellow and rotten teeth behind pallid lips.

"Are you sure that was his name?" Eric questioned Bill about the man he had escaped from, and where he was now. When he had finished, he turned to Argyle. They both started to talk in low voices. Bill couldn't hear all of what they were saying and what he did hear he didn't understand. Argyle turned to Bill and spoke.

"You'll have to come with me now, you have no choice." Argyle pushed Bill inside, closing the door behind them.

"That man is here to kill Eric, myself and anyone along with us." Argyle paused and Bill feared his name was the next word upon Argyle's lips.

"You." Bill stammered but failed to form a sentence. "You're a Keeper like me, and Eric is also a Keeper. Scaripdemus is a General for Ehmunnra." A thousand questions ran around Bill's head.

"We must leave now and once we are safe I will answer any questions you have. Come, we must leave." Argyle handed Bill a black bag and a single blanket, Bill however had other ideas about leaving.

"Why is he trying to kill me? Who are you? I'm still not sure what you are doing here and like I said before, I'm not going anywhere... this is my home and I have chores to do and my father will be back soon." Dropping the blanket and the bag, Bill slumped down on a stool near an open fire, he sat staring into the flames, watching them jump and flicker in the fireplace. He wished his father was here and then maybe this man would leave him alone. Together they could get rid of Scaripdemus and fix the hole in the roof. Times would be back to normal and if his mother were alive, then they could go down to the river for a picnic and go swimming or fish for their supper. Bill was soon jerked back to reality by a voice in his ear.

"You're a Keeper of Secrets, Bill, like your mother was and like your uncle Argyle." Bill turned to look at Eric. "You're wondering what sort of secrets do we keep and from whom?" Bill nodded. "You've heard of Troy and how for many years it was attacked because of one man's love for a woman? Well that's not why that war started." Eric sat down beside him and told him Ehmunnra and Scaripdemus were in Troy and that they were trying to raise a dark army to overthrow the powers of good.

"Ehmunnra had entered Troy in the hope of finding the Book of Demons and bring back his master Du'Ard and to raise his dead armies and lead them against the world." Bill stared into Eric's eyes but could find no lies.

"You must understand that if the Book of Demons falls into his hands, then darkness will rule again. The Keepers are the ones responsible for protecting the Book of Demons and keeping its location secret from those who wish to use it for evil. You are one of those. You have powers to help you carry out this duty." Eric raised his hand and spoke 'Karuck De Karuck.' At this, Eric's sword leaped from the door and across the room into his hand.

"You see Bill, we are not ordinary and we live for many hundreds of years and longer, until we find a new Keeper to do our job. Your uncle has lived for sixteen hundred years and it was to fall to your mother to take his place, but she was killed in the battle of Styx and so now it falls to you." Bill had always believed his mother had fallen to her death from Kantoruck peak. He had so many questions to ask but he knew that if he returned to his farm, he might fall foul of Scaripdemus.

"Ok, I'll go, but once you've dealt with Scaripdemus I'm returning to my farm and no one is going to change that." Bill was determined to return home once he knew it was safe. He stood up from the fire and walked towards the door.

"I want to know the truth about my mother and why it's been kept from me all this time." Bill didn't look at his uncle or at Eric as he walked to the door. He felt a hand on his shoulder.

"Bill you'll need these for your journey." Eric handed him a sword. The sword was made of silver and had a red flame running the length of the blade. It was much lighter than Bill had expected it to be. The flame flicked when he moved the sword. "Whenever you are in great danger, the dragon will protect you and the flames will give you the strength to overcome that danger but you must use them wisely." Bill didn't understand what Eric meant by these words.

"Where is the boy? Where is he?" Scaripdemus had returned to the farm and kicked in the front door. Turning towards the guard he had left in charge he drew his sword. "I'll ask one more time, Where... is... the... boy?" The guard had started to back away; Scaripdemus took this to mean that he had no idea where the boy had gone. Striking out with his sword, he cut the guard in two at the waist.

"Fools! We must find the boy; he's the one! Go search all the farms around here..." Turning to where he had cut down the guard he uttered words of a dark spell. Scaripdemus look down at the guard with disgust.

"Pull yourself together man!" At this the guard stirred on the ground, his body knitting back together where it had been cut in two.

"Burn it to the ground." Scaripdemus turned to the house and screamed out. "I will find you Argyle and I will kill you and the boy." He mounted his horse and watched the farmhouse burst into flames.

"Come, we have to find the boy." A cloud of dust rose up as they rode out of the gate and back towards the tavern.

From Eric's front door, the three saw the black plume of smoke rising into the sky from where Bill's farm was.

"My home! We have to go back there it's burning." Tears began to fill his eyes as he started to run down the road. Argyle ran after him grabbing him around the chest and pulling him back.

"Its gone boy, forget it." Bill struggled to get away from his uncle desperate to save his home. The last memories of his mother were in that house. "There's nothing you can do, leave it. We must leave, it won't take them long to find us." Argyle pushed Bill back towards the house. "Eric has a horse for you." Coming across the yard with Hermes was a large white horse, a golden mane hung from its neck. It flicked its tail and bowed in front of Bill.

"This is Athena and she was your mother's horse at the battle of Styx." Eric handed the reins to him. Bill patted the horse, his eyes firmly fixed on the black plume of smoke in the distance; his momentary silence was interrupted by Argyle's voice.

"Eric can you hold them off long enough for us to escape?" Bill now noticed several riders heading towards them along the road.

"As long as I can. Now waste no more time on me." Eric turned to Bill. "My time has ended here, but when you need guidance, I'll be there. Spread these in a circle and ask your question." He handed Bill a bag with silver and purple flames inside. "Now go and Argyle will teach you everything you'll need to know on your journey as a Keeper." Bill climbed onto Athena and followed Argyle out across the fields towards the unknown. When they had reached a safe distance, Argyle pulled Hermes up and turned towards the farm where they had left Eric. "Farewell my old friend I will see you again in a far better place and if you can't find the way, ask for directions, hahaha!" Argyle waved his hand over his head and gave Hermes a gentle kick urging him on.

Eric turned to face the riders bearing down on him. He knew that this was his time to join his fallen comrades from times past. As the riders came thundering into the yard, he drew his sword and stood firm.

"Scaripdemus, I challenge you under the code that binds all members of the Order of the Dragon and those who choose to oppose us. Stand and fight with swords and may the better man stand last." Laughter erupted as Scaripdemus stepped down from his horse and drew his sword.

"Eric my old friend, I would fight you in the old way, but I have neither the time nor the patience for games." He replaced his sword in its scabbard and walked towards Eric. "The boy, is he the one?" Eric stood his ground and didn't answer. "Eric! There is no time for you to play games, where is the boy?" Scaripdemus threw out his hands and from them a fireball erupted and flew at Eric, engulfing his body. Eric could feel his insides burning but he wasn't going to speak of Bill and Argyle.

"Last time and then you die. Tell me and I might spare your worthless life." Another fireball shot at Eric, this time penetrating his body taking hold of his heart.

"The boy, where is he?" Scaripdemus squeezed his fist tighter taking the life from Eric. Defying Scaripdemus to his last breath, Eric lay dead at his feet.

"Stupid man you could have lived out your life if only you told me where he was." Scaripdemus turned and mounted his horse. "I will find them that I promise."

Crown Jewels

"Cundra where are you? Come out and fight me, fight like a man."
Bill lay wounded on the cover of a tomb. The inscription on it was
just readable.

'*Here lies the body of a great warrior, who for many years gave great
service to his King, his brothers and loyal friends. He served without
question and gave his life for the Brotherhood of the Dragon.*'

Bill rubbed away the green moss from the tombstone so he could
read the inscription. 'Bill Brickton, Keeper of Secrets, killed at the
hands of the beloved CUNDRA.' Was this the effects of Cundra's
magic or was he already dead? Pulling himself to his feet, Bill
looked around the graveyard.

"Cundra, you'll not have your day, come and face me." Bill's voice
was full of hate, his palms dripping with blood.

"Oh Bill, how you make me laugh, you almost spilt my sides with
your humour." The shrill voice of Cundra floated across the air. "I
will face you but first know this, I killed your mother." The blood
boiled in Bill's body and every part that could hate was bursting
with malice. "Bill, friend, you know who I am and why you are
about to face me, but did old Argyle tell you about your father, how
he became loyal to Ehmunnra and fought side by side with him,
how he stole the Book of Demons and how he created me?" A laugh

echoed in the graveyard. Bill moved silently towards Cundra as he spoke. His sword was stained with blood from the battle.

"So tell me Cundra, you of great knowledge, where did I lose my father?" Bill lashed out with his sword striking Cundra in the shoulder. It cut right down to his bone but had little effect on him. Swinging out at Bill with his battle-axe he roared.

"Have you not seen it boy, can you not tell when you look at me?" Bill was flung to the ground hitting his head off a gravestone. Cundra stood laughing over him. "It's me boy, I'm your blood, your creator, the one who cast you into this hell. Keeping secrets from the weaklings, weaklings who think they wrote history, who think every little invention was created by them. They who think wars start, so they can rule more lands, so they have peace for their feeble existence."

"Fools! All of them fools. If they only knew what the truth was. Well once you're gone I'm free to let loose my Generals on the world." A shrill laugh echoed in the graveyard. "I'll make your end as painful as possible my son like that of your mother when I tortured her to find out where they had the book. Oh how she cried near the end, but I didn't kill her, no I kept her alive and all the others along with her."

Cundra pointed to the centre of the graveyard and to four pillars that were slowly rising from the ground. Strapped to each pillar were four hooded, blood stained figures. Bill couldn't see their faces.

"Would you like to see their faces?" Cundra grabbed Bill by the throat, his stale breath stinging his eyes. "Of course you would, because you'll want to save them or at the very least... try." Mockingly Cundra laughed, slowly walking towards them. Cundra drew his sword revealing the first of the hooded figures and Bill struggled to break free of his grip.

"Mother!!!" Bill cried as Cundra raised his axe and killed her before Bill could do anything.

"NOOOOO." Bill fell to his knees as his mother slumped over the stake. Looking up Bill tried to ask why. "Not quick enough Bill. Perhaps you should try again." Cundra pulled the hood from the second figure and again revealing Bill's mother! Bill opened his eyes and looked up from the ground to where Cundra was standing; a black shadowed hand was now coming down on his mouth cutting his scream to a muffled whisper.

"Bill it's me, Argyle, be quiet boy, we have unexpected company in the trees. Have your sword at the ready and stay alert." Argyle disappeared into the darkness of the trees leaving Bill to wonder about his dream. He watched as Argyle's shape was swallowed up by the blackness of the night. He lay watching the trees for signs of movement, his sword gripped in his hand ready to strike, his other hand pressing the ground ready to launch him into the attack. His dream was still racing in his mind wondering what Cundra had meant by his words and what the dream meant. His thoughts were quickly cut short by rustling in the trees.

"Argyle is that you?" His body tensed as he waited for the reply confirming that it was his uncle.

"Tis not boy, it is however your new companion for the rest of journey or till ye two get me safely to the King. Now, how long do ya think it will take the big fellow to realise that there is no one out there?" A small leprechaun stepped out of the trees, his white beard reflecting the moonlight. Little patches of white hair sticking out from under his green hat. He pulled open a single golden button that held his jacket closed revealing a bright red waistcoat underneath. A chain ran between two pockets on either side of the waistcoat. Pulling on one end he revealed a pocket watch, flicking it open he looked at Bill. "The big fellow, think he's realised that there's no one out there yet?" Bill opened his mouth to answer but the words failed to come out. Grasping at his throat he tried again to speak but nothing happen! He looked up at the leprechaun who was now laughing heartily at him.

43

"I forgot to tell you, I've temporally borrowed your voice." He held up a glass jar and began to laugh. "I'll give it back when the big fellow returns, which better be soon as I've not got all century to get my package to the King. A lot depends on it." At that moment Argyle emerged from the trees. "Aye and about time too. Don't you know you mustn't keep the King of the Leprechauns waiting?" A look of surprise hung on Bill's face while Argyle smiled and bowed in respect for their small visitor.

"Shamus Finnegan I haven't seen you since I was a young lad." Argyle walked towards him with a hand held out in friendship. "What brings you to these parts in such dangerous times?" Shamus held out his hand and shook Argyle's with all his might, which to Bill seemed a lot for his small size. Bill was sure that Argyle had left the ground at least once or twice while shaking hands.

"I'm on a peace mission to the King of Crintia with a gift from my people and a word of thanks for his help with those dragons that nearly destroyed my Kingdom. Crintia has a lack of crown jewels and my people wish to give your people some but not just any old jewels but ones with magical powers." Shamus tapped a bag that hung on his side.

"I wish to assure your people that these troubled times are not the doing of the wee folk. All of our tribes have sworn that they are in peaceful times and wish no trouble for themselves or for the big folk of Crintia. I need you to bring me to the King so I can give him our gifts, will you be my Keeper and take me to his castle." Shamus smiled at Argyle who was nodding in acceptance. Shamus stuck his hand out for Argyle to shake it.

"I'll bring you to his castle my small friend and protect you from the rascals that line the roads between here and there." Argyle turned to Bill and beckoned him forward. "Bill, meet the real King of Crintia and all the wee people in it." Bill pointed at his mouth and tried too speak but no words came.

"Oh be the hokey, man, I was forgetting, I stole his voice so I could surprise you on your return." Shamus opened the bottle and released the voice inside; Bill's mouth flew open and a scream shot from the bottle and into the back of his mouth knocking him over.

"Now you can introduce yourself to me boy and I to you. Shamus Finnegan the real King of all the wee people and lands in Crintia, and you my fine young lad are who?" Shamus bowed and held out his hand in friendship.

"Bill Brickton, nephew to Argyle the Horrid and it's my wish that you leave my voice where it's meant to be in the future!" Bill glared down on the leprechaun and walked away thinking of his dream and what it all meant. Early the next day, Argyle woke Bill and they set out for the King's court. They headed north until they came to the edge of a large forest.

"The Thieves' Forest, well we can go around or we can go through it." Argyle looked at Bill as if he was waiting for him to decide. "Into it we'll go and take our chances. Shamus I hope you have your package well protected."

"That I have." Replied Shamus. Shamus patted his waistcoat and walked towards the entrance of the forest.

"Well what are we waiting for, lets be on our way." Argyle led the way followed by Shamus and Bill. The forest was dark, not allowing any light to enter into its realm. The only sounds that could be heard were that of the trees creaking from the breeze whistling in around them. Bill saw hundreds of eyes peering back at him from the darkness.

Later that evening they made camp under a large oak, which Shamus said, was in the middle of the forest. Bill lit a small fire inside a circle made from rocks and watched as his uncle drew his sword and began to perform intricate patterns of defence and attack with his sword. His sword made graceful arcs, dive, slashes and controlled sweeps, cutting the nights air with silver dancing flashes. When Argyle finished he turned to Bill.

"Now Bill, repeat what I have done." Bill gaped at his uncle and then after a moments hesitation drew his sword. His sword wobbled through the air and managed to throw him off balance on a few occasions.

"You must practice until you can perform this routine with your eyes closed and then I will show you more." Turning he walked away, leaving Bill to fumble with his sword.

Argyle had disappeared into the darkness and returned several hours later with a wild boar slung over his shoulder.

"Aye, a feast fit for Kings." He announced as he dropped it at the edge of the fire. "Bill skin it and we'll have it for supper." Bill felt sick at the prospect of cutting up his own dinner.

"Oh, how I wish I was eating at the inn and drinking a tall cold glass of milk and eating their steak and kidney pie instead of cutting up my own dinner..." Grabbing the foot of the boar, Bill began to drag it towards the edge of the clearing.

"Ouch, do you mind not hitting me off every rock in your path young Keeper, I have after all, only one life." Bill dropped the foot and stumbled backwards watching the boar transform before his very eyes. A grin grew across the face of the man standing in front of Bill.

"I'm sorry young man, please allow me to introduce myself." He stood to his full height, which felt very high to Bill who had fallen over.

"I am Raymur of the Wood Elves, a friend of your uncle Argyle." The elf held out his hand to Bill who accepted it, smiling up at his new companion. He stood taller than either Argyle or Bill not to mention Shamus. Bill noticed a smirk on his uncle's face and before he could speak, the elf again spoke.

"You are to be my guests while you're in this forest." At that moment five more elves appeared from the trees carrying golden trays of food and large golden jugs of wine and fruit juices. All that night, they ate and drank their fill. Bill listened to stories of far off lands and great adventures that his uncle and Raymur had shared together, until he drifted off into a peaceful sleep.

The next morning Bill awoke to the smell of breakfast. To his great surprise he was no longer in the forest, but on its edge. He looked around to see who was cooking breakfast and more importantly, what it was? To his great joy, Argyle was cooking a large salmon on a spit over a freshly lit campfire.

"How did we get here?" He asked in a puzzled tone. "After you fell asleep the elves used their magic to take us out of the forest." Bill was glad that he didn't have to spend any more time in that forest and now just on the horizon he could see the start of a town. Soon he would have a bed or at the very least some straw to lie upon.

"They set us down here and then Shamus left with them to meet their King." Argyle looked around the trees. "He should be back soon and if you can drag yourself from your roll, breakfast is ready." Bill's eyes were still fixed on the edge of the town; he was wondering where it was and what it was like? He sat opposite Argyle and wolfed down his breakfast. Eager to travel on, he paced up and down on the forest's edge, all the time wondering where the leprechaun was and what was keeping him.

Shortly before the sun had climbed to its highest point, Shamus returned. Bill had already packed up the camp and they set off for the town. Leading the party Bill never looked back once to see if his companions had kept up with him. His eagerness had overtaken from the time they had left the outskirts of the forest. After what seemed a long time, they arrived at the first of the guarded gates.

Two towers rose high into the sky, blue flags dancing happily in the light breeze. Large black wooden gates blocked their way; each covered in metal spikes the size of Bill's head. Several tall men were standing beside a fire and came to life as they reached the gates. The guard in charge wore three stripes, indicating he was a sergeant. His gaunt features causing Bill to stare, watching the man's sullen eyes pass over each of the strangers standing in front of him.

"State your business in the city." His voice was coarse like the winter's eastern winds, chilling and harsh. After stating their business in the confines of the walled citadel, Argyle left Bill to roam at his own free will.

"Be at the Frog's Head when the sun starts to set." Telling him how to reach it, he let Bill set off in awe to explore his new surroundings.

Walking through the small crowded streets, a cacophony of sounds was filling his ears. The dull sound of the blacksmiths hammer, the sucking sound of his bellows, mixed with conversations, all whirled past his ears, strange and unfamiliar languages echoing in the streets. He sucked up the smells, aromatic and putrid alike the latter turning his stomach in knots. The stalls sold everything you wanted and things Bill never could have imagined. What uses could people have for dragon toes and troll spit? A man stood behind a small wooden box tempting people to find the jester hidden among the other three cards.

"If you find him Sir, you win ten gold pieces and if you can't, then I'll take ten gold pieces and lighten your pocket." Rubbing his hands with wicked delight when someone took up his challenge and when they said he had cheated, the man and his little boxes disappeared in a cloud of blue smoke, leaving only his fading laugh and a disgruntled person behind.

People sold all sorts of food and drink, including sheep eye soup and lizard tongue buns, all with bird beak or toe of dog if you wished. Bill's curiosity led him to try an eye of newt scones and dragon breath tea, foul and sulphurous. As the day wore on, he headed for the Frog's Head, where he would meet Argyle.

On his way he saw a swordsmith's shop and wandered towards it. As he got closer a man exited in a long black cape, knocking Bill to the dusty ground as he stormed by. Picking himself up, Bill walked into the shop. The smith apologised for the man who had knocked him. "Lord Termagil, a champion of Crintia's jousting tournaments."

The smith ushered Bill to a small basin where he could wash the dust from his face and hands. Bill saw weapons of familiar shapes and some he had never seen before. He walked around trying some for size and looking at others. The smith watched him as he examined the weapon in awe and amazement; his fingers gently sliding over the masterly creations.

"And what can I do for you young master?" A tall smoked man covered with a long brown leather apron, stepped in front of a large suit of armour that Bill was staring at. It was the first time he had seen such a beautiful piece of armour. His father's was war weary and held many dents from the battles won and lost at his King's side. Bill shook his head.

"Just in for the looking young man? Well it's your lucky day son." The man rubbed his hand against his leather apron and walked out of the shop returning shortly afterwards with a folded calfskin in his hand.

"The man, that knocked you as you came in had ordered this and paid for it. Now he tells me it's too small and that I'm to remake it bigger. Champion or not he should not have knocked you." Unwrapping the skin he revealed its contents.

"It's the best I've ever made. I can see you're destined for great things. Please accept this as way of apology for our gracious champions rudeness..." Bill's eyes lit up as a golden dagger was revealed before his eyes. "For you young man, a gift. Will you accept it?" The man shifted his gaze from Bill to the dagger as he handed it to him.

"I cannot Sir, for such a dagger must be worth far more than I could ever give you." The handle of the knife fitted perfectly into Bill's hand. He held it out and swished it in a defensive motion.

"It's so light! You must accept something in exchange for it!" Bill searched his pockets for any amount of silver that he had. Finding only one small piece, he offered it to the armourer. His hand held many scars and now along with them he held the only piece of silver Bill had.

"I accept your offer if you accept mine." Nodding Bill watched as the smith dropped the coin into his pouch a smile on his lips. Bill left the shop and walked along the streets towards the Frog's Head. He turned down the street where his uncle had said he'd find the tavern and there it stood.

A small wooden door with a Frog's Head on its front marked the entrance to the inn. The building itself looked like a shed where you'd find cows or pigs. He walked towards the door avoiding a steaming pile of horse waste on the way.

As he opened the door, the smell of stale sweat, ale and tobacco smoke hit him in the face. Just inside, a creaky wooden staircase fell towards the main drinking area of the bar. As Bill's eyes adjusted to the smoky darkness, he saw his uncle and Shamus sitting near an open fire. A small stocky man was in conversation with them. As he walked down the staircase, he noticed a man staring at him. He sat in the shadows, only the whites of his eyes revealing his presence. Bill sat down next to his uncle and picked up on the conversation.

"That's the guy over there." The barkeep nodded in the direction of the stranger that Bill had seen on his way in. "Been here oh, two, three days now. When he came in first he asked about three travellers one of whom was a young boy, wanted to know if you had passed here yet. When I said you hadn't, he ordered ale and has been sitting there since, never moved, not once." At that the barkeep turned and walked towards a man standing, shouting for ale at the top of the bar. Argyle nodded at the stranger in the corner and then turned his attention to Bill.

"Watch him and remember his face, he's a thief." At this Argyle stood up. "Come on we're leaving, less than a day to the King's court." The party bid goodbye to the barkeep and walked back up the stairs, Bill couldn't help feeling that the thief was watching them as they left. They entered the street outside the inn and Argyle searched the street for a spot to watch the inn door.

"You two hide down that alley and keep your eyes on the door,

I'm going around the back to see if he leaves that way." Argyle disappeared around the corner and out of sight; Bill and Shamus dropped down the alley and stood concealed in a doorway waiting for anyone to leave. Several minutes passed and then his uncle returned.

"He's left and riding in the direction we must travel, we'll have to go another way and get there ahead of him if we can. That's the only way we can be sure that the jewels will be safe from him."

Late the following afternoon the castle came into view, towers at each corner rose from the landscape breaking the blue skies with purple and green flags waving out towards the lands around them. As they came closer, Bill was dwarfed in its presence; the towers rose higher than he thought possible. The flags were almost out of sight. Guards patrolled the walls, carrying long pikes and clad in silver armour, their helmets topped with green plumage. The castle gates rose from the ground like two great oaks, topped with steel bands covered in spikes but they remained closed when they stopped outside.

"Friends loyal to the King who have travelled to present him with gifts fit only for a King as great as King Arnon." At these words, a guard exited from a small stone door beside the gates his armour reflecting the afternoon sun; his breastplate was engraved with a red dragon encircling a sun. The red plumage was shivering in the light breeze that was blowing about the castle walls. He eyed the new comers and Bill saw a smile spread over Argyle's lips as he recognised his friend Fionn of the Wooden Toe.

"My old friend Argyle, I've not seen you since the war of the Great Sands but old tales can be saved for later, the King is expecting you." The guard turned before Argyle could answer him. "Masahura, if you're not too busy the gates, if you please." Masahura jested at the Captain of the Gates, his laugh slowly descending from the castle walls. Bill raised his eyes to the top of the wall where the head of Masahura, the Man at Arms appeared and replied in a mocking voice.

"Would ya be asking me to open the gates then is that what ya want? Avast ladies, tis not on the sea you are now, open them gates or I'll have yer livers for me supper." A loud roar of laughter erupted from inside the gates and then came the loud creaking of the gates being pulled opened. A hive of activity was revealed on the other side.

As the companions entered the citadel, Bill saw Jesters cart-wheeling and playacting with wooden swords to the roars of ela-tion from on lookers. A man was lifting a stage with ten people on it and held it above his head with one hand while the other hand played a whistle. Bill saw a man swallow an apple and then a sword right down to the hilt, pulling the sword back from the pits of his stomach with the apple pierced on its end. A woman spat fire out over the crowd, as if a dragon had taken hold of her insides. The crowds were going wild for the activities of those who entertained them. As Bill surveyed the crowd, he saw the thief from the inn and turning to tell his uncle, he was greeted with a nod from him.

"I see him, he overtook us yesterday." Turning back to see if he still watched their movement, Bill saw a gnome watching the thief from the back of a hay cart. The thief saw that Bill's eyes had fallen on someone behind him and turned to see the gnome disappear into the crowd. A look of panic flashed in his eyes and he too dis-appeared into the crowd. Bill wondered who the gnome was? He thought to himself that the sooner these jewels were in the hands of the King, the better.

That night a lavish banquet was held in the castle's ballroom. Bill had never witnessed anything on such a grand scale before. Tables ran along the length of the walls, each table surrounded by deco- ' rated high back chairs. There were silver plates, silver goblets and food piled high in the centre of the tables. Large candle lit chan-deliers hung from the wooden beams that capped the great hall; each beam had a large serpent craved into it. The guests littered the edges of the hall, talking, laughing, and pointing at the other guests and then a silence fell across the room. Bill and the guests all turned. A man, dressed in a green ruffled collared shirt and green trouser starting shouting.

"My lords, ladies and all guests of his Highness and most esteemed King of Kings in our fair land; I give you his Royal Majesty King Arnon." Five dwarfs ran into the hall throwing green plants into the hands of the guests, then, as if by magic, a tall man appeared in the centre of the room, a long red robe floating softly to the ground behind him. A great cheer erupted from the crowd, as King Arnon spun around, flowers and sparks of silver and gold shot from his fingertips. Then from across the room shot a dragon of green and orange with white smoke streaming from his nostrils, Bill dived underneath a table fearing the dragon would pick him from the crowd and fly from the hall with him as a midnight snack. Argyle bent down and pulled Bill out from beneath the table.

"It's not real, just Arnon's magic." Bill slowly crept out just in time to see the dragon burst into flames. Much to his relief, it was gone and no one had noticed his cowardly dive for cover.

As Bill pulled himself to his feet, he saw the thief in the crowd. Bill pushed through the crowd excusing himself as he went, watching the thief as he moved closer to the King. As the ceremony began, Bill kept watching the thief but became aware that he too was being watched. Looking around, he saw the gnome from earlier watching both the thief and himself. Bill decided that it was time to find out who that gnome was. Dropping down to the ground, he crawled under a table. Peeping from beneath the tablecloth, Bill saw the gnome move closer to the thief. Now it was his chance to get closer to him. Slipping from under the table, Bill moved through the crowd. He could hear Shamus talking about how his people wanted the King to accept his gift and then to the gasps from everyone, he unveiled the jewels. A silver crown encrusted in green emeralds and red rubies surrounded by diamonds, it was companioned by a brooch of silver with emeralds set into intricate carving of a serpents. The King accepted them and in return asked Shamus to be his guest for as long as he saw fit.

Four tall men clad in long white robes took away the jewels, followed by five armed soldiers. Bill followed the thief along a narrow hallway after the soldiers; the hallway turned and fell down a stairway into another hallway lit by burning sconces on the walls. As he moved slowly along it he could hear voices in the distance. It was the guards returning but where had the thief gone? Bill decided he had to tell his uncle about what he had seen. Turning back towards the great hall, he saw the gnome disappear back up the staircase. Bill climbed back to the top to see the thief and the gnome fighting at the entrance to the courtyard. Running towards them Bill drew his sword from its scabbard and thundered down on the fighting men who turned just as Bill drew up upon them. The thief flung a ball to the ground and disappeared in a cloud of smoke. Holding out his hand to help the gnome to his feet, Bill asked.

"Who is that thief and why were you fighting with him?" Bill found no hand or answers to his question. The gnome too had disappeared into the smoke. Staring into the darkness of the courtyard, Bill wondered what had happened and who both these strangers really were. Up to this point, Bill had heard the crowd celebrating the King's new gifts and the music that was playing in the hall but now he could hear neither. Had the guards alerted the King and his guests to the fighting in his castle or was someone else about to give salutations to King and country? Walking back to the hall, Bill saw its wooden doors open and to his horror, revealed his uncle in shackles, trapped between several of the King's guards. Shamus came running towards Bill, who was now grasping his sword ready to free his uncle.

"No Bill, you must not draw your weapon or you too will be placed in manacles. Listen to me and I'll tell you what has happen." Shamus told Bill of the jewels being stolen and how Argyle was accused of helping to steal them. "You must ask the King for time to save your uncle by finding the thief and return them to him."

"Can I speak to my uncle first before I see the King?" Bill was led to the dungeon and to the cell where Argyle was. He relayed the entire story to his uncle and of the fight in the entrance to the court. Argyle sat on a bed of straw and looked up at Bill.

"That's everything you saw?" Bill nodded and sat down beside him. After a few moments Argyle started to speak in a low but firm voice. "You must first ask the King for permission to save me and then you must take Hermes and return to the Frog's Head to see if the thief was there. Ask the innkeeper if he overheard where he might be going and if he won't answer show him this." Argyle handed Bill a golden chain with a moon encircled by a red dragon.

"Anytime you need help show this to any innkeeper and they'll help you. Once you find out where he's gone, follow him there and then send word back to me. Once I receive word I'll send my old friend Sven to help you. Now go." Bill did as he was told and left the cell.

"Take me to the King." He spoke firmly to the guards outside his uncle's cell. He was led to the private chambers of the King and was given time to speak and state his reason for believing his uncle was wrongfully accused. The King granted him permission to recover the crown jewels and gave his word that Argyle would not be executed until Bill returned. Leaving the King's chambers, Bill raced out across the courtyard to where Hermes was stabled. Taking the reins, Bill guided the horse towards the castle gates explaining what had happened to Argyle.

"So Hermes, you see why we must be swift like the wind to find the thief!" Hermes shook his head and when Bill had mounted him they took out across the castle grounds like the winds of a hurricane.

55

The Chase Begins

"Finally I've caught up with you." Flashes of blue steel lit the halls in King Arnon's castle. "I've been onto you for some time now Chaykin and this time I have you. Where is he and what use has he for those jewels?" Suddenly a shadow appeared in the corner of the Chaykin's eye. Turning he saw the young boy bearing down on him, sword drawn for battle. Turning to face both opponents Chaykin smiled and smashed a ball between them, releasing a cloud of smoke. Chaykin turned and ran across the courtyard.

"That was too close Shadow." His black horse was ready and waiting for the escape. "Quickly now and leave no trace of our path." Pulling the hood of his black cloak over his face, they galloped across the castle grounds and along the road for Thornburg city. "He'll pay kindly for these jewels Shadow and I think I've found the boy he's been asking about too!" A smile fixed firmly on Chaykin's face at the prospect of more reward for the information he now had. "Two days and we'll have our reward, ride now for the Frog's Head and then at first light tomorrow, for Thornburg city, Shadow."

The moon was already high in the night sky when Chaykin got to the Frog's Head.

"Innkeeper, a room and stable for my horse and a call at sunrise or you'll not see a penny of what I owe you for your service!"

Slamming the door behind him, Chaykin pulled off his tunic, revealing a gash in his side.

"Old Sven, you are not so slow for an old fool and I should not have thought you to be!" Bathing his wound in cold water and then placing some maggots in it, he wrapped it in a leaf bandage and settled into a chair near the fire in his room, his sword firmly clutched in his hand.

"FIZZZZZZZZZ." The innkeeper slid a match across his grey piece of flint, its yellow flames cracking the blackness of night. Placing the match to his withered candle he watched as his surroundings stood out yellow in the night. Pulling himself from his bed he made his way up to where his only guest was sleeping. The stairs moaned beneath his feet as he made his way to the guest room. Two loud bangs rang out in the dark room, the only light rising from a few embers glowing in the fireplace.

"Sir, it is just dawn and your horse is saddled and ready for you at the tavern door. Sir! Are you awake?" The door jerked open and Chaykin pushed the innkeeper to one side. "Sir, payment for the room is..." Before the innkeeper could finish his words, two gold coins hit him in the face and fell to the ground where they rolled before falling over to rest.

"Well, some people are full of good cheer at dawn. I should call people more often at this early hour." The innkeeper heard the inn door close with a thud. "And have a nice day Sir. Didn't I tell you the greeting was free of charge..." He rolled his eyes to the roof. "Well back to bed for me and..." Biting down on the coins he remarked. "At least the gold is real." The sound of the horse beating down the cobbled street outside soon faded into silence, and only the chorus of morning birds could be heard.

"On Shadow and don't slow till we reach the Devil's Hide and our reward." Chaykin rubbed his hands together at the prospect. The sky was grey as noon approached; Chaykin saw the first signs of Thornburg city and the tall ships on the Lufta.

"There it is Shadow, the first sight of our money." Chaykin spotted a tall ship slowly moving up the river, its seven masts stripped of their black sails, only a red flag flying on the top of the middle mast. Pulling out a telescope, Chaykin pulled the flag into view.

"Ah yes, that's her alright Shadow!" The flag's red colour surrounding a dog's head with a snake coiled around it. "Quickly now Shadow and ride like the wind that fills its sails on the high seas." Within minutes Chaykin and Shadow thundered down the streets of Thornburg city, towards the Devil's Hide.

"Is this what you wanted?" Chaykin walked towards the table in the middle of a darkened room, a solitary candle burning in the table's centre. Two shadows moved just on the outside of the candle's light. Chaykin placed his bounty on the table spreading the jewels out.

"And the boy you've been looking for is on the way here, he's about a half day's ride behind me. That has to be worth extra?" Scaripdemus walked into the light and picked up the crown and then placing it on his head, turned to the thief.

"You're sure it's the one I seek?" His eyes fixed firmly on Chaykin and he continued to fix his crown. "If it's the boy then, I'll double your reward but you must bring him to the Lucipher, alive." Chaykin took the jewels and handed them to the stranger, raising two fingers.

"Two days on the ship." And he left. Taking the jewels and pulling the dog after them, the men left watching to see if they were being followed.

* * *

"Hello again young master, not with your uncle today?" A small stocky man stood watching Bill, as he walked towards the bar. "What will it be, milk?" As he waited for his answer, he began to rub his hands in the blood soaked apron hanging around his barrel like belly.

"No thanks but that man that you spoke of to my uncle has he been this way?"

"He left in the direction of Thornburg..." The innkeeper watched as Bill ran back up towards the street and returning to his work remarked out loud to himself.

"How rude people have got, times are a changin'!" Bill jumped back onto Hermes and kicked him to urge him off his resting spot.

"He's been here, do you think he's heading for Thornburg or somewhere near there?" Hermes sprang forward and nodded.

"I see we still have company shadowing us." Bill was watching a rider not far behind him. He had noticed him shortly after they left the King's castle but had decided not to do anything. The sun was already starting to set when Bill left the Frog's Head.

"How long is it to Thornburg city?" Turning his head for a moment, Hermes shrilled.

"Two hours if you can stay quiet and hang on." Bill placed his hand across his mouth mocking Hermes' request.

The sun gave way to the moon as it climbed steadily into the darkening sky. Bill could see the outskirts of the city as the first of the gas street lamps were lit.

"We can't look for the thief until morning so we need somewhere to stay. That barn looks good and then at first light, we can head into the taverns." Soon after Bill had spread out some hay for Hermes and lit a fire. Staring out into the darkness of the night, he became aware of another fire burning in the distance.

"Hermes it looks as if we still have company, should I go see why he is following us?" Hermes shook his head and returned to eating his fill. "Guess we should keep our distance and see if he approaches us." Bill tucked into his rabbit and then settled down to get some rest. Early the next morning, Bill was woken by Hermes hot breath on his face.

"Is it morning already friend?" Stretching out, Bill rose slowly to his feet, looking to where the other campfire had burned the night before. "He's gone, perhaps he isn't following us after all." Packing up their few things, Bill and Hermes set out for the taverns of Thornburg.

Bill had never seen so many buildings in one place before, tall ones, and small ones, round ones and so many horses and carts, all full of strange looking foods. People of all shapes and sizes, wearing clothes he had never seen before.

"Hermes where are we going to find the thief?" Hermes shook out his mane refusing to answer. "Not speaking or just won't because of all the people?" Bill leaned out over Hermes shoulder to see if he would answer. "Ok, we'll start out with some taverns at the castle, where is the castle or is there one?"

Hermes walked slowly through the crowds of people to the hill that led up to the castle. Just before the castle entrance was a tavern called 'Gabriel's Well'.

"As good as any place to start, I suppose." Bill dismounted and walked towards the oak entrance door, carved into it were sets of wings, and above the door, a face, sunken into the stone, weathered and discoloured. Just as Bill reached for the brass door handles, a man came crashing onto the street; Bill just managed to avoid him.

"Don't come back, we don't need your type here." A tall man blocked the doorway to the tavern. Rubbing his hands together, he turned and slammed the door in Bill's face. Picking up all his courage, Bill pushed the door open and walked into the darkened room. As his eyes adjusted, he began to see clearly people in the tavern and standing at the bar staring straight at him was the innkeeper.

"What do you want boy?" The innkeeper stood waiting for his answer. Bill looked around and thought; maybe the type of person he was after wasn't to be found here.

"Well I'm looking for a thief, Sir." A lump swelled up in Bill's throat, he watched as the man came from around the counter and walked towards him. Bill found himself slowly moving back towards the door, fumbling in his pocket he pulled out the chain his uncle had given him. He held it out in front of him; the man stopped as if stunned by some form of magic and grabbed Bill pushing him into a small room. Sticking his head back out the door he shouted at a young maiden.

"Sylvia, behind the counter now and look lively!" Closing the door he looked at Bill and exclaimed. "You're a bit small aren't you lad?" Not knowing exactly what he meant, Bill thought it best to remain quiet. Scratching at his head, the man looked at the chain, then at Bill and then at the chain again.

"Where did you get this boy?" The innkeeper stared at Bill.

"From my uncle. He told me that any innkeeper who saw it would be a friend and lend me aid or information if I needed it." Bill looked at his face trying to decipher his expression. "So, I guess the question now is can you help me? If you cannot, then I shall bid you good day Sir." Bill moved slowly to the door and found it blocked by a large arm.

"Now don't be so hasty young man, who is your uncle and what help can I give you assuming I know him?" The man stood looking at Bill.

"Argyle is my uncle." Watching the innkeeper's face, Bill began talking. "I seek a thief who has wronged my uncle at the King's court." The innkeeper smiled down at Bill and patted him on the back.

"I can help you, but first some food, and then you can tell me your story and who it is you seek." Pushing Bill back into a chair, the innkeeper popped out to the tavern and pulled a large leg of meat from behind the counter and put it down on a table. "Now, tell me all you can young man, and start with your name so I know what to call you. I'm Gabriel." Bill told the story to the innkeeper and all that had occurred from the first day his uncle arrived at the inn near his home.

"Well, you've certainly had quiet an adventure haven't you, and how is old Eric anyway?" Bill told him about leaving Eric to fight

Scaripdemus and his men on his own and they had not heard news of him since that day. Gabriel wiped some ale from his chin and tore another chunk of meat from the bone.

"Well if it's a fight they were looking for, then Eric was their man." Pausing to take a drink from his ale jug, the innkeeper continued. "You say you're after a thief, well then I'd say you best head for the Devil's Hide. Mostly full of cut throats, pirates, brigands and thieves, but you had better not go flashing that pendant around in there or you'll not see another day!" That was the last thing Bill wanted to hear. Gabriel told him that the inn could be found down where the ships were moored, but he'd have no problem finding it if he followed the line of drunken men lying in the gutters. Bill thanked Gabriel and left the inn.

As he sat on Hermes thinking of what he had just heard, he noticed that the head above the inn door was remarkably like the face of Gabriel the Innkeeper. Turning Hermes towards the ships, he left Gabriel's Well behind.

The smell of the sea and the freshly caught fish began to fill Bill's senses as they rode down towards the ships. Two cloaked riders approached as the ships came into view. They looked at each other and then at Bill again. Hermes turned down a side street leading away from them. As Bill looked back, he saw that one of the rider's legs was dragging underneath his horse. The two riders stopped, their lips moving as a silent conversation took place. Their gaze made Bill feel uncomfortable.

"Who are they and why did they come this way?" Bill whispered into Hermes ear but got no answer. Hermes turned again and they came out onto the docks and now for the first time, Bill became aware of the true size of the ships he had until now only seen from a distance. Sitting on the water in front of him was a ship with five tall masts and its crew was busy preparing to set sail for what Bill could only imagine to be an adventure out in some strange and unconquered land.

Dismounting Bill took in the true splendour and size of the ships in the docks. Nudging him from behind, Hermes drew his gaze towards a tavern not far from where they stood. Turning Bill saw the thief entering a tavern at the end of the wharf.

"Go and hide somewhere and watch for him leaving." As Hermes walked off, Bill headed for the tavern with what Gabriel had told him in his thoughts. As he approached the door, his attention was drawn to a carved head of the devil and written within his horns were the words in blazing red, 'Enter and you may not leave.'

Slipping quietly inside Bill focused on the patrons of the Devils Hide. The only light was from small knotholes in the wooden walls. The smoke whirled up through the light, dimming the room even more. Pipes being sucked upon glowed in the corners and Bill felt a thousand pairs of eyes on him. Plucking up his courage, he slowly made his way to the counter. He made out the battle-hardened face of a pirate with half his ear missing and the end of his nose was gone too. A wooden eye had been thrown on the table, and a black bottle lay on its side with a drop of green liquid hanging on the lip's edge waiting to fall onto the soaked table. When he reached the counter, he looked up at the innkeeper. In a very low and feeble voice, Bill said.

"Sir, my master just came in, where did he go?" The innkeeper turned, spit dripping from the corner of his mouth, a scar ran the length of his face and his single eye peered at Bill. From the side of the counter, two large black, hairy dogs appeared, both carrying meat in their mouths. Bill's expression changed from fear to terror.

"Don't worry boy, the only way they'll kill you now is if you took their meat away and you don't look hungry enough to do that. Your master is in the last room on the right." He turned and went back to cutting up the raw meat that lay on his counter.

Walking slowly down the hallway towards the room, Bill could see the innkeeper watching him and waited till he turned away.

63

Bill slipped into the room next door. The room was dark, its only occupants a bed and cupboard. He looked around for a hole or crack through which he could look through and spy on the activities in the next room. Beside the cupboard was a knothole, and he could see and hear everything taking place in the thief's room. As he listened to the conversation, he saw the black, hairless dog from his farm walking around and then he saw the red cloak of Scaripdemus. As he watched the red cloak move in and out of the darkness, he saw the dog staring intensely at the knothole. Then, without warning, the dog jumped for the hole. Bill's heart jumped into his mouth, as a hand grabbed him from behind and pulled him into a secret passage near the bed.

The dog came crashing through the wall and into the room just as the stranger's hand closed the passage behind them. Bill watched as the thief and the others left and he felt himself being unrepentantly shoved back into the room turning to face the hands that pushed him.

"You fool, you almost got yourself caught and what use would you be to your uncle then?" The gnome from the King's court was standing on a chair in the room. "Come on, we're leaving." To Bill's amazement, the man stood barely taller than a cat and wore the strangest assortment of coloured clothes he had ever seen.

"Where's Hermes hiding? We can't afford to loose Chaykin this time." The gnome ran from the room and towards the street outside with Bill racing behind him.

"Hermes, which way did they go?" The horse was already waiting outside the tavern. "Hurry boy or we'll lose him." Bill and the gnome jumped onto Hermes's back and they galloped up the street after the thief. After sometime, it was agreed that they had lost the thief in the growing darkness and would resume their search in the morning.

Bill looked at the fire that had been lit in their new campsite. The old tower must have been deserted for many years now and its new owners, the pigeons, didn't seem to mind that they had guests.

"So you know who I am but I don't know who you are." Bill had decided to break the silence. "The only time I've seen you before was when you were fighting with the thief!" Bill's new companion said nothing for a few moments and just as he decided to repeat his question, the stranger looked up from the fire. Pausing the gnome took a draft from his leather bound canteen.

"Sven." The gnome paused, a look of pain and sadness on his face. "I'm one of the few free Gnomes to wander around without the weight of a collar and chain." Bill stared at him wondering what he meant. "I've been tracking Chaykin for over a year now and the castle was the second time I've gotten close enough to capture him but again, someone allowed him to escape." Sven looked up at Bill wondering if there were any more questions.

"Hermes!" Sven turned towards Hermes who was ear deep in oats. "Did Shadow say anything to you or did he recognise you?" Hermes lifted his head long enough to inform his companions that Chaykin was staying near the ships in some tavern. Sven turned back to Bill.

"Well that's where we go then, back to the ships and hope we spot him before he spots us. Now get some sleep, we leave before sun up." Sven dropped his head onto his roll and was asleep before Bill had settled down. It took Bill a while to go asleep as he had been thinking of the dream he'd had the past couple of nights and wondered if that's all it was, a dream?

The first orange rays of sunlight pierced the morning darkness as Bill woke to the smells of cooking. Sven was cooking a feast over the fire.

"Come on lad, food is ready and old Hermes is eager to get on the trail of the thief." Bill stretched out and sat up just in time to catch a plate of fish flying at him. He wolfed it down as Sven sat waiting on Hermes' back.

"No need to rush on my account, I'm sure Chaykin won't mind us being late to follow him." Tossing the bones of his fish away, Bill jumped up onto Hermes, and no sooner was he sitting than they were galloping towards Thornburg city.

The streets were all quiet with only the castle guards moving, all the buildings were in darkness. A large brown rat sat gnawing on the remains of bread and when it saw Hermes' large hoof crash down not far from him, he scurried into a crack in the wall and disappeared. Bill saw a ship sail over the horizon catching only a glimpse of its white and red flag as it disappeared out of view. Hermes turned down a side street near the Devil's Hide and stopped waiting for signs of life.

It seemed they had spent all day watching the tavern and the gulls flying overhead. Only once had Bill been caught by one of those birds relieving themselves, his shoulder was home to a white mark. Hermes and Sven had laughed heartily at his misfortune but had been interrupted when they saw Chaykin leaving the tavern and walk up the gangway of a small ship nearby.

"That's him, stay alert and maybe we can get those jewels back today and then you can free your uncle." Bill watched as the thief left and mounted his horse and rode back out towards the tower where they had camped the night before. Following at a safe distance, Bill spoke to Sven.

"Last night you said you were one of the few Gnomes to wander about free, what did you mean?" Sven placed his finger to his mouth and didn't answer. Bill stared intensely at the back of the little head in front of him.

"Will you tell me later then, once we've finished with Chaykin?" Sven nodded his head and Bill accepted this but was still determined to get to the bottom of Sven's past. They rode out into the forest at the back of the tower where they had spent the previous night. The trees grew tall and straight in the forest as the animals went about their business. Hermes came to a stop and they watched as the thief dismounted and drank from a stream. Then taking a bag from his horse's saddle he buried it near the edge of the stream, marking it with a stone covered in moss. Bill thought that this bag surely contained the jewels and now, he could return to free his uncle.

The thief led his horse back along the stream in the direction of the tower. As they followed him, Bill saw a third rider in the trees.

"We have more company over there in the trees." Bill pointed in the direction of the third rider.

"It's ok, he's a friend and has been with me since we left the King's castle." They followed the thief back to the edge of the forest where they saw him leave his horse in the trees and watched as he searched their camp and bags.

"Why aren't we stopping him or digging up the bag he buried back there?" Bill was hushed into silence and told to be patient, that they would get a far greater victory if they waited. Bill didn't understand but decided to wait, not that he could do much without Hermes who now seemed to be on Sven's side.

The thief searched everywhere in their camp and returned back into the woods with Hermes, Bill and Sven following him. After several hours of going around in circles, the thief entered an opening where a large dead tree resided at the bottom of a cliff. The thief settled down under the tree and appeared to go to sleep. Shortly after he had sat down, three other riders entered the opening and greeted Chaykin, all with the same handshake.

One man towered over Chaykin and was dressed entirely in green the other two were much smaller but were bigger in girth than either Chaykin or the tall one. After speaking in the opening for a while, the four thieves turned to walk into the forest but to everyone's surprise, entered the dead tree's trunk.

"It must be their hideout, now what can we do?" Bill looked at Sven to see if he had a plan but Sven was staring at a tree on a ledge halfway up the cliff face.

"There, behind that tree." Bill looked up at the tree and just visible was a cave entrance. "We'll get in there and see what's going on inside." Bill shook his head.

"There isn't a chance I'm climbing up that cliff face, I'll use the front door and hope I don't meet any of them inside." Sven set out for the cliff face and the long climb up, while Bill crawled down through the bushes and up to the dead tree where he slipped inside.

The inside of the trunk opened onto a staircase that lead down and then back up into a chamber surrounded by stone pillars rising high into the belly of the cliff. He looked around for a hiding place, and slipping in behind a statue he saw the thieves standing around a table. They were looking at a large piece of parchment and talking about where they would place themselves when they arrived at Scaripdemus's campsite. Bill saw Sven drop onto the head of a tall statue at the far side of the room and slipped down along its ear eventually hiding in the ear hole. Bill gripped his sword ready to draw it, should the need arise.

As Bill watched the thieves, they began fighting among themselves. Bill's attention was drawn away from Sven and back to the table. Watching them, he saw Chaykin draw his sword and threaten one of the shorter thieves with it and at this the thief turned and left the room, followed by Chaykin. The other two men began to laugh at their display of temper. As they were talking, Chaykin returned with blood on his sword, followed shortly by the small thief carrying a dead deer on his shoulder. "Dinner lads, and guess who's cooking!" Pointing at Chaykin, the small thief began to laugh. "Told you I was better with a bow than you were. A better thief you may be but you'll never hunt as good as me." Bill saw Sven climb back out through the hole and disappear from view. This was Bill's cue to exit from the thieves' lair and get back to the others.

Leuchter

Scuttling across the sandy wasteland, a small green lizard searched for some food, spotting a beetle it dived at it only to be interrupted by the crashing of hooves. A rider on a small white horse shot by; narrowly missing him, white foam dripping from the horse's neck. The rider's red and black armour shimmered in the sun as he pushed the horse to its limit. The rider saw his destination come into view and he sunk his spur into the animal's side, urging it on. A large rock jutted from the sand, its shadow protecting a large red tent from the burning midday sun. As the tent got closer, the rider jumped down from his mount just as the horse took its last breath and collapsed dead on the sand.

"Master, word from the west." The rider rushed into the tent and handed a parchment to a tall-silhouetted figure standing just inside the door. Stepping forward his golden armour reflected the burning sun across the riders face blinding his view, forcing him to shield his face with his forearm. Dismissing the rider with a wave of his hand, he opened the parchment and read its contents:

Trap set, the boy will be arriving as planned.

Argyle's recovered and ready to board the ship when the boy arrives in Thornburg city.

Your loyal servant,
Scaripdemus.

"I have waited a very long time for this moment Keeper, and now I will have my prize." Turning, the silhouetted figure disappeared back into the belly of the tent. At the centre of the tent stood a large stone cauldron filled with a murky black liquid. Walking towards the cauldron the stranger opened a small glass bulb and poured its red contents into the cauldron. The red liquid congealed on the surface and as it settled a face slowly formed in the liquid.

"You have news for me?" Erasmus Reich spoke across the paths of time. Nodding the stranger smiled.

"I will have the boy shortly and then you will be able to bring me to you so I can rule with you at my side. Are our plans on schedule in the future?" Du'Ard stared across time as Erasmus smiled and nodded as his image faded from the cauldron.

Bill slipped back up the stairs and outside to where he had left Hermes. Sven was already there waiting for him. They slipped back through the trees and out of sight of the dead tree and the opening.

"We have to get a look at the map they had, it looked like a battle plan for an attack on..." Sven stopped talking and began looking at Bill. "Like an attack plan for where the Book of Demons is held!" Bill waited for Sven to continue and then from the trees behind Sven, a tall dark figure emerged, Bill jumped up, drawing his sword poised for the attack but before he could, Sven had stood up and held his hand out to greet him.

"Drego, have they left?" The stranger nodded and walked back into the trees, disappearing in the shadows. "Ok, let's go." Sven walked back towards the tree. He dropped into the bushes and crawled to the entrance, Bill followed him and they cautiously slipped into the hideout. Slowly making their way down the steps to where Chaykin and the three men had been earlier, Bill saw the map still on the table.

"You wait here and listen out for their return." Sven walked across the room to the table. Jumping up onto the table he looked at the map. A few moments had past when Bill heard voices at the top of the stairs. Turning to warn Sven, he saw him slip into a door at the far side of the room. Bill ran and hid in the shadows where he had watched from earlier. As he crouched down the four thieves returned. Bill wondered if Sven could hear them from the other side of the door. He watched as they gathered at the table and listened to the bits of conversation he could hear.

"This is where we're to gather our men, just south of the castle and wait there for the signal." Chaykin was leading the conversation while the others pointed every now and again to the map.

"When we get the signal, we're to spilt into three groups and attack at intervals. The main force, lead by Scaripdemus, will attack head on at the main gate. Our job is to create a diversion on the sides. Thorsen will lead another force to draw the guards from the rear wall. I've been told that Scaripdemus has a surprise for those inside." Bill listened to everything that he could hear.

"The jewels and Argyle are on the Lucipher and once we find the boy, he's to be brought there without delay. If we don't catch him, then one of us has to remain behind and bring him across later."

Bill decided now would be a good time to leave before they became aware of his presence, and while the thieves were looking at the map, he slipped onto the stairs and back outside to meet up with Sven and Hermes. When he found the others, he relayed everything he had overheard and they agreed that they should get on the ship in Thornburg; the ship known as the Lucipher.

The rain fell in sheets as Bill walked along the docks towards the Lucipher. He saw Sven pull some rags over his shoulders as he sat in a doorway near the ship. Bill walked a short distance beyond the ships gangplank that lead onto the deck, and picking up a piece of wood and an empty cup, he propped himself against the wall of the Devil's Hide. Two guards walked towards him, eyeing him suspiciously. Bill shoved his cup forward.

"Alms for a blind boy... Spare a few shekels kind Sirs." The two guards pushed Bill out into the street laughing. Picking himself up out of the mud, he saw Sven laughing from his doorway. Bill shrugged his shoulders and leaned back against the wall watching out for the thief or Scaripdemus.

The rain seemed to be falling heavier now. The minutes dragged into hours and the hours slowly grew into most of the day. The sun had started to set before Sven moved from his spot in the doorway, something had caught his eye and he slowly moved towards Bill. As he came closer, Bill saw him beckon to follow and not to look back. Bill followed Sven up the street and down a small alleyway near the Devil's Hide.

"Witch hunters." Sven peered back around the corner of the alley. "The first people they'd pick on are street beggars and gnomes, better off staying out of their path." Sven watched as three tall men clad in long black robes stepped onto the docks. Two of them were carrying banners mounted on poles of gold with the words, 'Repent ye sinners, for he sees all sins', written in tall red letters. Their hoods hung low over their eyes casting a shadow over their slender faces. The third was walking slightly to the front reading from a black leather bound book, covered in gold writing, his shrill voice lashing at the salty air like a serpent seeking out its prey. A large sliver war hammer swung from his side, the word 'REPENT' raised on its side. His robes were splattered with mud from the wet streets. A white tunic, home to a red cross, covered his shoulders and chest. A stovepipe hat cast long shadows that hid his face.

"Theobald Rheims, and the Angels of Mercy, we need to get out of here before he sees us." Sven turned and ran down the alley. Bill took this chance to get a look at the witch hunters he had heard so much about. As he watched them moving slowly up the street, he saw it to be empty and the people who had been so busy trading moments before were now nowhere to be seen. Sven's voice whispered in his ear.

"Move or you'll be a witch at the stake whether you like it or not!" Reluctantly, he turned and ran after Sven. Witch hunters had plagued the land since the short reign of the Goblin King, Seratouse. Some humans had come to aid a city of Gnomes during the battle of Evermore. The gnomes had withstood everything the goblins had thrown at them. Their mechanical ingenuity was more than a match for the primitive weapons of the goblins. But when a fanatical group of humans known as The Rama Divine arrived from the north, Evermore fell within hours. The goblins enslaved all the captured gnomes in their mines and hired the Rama Divine to hunt and capture those gnomes that had escaped.

The Order had attacked the newly formed goblin fortress at Evermore and defeated Seratouse. Banished to the lands of ice in the north, the goblins kept in contact with the Rama Divine leader Harold of Potsburg to keep their contract in place. Harold agreed and sent out a decree to his followers stating that they should identify themselves as Witch Hunters in service of the One God. The Witch Hunters continued capturing the escaped gnomes delivering them into the goblin mines. They also took on the wizards and witches of Crintia saying that the One God took offence to magic and all races who were not human.

The preaching of the Witch Hunter soon faded behind Bill and now only the sound of his running and his heavy breathing echoed in his ears. Sven had slowed down and stopped at one of the town's drinking fountains. Bill noticed that the street was empty of people and the silence was deafening.

"Where is everyone?" Sven looked up from the fountain, seeing for the first time the lack of people in the streets. A shiver ran through Bill's insides, as he watched Sven jump down from the fountain. Then, as he waited for Sven to say something the silence was broken by the shrill voice of Theobald Rheims.

"Repent sinners and seek forgiveness for the greater good." His words cutting into the air like a butcher's knife into meat. "Take time and be saved Sven Thorsen." The witch hunter rounded the corner at the end of the street, his war hammer in hand and his book swinging at his side.

"I know your crimes and shall help save your soul and return you to your people. I shall reunite you with your family and friends." Bill felt Sven's hand pulling him back towards the fountain.

"We must go now, back to the ship." Sven's voice was calm, his gentle but firm grip on Bill's arm. "Run!!!" Bill turned and grabbed Sven lifting him clear off the ground.

"My legs are longer." Bill grinned at Sven as they hurtled down the streets away from the witch hunters. As they ran Sven spotted an open sewer.

"Quickly, through that hole." Bill dived onto his belly and slid into the sewer. Bill's eyes slowly adjusted to the darkness and to Sven's movements.

"What now?" Sven beckoned him into the darkness of the sewer and as they walked further into the belly of the city, he turned to peer into the darkness. "Sven, someone is following us!" Sven remained silent and stayed on his course. Bill was sure someone or something was behind them, hidden in the darkness.

The sewers rose into high gothic arches, gargoyles peering into the darkness. The sewage flowed swiftly past them, its stagnant green colour reflecting the small amount of light on its surface as it followed its predetermined course to the bay. Bill followed Sven down along the path that followed the flow of water; the uneasy feeling of someone following them grew in Bill as they walked further into the darkness. He turned at every sound he heard, searching the darkness for any movement.

When Bill turned back to follow Sven, he found himself inside a great hall that rose a hundred feet above his head. The hall itself was filled with the sewage from the city above, all flowing into seven tunnels on the far side of the sewage lake. A green gas cloud hung on the lake surface, its pungent smell stinging Bill's nose. A slippery path covered in green slime lead around the edge of the lake, stopping halfway. Three small boats were tied to wooden poles rising from the stagnant water. Sven was already halfway to the boats when Bill set out after him. Just as he caught up with him, he heard a splash coming from behind. Bill turned to see the last of a tail disappear into the sewage.

"Sven, what was that?" Sven was untying one of the small boats from its mooring.

"Come on. Get in before it comes to the surface again. We need to get to the other side of the lake and into the middle tunnel." Bill stared at Sven in disbelief. Surely he wasn't serious. Bill jumped into the boat and grabbed one of the oars and began rowing.

"Easy, we need to be quiet. Leuchter can't see. When the Elders put him down here to protect the city from attack from the sea, they blinded him in order to trick people into thinking that they could sneak past him. When they blinded the hydra, they cast a spell on his hearing and his sense of smell to make up for the loss of sight." Bill pulled back slowly on his oar trying to be quiet and to cause as few ripples as possible. Slowly they proceeded across the lake of sewage, Bill almost forgetting to breathe along the way.

Bill looked back at Sven, but his focus was drawn towards the two heads moving slowly towards them. Bill's mouth fell open and before he could force the words out. Sven had sprung into action. Releasing two arrows from his bow, Sven turned and yelled. "Row as fast as you can..."

Bill pulled on his oar with all his might. He could hear Sven releasing arrow after arrow from his bow, and then it stopped as quickly as it had begun. The small boat jerked to a halt at the mouth of the tunnels. Bill jumped onto the shore and ran for the middle one. Silence followed him. Dropping to the ground, his heart beating faster than it had ever done before, he turned to see Sven locked in combat with the hydra. Sven fought for his life, his bow had been knocked from his hand and lay out of reach. Pulling himself to his feet, Bill charged down on Leuchter.

As Bill drew closer he saw for the first time how enormous Leuchter was. Its blue scales reflecting the green colour of the sewage, both heads snapping at Sven's every move, hot vents of green gas blowing from its four nostrils. Drawing his sword, Bill let out a fearsome roar to draw the attention of Leuchter to him away from Sven. Leuchter raised its left head and stared eyeless towards Bill. Its nostrils flared, sniffing for his scent while the right head continued to attack Sven.

Bill raised his sword over his head and brought it crashing back down; slicing Leuchter's toes clean from its foot. Raising its heads to the caverns top, it let out a dull roar of pain engulfing Bill and Sven's senses, stunning them where they stood. And then with all its might, Leuchter struck out at Bill knocking him to the ground. Bill watched as Leuchter dragged the rest of its enormous body onto the wharf, noticing the sewage level dropping several feet as Leuchter stepped out.

It now stood twice its size, its tail reaching halfway across the lake, powerful and whip like. Bill scrambled for his sword, just as Leuchter's tail swept him into the lake, filling his mouth with the green murky sewage. Pushing himself back towards the surface he saw Sven being picked up by the foot and tossed from mouth to mouth like an old ball. Bill began to thrash about in the water, hoping this would encourage Leuchter to drop Sven and attack him once more.

He began to move back in the direction of the wharf and to his sword, kicking his legs and splashing his arms about. Leuchter still played with Sven despite Bill's efforts to draw his fury down on him. Floating across the surface of the lake, Leuchter's tail stalked Bill, only pausing as Bill pulled himself from the sewage. Bill's sword lay a foot away from him.

Walking slowly across to where they lay, Bill flicked his sword up with his foot, grabbing it in mid air. He spun around and cut off part of Leuchter's tail. Dropping Sven, Leuchter now turned to where Bill was. His wounded tail lay in a pool of black blood. Bill stood firm waiting for the attack, sword gripped with all his might, summoning all his courage. Leuchter flicked his blood drenched tail, Bill drew his sword into the attack stance he had practiced so many times, and waited. The cavern filled with the mighty roar of Leuchter, as it turned back towards the green sewage disappearing back into the blackness of Thornburg's underworld. Bill looked towards Sven to see him brushing himself down.

"You truly are a Keeper Bill Brickton, and I am forever at your service." Bill stared at Sven, not sure of what to say. Just glad to be alive, he nodded and smiled. "Come on then young Brickton, our quest has just started." Bill was glad that they had finally emerged from the sewer and had started to follow the streets leading back to the ships.

"I guess its time to get on board and take that journey, but you are going to have to tell me why that Witch Hunter is after you, once we're on the Lucipher." Sven didn't answer and Bill said nothing else.

The Lucipher soon came into view but now it stood differently on the water. Some of its sails had dropped into position and the deck was a hive of activity, its crew working franticly to prepare her for the voyage. Bill quickened his pace along the docks, he knew that Argyle could be on the ship and he had no idea what his fate was to be. As he drew closer to the ship's gangplank, two black horses drawing a large coach thundered past them, knocking them into barrels lying on the dock side. Picking himself up, Bill saw that Sven had already brushed himself down and was climbing up the mooring ropes. Bill's attention however was drawn to the coach. Scaripdemus stepped down from the carriage leading a man in manacles and chains, whom Bill instantly recognised as Argyle. He watched as his uncle was led onto the ship and out of sight. Turning to see if Sven had seen what happened, he saw Sven slip on board and out of sight.

Gripping the rope, Bill began to shimmy up towards the deck. The rope was wet and slippy however, making it hard for him to move swiftly. Then as he neared the top, it came loose and he found himself crashing towards the cold water below. The water was colder than Bill had expected, his body becoming rigid as he splashed into the bay. Forcing his body to react, he pushed off the wooden legs of the dock and back to the surface, gasping to catch his breath. He watched the anchor chain begin to rise from the depths, the links covered in green slime. Swimming towards it, he grabbed the first link that came into reach and hung on till it reached the top. He heard the chain click into its locked position, and from below he heard the sound of portholes opening along the ships side, each one producing a long oar. Now he just had to wait for his chance to slip aboard.

The distant sound of witch hunters chasing down a witch drifted onto the deck of the Lucipher.

"That's it old Theobald, you catch that heretic and then you can call over here to your favourite ship." A tall man stood looking out over the small houses on the dockside, the ends of his knee length pants dancing on the light breeze blowing across the ship's deck. He tossed his cutlass in his hand, handle to blade, blade to handle, always keeping his hand to the inside where the blade was dull and not sharp.

"Come on you dogs, get this ship into shape, we set sail before night. Look lively ye vermin pups, pull them sails and check 'em for holes or rips." His gruff voice matched his rough exterior, his half jacket stained with stories of a thousand boarding's, its colour faded and ripped away. His beard hung far below his chin and led many a man to a broken jaw or a lost tooth. His head was as bare as the day he entered into the world, with a third eye tattooed at the back of his skull for company. Watching his men prepare the ship for the voyage, Guts McCracken had his attention drawn out over the city to a shaft of light shooting into the sky near the distant mountains.

"Make lively lads, the package is on the way back to us. Get them sails ready for work. Greedshank get them slaves to the oars and be ready with the drum..." McCracken watched as a black coach thundered through the streets towards the Lucipher, foam blowing from the two warhorses pulling it.

"Get that plank into place." The gangplank slid onto the wharf and was locked into place with large brass bolts. The familiar coach stopped at the foot of the gangplank and four steps fell forward, coming to rest on the ground. As the carriage door swung open, a black boot landed on the uppermost steps and paused.

"Has the boy arrived?" Scaripdemus stood in the door of the black carriage. McCracken nodded and shifted his eyes to a darkened figure at one end of the docks. "Good, its time to bring out my bait!" Turning, he pulled on a rope and the clank of chains could be heard inside the carriage. "Come Argyle, its time the boy thinks he sees you being dragged onto my ship."

A smile ran from corner to corner on his mouth as he brought his prize catch from the darkness. Stepping out as best he could, the setting sun hit Argyle's face. Scaripdemus led him up the gangplank, onto the deck. Argyle looked down the wharf to where the figure stood watching the occupants of the carriage climb on board. He tried to yell out to warn his would be saviour but a spell had been cast to take away his voice.

The gangplank was drawn back on board, the anchor raised and the sails hoisted and slowly the Lucipher moved out into the bay. As the water steadily got deeper, the oars moved into life accompanied by the slow beating of a leather drum, stroking the water and urging the ship forward.

Bill climbed up the anchor chain towards the deck and to where he could plan his boarding with the help of a better view. He watched the crew as they went busily about their work, suffering the lash from the cat of nine tails if they slowed or didn't pull the sails high enough on command. He watched as the new arrivals disappeared down the stairs and into the belly of the ship. Bill turned to look back at his homeland and wondered if he'd ever see it again, or how long would his quest for the stolen jewels take and where was it leading him. As he watched the houses grow smaller and smaller, he saw a familiar figure step onto the wharf followed by two banners. Theobald Rheims had found them and in the same instant lost them. The witch hunter walked up the pier to where other boats were moored, Bill wondered what the hunter wanted with Sven and what he had meant by 'I know your crimes and shall help save you and return you to your people, to reunite you with your family and friends.'

As Bill watched he saw Theobald approach a sailor sitting on a small sailboat. There he paused and then after a few moments Theobald and the Angels of Mercy got aboard. Bill shifted to get a better view and as he watched, the sails rose out of the boat and grasped the wind.

"Theobald must have seen us get on the ship." Bill saw that one of the ship's portholes for the oars was empty. This might be his way into the heart of the ship and one step closer to Sven and his uncle. Shifting slowly down the chain, Bill carefully peeped into the ship's porthole. The inside of the ship lay in darkness, just a small shaft of light dividing the two halves of the room in darkness. Pulling himself into the darkened room, Bill saw a familiar face staring out of the darkness at him.

"Sven, Rheims is after us and Argyle is on..." Before he could get all the words from his mouth, Sven had clasped it shut with his hand. Pointing into the darkness, Bill saw the shape of a man moving but Sven had again disappeared leaving Bill trapped. Bill reached for the hilt of his sword, preparing for the fight. The figures stopped next to him and then collapsed to the ground.

"Quickly tie his feet and hands." Sven was already stuffing a rag into his mouth. "Pull him behind those crates there." Bill told Sven what he had seen on the wharf and how he had moments before seen Theobald Rheims board a smaller ship and set sail after the Lucipher.

"The boy was spotted on the anchor chain as we pulled it clear of the water." McCracken was standing in a small cabin below deck, two other men with him. "Should I have him brought to you my Lord?" Placing his hand nervously on his cutlass he added; "Rheims was spotted boarding a small schooner moments after we set sail." McCracken watched as the two men pointed at locations on his charts.

"No, leave the boy for now and as for the Witch Hunter, forget him, we'll lose him in the darkness." With a wave of his hand, McCracken was dismissed only to be stopped as he reached the cabin door.

"And Captain, full sail and oars till I say otherwise." Scaripdemus turned back to his charts and the conversation with his companion. "The boy is of no importance to us until we reach Zen Zarrif's stronghold in the desert, the only question is will he try to save his uncle?" Scaripdemus smiled into the shadows of the cabin. Scaripdemus watched as his companion revealed himself, stepping out of the shadows.

"He'll try, but not just for his uncle but for these as well."
McCracken watched as he held up the jewels that were presented
to the King a few days before. Smiling McCracken closed the door
behind him and headed back up on deck, where he passed the
orders to his first mate. A small grey haired man stepped up to
McCracken, his eyes searching the shadows leading down to the
captain's cabin.

"What about that shape shifter, can we trust him?" His voice full
of hate and suspicion of their passengers, gripping his cutlass he
watched McCracken's face. "Say the word and I'll splice him from
head to toe or heads to toes in his case. Scurvy dog."

"You leave that one to me and remember the boy and the gnome
are not to be touched. Now get this floating coffin moving faster,
that Witch Hunter is making me nervous." McCracken turned and
watched as the city became smaller, drifting away on the waves.
He could see Theobald Rheims crossing the water behind them,
the white sail of the schooner growing smaller and dimmer in the
fading light.

"What now?" Bill turned to Sven and spoke. "Now that we're on the
ship surely it wouldn't be long till we are discovered?"

"Nothing, we sit and wait to see where the Lucipher takes us."
Sven sat down behind some crates out of sight of anyone that could
enter the cabin. "They know we're on board so either they'll come
get us or they'll leave us be, so make yourself comfortable." Sven
patted the corn bags beside the crates, small clouds of white dust
forming over them. Bill made himself comfortable or as comfortable as he could. He knew he was in reach of the jewels but more
importantly, his uncle's freedom. Bill's thoughts were drawn back
to another problem.

"Theobald Rheims! What about him, he's already on our trail and
I saw him board a smaller ship as we sailed from the dock." Sven

had forgotten that the witch hunter had caught up with him after all these years. "Well, the Witch Hunter, what does he want with you?" Bill saw the pensive look on Sven's face and waited for his answer.

"That's a long story. It started back in 1431, in a small village near the Northern Provincial town of Wolfenbuttel. I saved a girl from being burned at the stake by Theobald. He said she was a witch, along with two other schoolgirls, but I know that not all witches are bad and she had just saved the people from the hoards of Merkluff the Goblin." Sven paused watching some clouds drifting by the small ship's porthole.

"So it all started one summer's day in July, hmmm that was a hot day!" Sven paused as footsteps passed the door of their hiding place. Bill almost forgot to breathe, when the footsteps stopped a short distance from the door. The creaking of the boat seemed to go quiet as Bill sat still on his bags of corn waiting for the moment when the door would burst open, revealing the stow-a-ways on the Lucipher. Then he noticed a shaft of light, piercing a small knothole beside him. Slowly Bill peered into the galley next to their hiding place.

Bill watched as a tall white shirted man with a belly hanging over a large fading silver buckle, took live eels from a barrel striking each eel with his wooden hand as he placed them into the bucket. Bill watched as the light from the swinging oil lamp threw shadows across his face, revealing a scar dividing his upper lip into three pieces, each one more chapped than the other. Bill never thought it could take so long to fill a bucket with eels, feeling as if it had taken a lifetime to do so. As the man turned to leave he paused, picking up his oil lamp, he looked directly at Bill's eye peering from the hole and then turned leaving the galley in darkness. Bill pulled away as his eye met that of the sailor. His heart beat faster as he imagined the sight of ten sailors come rushing into the room.

"Bill, he's gone you can relax now. They know we're here but they'll not try to capture us until we're getting off the ship." Sven's voice brought Bill back to the increasing darkness of the Lucipher and it's creaking galleys. "They have no use for us until we reach land, get some rest, I'll take first watch." Sven moved closer to the galley door.

"What about the girl in Wolfenbuttel?" Bill inquired as Sven sat down at the galley door. Sven looked across at Bill, his face starting to disappear in the darkness. Sven turned and stared at the splashes of water jumping through the ship's porthole and then rushing across the floor desperate to find a crack to slip back out to the open ocean and freedom...

Maisie's Rescue

Sven sat at the edge of the darkening cave overlooking the town of Wolfenbuttel, his eyes scanning the gothic shapes for signs of goblin standards. The sun had begun to set as the dark storm clouds gathered overhead and the first few drops of rain touched Sven's face as he turned to enter the cave. Sitting down beside his fire he thought it best not to enter into Wolfenbuttel till the next morning. He had only just escaped from the goblin mines in the frozen lands of Stanoss. His mission now was to get back to his own people in the forests of Abnos, and to help the rest of the gnomes whom he had left behind.

Watching as the sun sank behind the rising spire of the cathedral in the centre of Wolfenbuttel, Sven's thoughts drifted back to his wife Leona, who he had left behind in Stanoss. If he had been a little quicker maybe he could have saved her as well but the guards had come back earlier than normal, almost catching him entering the tunnel. He had watched as Leona was dragged back to the cells kicking and screaming, trying to catch a last look of her Sven before he escaped, leaving her at the mercy of Eagleton, King of the Goblins. He had considered returning for her and leaving his escape till the next night but the elder gnomes had told him of the risk of bringing Leona with him and this was his only chance to do it. Stoking the fire one last time, he pulled his sheepskin blanket over him and drifted into a deep sleep.

Covering over the small hole where he had lit his fire the night before, Sven set out for Wolfenbuttel, erasing all trace of his presence in the cave. If the goblins knew he was missing, then the Slannock riders would be on his trail or worse still, Sarkop the bounty hunter!

Slipping into the city before it came to life would allow him to check for goblins or the feared Slannock riders. As the sun rose over the city, the first of its citizens began to move, the streets filling as the day grew older. Sven had entered the first tavern he found near the city's market square, 'The Bleating Yew.' Some of the occupants looked as if they hadn't left the tavern in several days, possibly weeks, their eyes sunken into the back of there heads; spittle stuck to their chins, beards filled with dirt and grease from rotting food strewn about table and floor.

A large black cat was fending off two rats that had tried to steal a rotting hand from its tray, its yellow and red stained teeth ripping at their furry flesh. Sven searched the shadows for goblins, but all he could find were deep yellow suspicious eyes staring back from the shadows. Placing himself at the cleanest window the tavern had to offer, Sven watched the streets leading to the square come to life.

The cathedral cast its tall shadow across the square and surrounding buildings. The grey clouds sat above its spire, swollen with water. A vendor set up his stall in the centre of the Market Square, selling fish, lizard tongues and dragon feet. Shortly after a shop opened beside the tavern. Sven watched as the short man carried his sign out and placed it beside the now busy street, upon it the words 'Apothecary' written in gold letters. Disappearing back into the shop, the man returned with a rack of green, red and white dragons feet, for ten shekels each or four for thirty shekels. From the corner of his eye, Sven saw a wanted poster.

'All Witches and Heretics handed over or revealed to us shall yield a reward of one hundred shekels.'

Signed Erese High Priestess

Sven turned his attention to the poster that was hanging beside it.

"Public trial of Maisie DuPont, for the crime of witch craft. Followed by public burning of afore mentioned witch, at three bells in the market square."

Getting up from his window seat, Sven left the tavern and headed towards the cathedral. Rising from the ground, the cathedral with its gargoyles, sat spying on the people of Wolfenbuttel as they went about their daily chores. Its steps dropping from the entrance down to the market place, pillars rising out of the steps like teeth in a hungry animal. Shadows hiding a thousands eyes, all watching for your crimes.

At the top of the steps, a pyre stood awaiting its victims, young or old. It didn't care as long as it lit up the shadowed interior of the cathedral and cleansed you of your sins. Sven's thoughts were interrupted by a creaky voice.

"It'll be a good show today, it's Rheims and his crones doin' the burning." His voice was full of excitement. "Never fails to entertain does Rheims, aye never fails..." Sven turned to gaze up at the crooked old man standing beside him. His clothes were reeking of stale ale and vomit. He had a grey beard half eaten with fleas and his brown wooden teeth showing. Sven's stomach lurched from the smell of his breath as the old man bent down closer to Sven's face.

"I sssaid, he always givesss a good show, nevvv." A sneeze exploded into Sven's face, covering him in warm green slime. He ran for the nearest water font to wash it off, his stomach lurching from the feel of the slime slipping down his face and touching his lips.

As the afternoon wore on, a large crowd formed at the base of the steps leading to the cathedral. Several priests of mixed Orders had gathered at one side of the cathedral and were deep in prayer for the young girl's soul, hoping that they could save her from the fiery end she was headed for. Opposite the praying priests was a hay cart, where some dwarves were watching jugglers performing at the top of the steps. Sven approached the cart and was helped up by the smallest dwarf.

"Come to watch the festivities have ya? First time I've seen Rheims. He puts on a good show or so I've been told. Old Van Der Burg here has seen him few times, ain't that so?" The dwarf tugged at a slightly taller, red haired fellow standing beside him.

"Aye, I'ver err seen him before, very good he is, very..." The dwarf turned his eyes back to a juggler tossing a piglet and three knives, not bothering to finish his sentence. The smaller one flicked his blonde hair from his face and pulled Sven the rest of the way onto the cart.

"Looking forward to this one, she is a right nasty piece of work, eaten babies and was seen flying around on a broom last Monday night, she was..." The dwarf nodded his head in disapproval of her activities.

"You don't say much for a gnome do ya? Last gnome I knew talked the hind legs off old farmer Winker's mule." The dwarf tilted his head to one side and winked his eye in a joking kind of way. Sven smiled up to him, still watching to see what else was happening nearby. Sven had heard of these witch trials and knew that most of the victims said they were witches just to stop the torture caused by the Witch Hunter General, even if that meant the end of their life.

The boom of the cathedral bells suddenly interrupted Sven's thoughts. The crowds erupted into screams of excitement, drowning out the clang of the bells. Sven watched the two large wooden doors, waiting to see this terrible person, this bringer of destruction. As the last sounds of the bells died so too did the excited roars of the crowd. The King's guard struggled to hold back the crowd from the steps. Then as if an enchantress stole every voice in the city of Wolfenbuttel, silence became the unspoken ruler. Children hid behind parents, clinging to aprons, watching for the witch Maisie DuPont and her accusers to emerge from the cathedral. Sven felt the small dwarf grab his arm as the first creaks came from the opening doors.

As the doors cracked opened, the black interior of the cathedral shone out on the crowd causing them to burst into cheers at the prospect of that day's entertainment. Two priests emerged from the darkness drawing the doors in a wide arch to the open position. Their black frocks topped by a black cross embedded in white vests. When the door was opened to its full they stood in silence, heads bowed and small wooden crosses pulled close to their chests.

Silence found its way in amongst the crowd. The sound of the praying priests rolled down the steps shattering the deafening sound of silence. Then shadowy figures began emerging from the dark belly of the cathedral, their black frocks and brimmed hats concealing their identities. Some carried books of worship; others carried crosses while others carried bowls of holy water. Standing at each side of the pyre they too dropped their heads and placed their possessions close to their chests. Sven watched, as the doors remained empty filled only with darkness.

Sven waited for any sign of movement from inside, tension was building up inside him, his palms started to sweat. Sven watched the faces around him; the look of excitement creeping across them while others cried out loud, possibly friends of the alleged witch.

A low mournful chant started just inside the doors, somewhere deep inside the darkness, shadows moved. Louder and louder, the chant filtered down through the crowd, drowning out their whispers. Expectant eyes watched the entrance of the great cathedral. Two men clad in red robes stepped into the light, followed by a tall woman dressed in long flowing scarlet robes, her silver cross reflecting the few rays from the sun. As she stepped forward, the crowd burst into screams of excitement.

"This is it my little companion, the moment we've waited for." Sven was drawn back to the market square by the yelling of the dwarf. "Maisie DuPont, come on down…" Sven turned to look again at the scarlet woman. "That there is the High Priestesses Erese, she brought the witch hunters here after some of the wealthy business men lost a lot of money. They said it was magic that had brought them misfortune, brought on by a jealous person." Sven nodded pretending to agree.

"All of them said they had seen her hanging around their houses at night and they pointed the finger at her as soon as they lost their money…" The dwarf turned back and continued to scream with the crowd.

Sven looked back to the steps just in time to see, a small girl walking from the cathedral in chains, the crowd booing and hurtling rotten vegetables at her. The girl was surrounded by four tall men dressed in black frocks, their faces hidden by tall pointed hats, the brims casting long shadows down their faces. None would look at the young girl for fear of being infected by the witches curse. Sven watched as the procession slowly made its way to the pyre. The scarlet robes dancing in the gentle breeze as Erese stood and watched the young girl being tied to the stake rising from the centre of the pyre.

The young girl stood frozen as she was bound. Her light red hair clung to her face, held there by tears and small patches of dried blood. Sven's heart swelled with pity and sadness for her. He knew what she possessed was a gift and not a curse. He looked at her wondering if she really was a witch or the victim of these rich people. Either way he couldn't let them hurt her even if she was a black arts witch. Sven watched the top of the steps waiting to see Theobald Rheims emerge from the cathedral. The crowd's roars had grown to a screaming silence as they waited for the man of the hour.

The Angels of Mercy walked slowly from the cathedral, the crowd watching in awe. Their long black garments trailing along behind them, their hoods hiding their faces from view. Rheims followed slowly, reading from a black leather book, its cover filled with gold writing surrounding a white cross. His pale white skin shone in the grey sunlight. His black eyes sunken deep in their sockets, cold, unforgiving and filled with malice. The crowd remained silent as he walked across the top of the steps, his shrill voice piercing every person's courage. Placing his book on a small table at the pyre's side he raised his face towards the sky and spoke in monotone.

"Save this condemned soul from the pits of evil. Born a child, cursed by the black arts of the underworld, servant to an unholy God." His words struck fear into every heart. "Now child, do you ask for forgiveness? Is it with a pure heart or with deceitful lies?" Turning his attention to the jerking body of the small Maisie, tears flowing down her white skin and she was shaking uncontrollably.

Sven moved towards the steps, watching the burning torches and the movements of Rheims, all the while wondering how he would rescue the young Maisie DuPont from the flames. Sven's attention was drawn towards the stage and the shrill voice of Theobald Rheims.

"Well, it seems she has lost her tongue and refuses to answer." Rheims turned to Erese and spoke. "What say you High Priestesses?" Sitting back against her chair, Erese spoke softly, her voice steady and calm.

"Continue Witch Hunter Rheims, these people have gathered here for nothing less than a confession and justice." Waving her hand towards Rheims she urged him to continue. Holding his hands to his front, and then raising his black book from the table, he began to read from it.

Sven had made it halfway to the steps when he saw the answer to how he was going to save Maisie DuPont from the hands of Rheims and his Angels of Mercy. If it were magic they wanted, then magic they would have…! Sven had seen a shop just on the edge of the square early that morning, the sign at the door reading 'Apothecary' in large gold lettering. It had closed like all the other shops in the city; all the residents it seemed had turned up to watch the young girl burn.

Sven slipped down the alley next to it, hoping to find a way in. A short distance from the squares edge, Sven saw his way in, a small window had been left open. Plumes of green smoke drifting slowly out onto the street; a potion left brewing by the apothecaries for a client or perhaps himself.

The window stood at least three times Sven's height from the ground. The voice of Rheims still echoing in the background and Sven wondered how much time he had to save the girl. A rush of hot air on his neck interrupted his thoughts.

"A bit small to get in are you?" Sven turned around expecting to see a city guard or a goblin standing behind him. As he turned he saw that it was the old drunk from before.

"I can lift you up if you like, make up for the sneeze earlier!" Sven looked up at the old man and nodded.

"Ok, just to the window and then you have to go back and look as if nothing is happening." The old man nodded, answering Sven in a whisper.

"Good, here we go then, up and in." As Sven climbed in through the window, he heard the old man's voice again. "GUARD, GUARD, I've been robbed." Two city guards came running from the square and stopped right outside the window.

"There was two of them, ran down that way…" Sven watched as they ran off down the street and out of view, the old man following behind them. Sven dropped down from the shelf and looked around the shop. The plume of green smoke was coming from a beaker of boiling liquid on the shelf where he had dropped down from; a small yellow and red flame flickering under it. As he dropped onto the floor under the shelf, Sven saw a cat's empty basket. He scanned the room for the cat and finding no sign of it walked slowly toward a cupboard marked 'Potions, Agents, and Roots'.

The door gave a creek as Sven pulled it open revealing bottles of multicoloured liquids and powders on its uppermost shelves, and boxes of roots, some Sven knew and some he didn't. Running his finger across the labels, Sven read off some of the names. 'Dragons Spit'- a yellow liquid, with a pungent sulphurous smell, that hit Sven in the face as he poured it into a small bowl. 'Devil's Powder' small black granules that slowly found their way down to the bottom of the liquid, and finally, Sven took down a small bottle with a fine red powder in it. The label read 'Dragon's Breath- Beware'. He threw a pinch into his mixture and stirred it, until it began to thicken.

He poured the mixture into an empty bottle and tightened the cap. As he turned to face back towards the window he noticed how dark it had become in the last few moments and the sudden feeling of being watched from the shadows came over him. Pausing to scan the darker areas of the room, Sven caught a flash of a yellow eye under a cupboard on the far side of the shop. Moving slowly towards his escape route, he saw a large black cat creeping from underneath the cupboard.

"So you come in here, take what you want and then just leave, purrrrrrr." The cat walked slowly towards Sven. "I've seen what you mixed purrrrrrr, so leave your eight shekels and I'll let you go." Flicking its tail and stretching out, it licked its lips.

"Just the right size for an afternoon snack, for little old me. Oh, Griswald, a break from rats and mice, you've earned a nice Gnome." As it poked Sven in the tummy and said it in a very delicious sort of way.

"Mmmm not too plump but not too much bone either, a nice meal... purrrrrrr." Sven pulled his coin bag from his belt and placed the eight shekels on the ground in front of him. "Gnome, dear Gnome, I need human shekels not these small things. I'm afraid you'll have to be a tasty snack!" Bearing his pearly white teeth, he stalked towards Sven, his claws ripping into the soft earth floor of the shop.

"Wait, these shekels are those used by the humans. Watch and I'll show you…" Sven pulled a silver disc from his pocket and tossed it into the air. The cat watched as the disc rose high above the ground, his paws twitching as it rose and then Sven had his chance. Before Griswald realised what he was doing, his paws had left the ground and he sprung to catch the disc. Sven was already halfway to the window when Griswald realised what was happening. Turning as he landed, he sprung at the shelves where Sven was climbing, crashing into them as Sven pulled himself to the window ledge. Sven turned just before dropping back to the street and tipped his hat to Griswald.

"Later my friendly cat and your money is now the right size…" Sven dropped down onto the street, leaving Griswald dazed and confused with his eight shekels for lunch. The street outside was still empty and the sound of the crowd still quiet. Only the voice of Rheims could be heard. Sven checked that his bottle was still secured to his belt and once he found that it was, he set out for the cathedral.

Sven reached the edge of the square, he saw that the old drunk had returned and was standing at the bottom of the steps watching Rheims question the young girl. Looking around the steps and the edges of the cathedral, Sven searched for his way in and found it in the form of a small wooden door on the buildings side. He slid through the slit in the door and out of view.

The inside of the cathedral was illuminated by hundreds of candles, all placed around the edges. Small wooden mats were placed side by side on the floor and the altar had the only seats. The altar was raised up above the main praying level and rose almost from view only stopping to meet the ceiling of paintings and swooping gargoyles hanging from the rafters. The stairs to the belfry weaved its way to the landing just under the copper bell. Sven climbed to the top and sat just below the bell itself, watching the crowd and Rheims far below. He could see the old man staring up at the belfry, then at Rheims and then back to the belfry. Wondering who the man was, Sven watched for his opportunity to save the girl.

"Witches." The old man had climbed halfway up the steps towards Rheims and the pyre, shouting at the top of his voice. "Witches, Witches, sure aren't we all witches. Haw, what do you think?" Bending down he shoved his nose into a guard's face. The crowd were pointing and laughing at the old drunk on the steps.

"Oh, well ye can laugh." All the time he was pointing at the crowd. "You butcher, with your money, stealing an extra bull or two from farms, so you'll have more to sell than the others..."

Sven looked down at Rheims who had stopped talking, his stare fixed firmly on the old drunk, disgust dripping from his expression. Sven watched as the Angels of Mercy descended the steps leading down to the crowd and watched as the old man dodged their attempts to grab him. The crowds heckled and cheered with every evasive move the old man made, slipping just out of reach as they got close to him. The old man continued his line of accusations while being chased.

"Who was it that really stole your money, was it truly Maisie here?" He pointed back at the young girl on the stake. "Or was it your own greed that stole it and now that you have nothing, you blame it on something that no one wants to understands. Magic, the black arts or it is Devilry..." The drunk began to dance a merry dance, pretending to cast spells on the crowd and avoiding the Angels of Mercy and their attempts to catch him. The crowd gasped as the drunk spoke, whispers running rampant amongst ears and then silence as the thunderous voice of Theobald Rheims rained down on the heads of men and women alike.

"Blasphemy..." His voice sending tremors through the strongest and weakest alike. "Heresy, I command you not to listen to his words. Angels take him to the Room of Repent." As the Angels of Mercy closed in on the old man, Sven knew that he wouldn't get a better chance than this to rescue the girl from the witch hunter. Taking the bottle from his belt he threw himself out of the window and threw the bottle at the torches at the base of the pyre.

"Look a witch flying from the cathedral!" The voice of a woman drowned out the shouts of the crowd, drawing Rheims away from the pursuit and to Sven falling towards the ground. A bright flash blinded Rheims, causing him to cover his eyes and stumble down the top two steps. The crowd began to panic, running from the edge of the steps, cutting the city's guards off from the commotion. Rheims regained his balance just in time to see Sven hover over the young girls head.

"What magic is this? Who are you?" Rheims voice trembled as the words spilled out. Grasping his war hammer in his hand, he called his Angels of Mercy to his side. Sven remained silent and watched as the old man fell to his knees behind Rheims watching what was happening, then Sven spoke.

"Silence." His voice swallowing the crowds sounds of panic. "Old man, release the girl." Sven looked down at the old man as he picked himself up from the ground and walked to the pyre to untie the girl. His hands had just touched the ropes binding her when Rheims spoke in a commanding voice.

"Do not release that witch or you too shall feel the cleansing touch of holy flames upon your skin." The old man stopped and looked up at Sven and winked.

"Oh, Theobald I don't think I'll feel the flames." The man tugged at his hair and it came away in his hand revealing a smoothly shaven head. Sven watched to see how Rheims would react. "Don't you recognize me?" The old man dropped his tattered coat to the ground revealing two swords at his side.

"You..." A look of disbelief fell on Rheims' face. But I burned you in Stanoss last year." Rheims mouth dropped as he saw the man now revealed in front of him. "How did you survive the flames?" Theobald drew up his hammer to his chest, readying himself for the attack.

"The next time you try to burn Miguel Hernandez Juan Raul Pablo Carlos Alejandro Fernando Pedro De La Cruz, I suggest you stay till the fire burns out." De La Cruz flicked his knife cutting through the rope holding Maisie. Miguel guided Maisie back towards the cathedral door.

"Don't be afraid we're here to help you." Miguel looked up at Sven. "What now gnome?" Sven returned Miguel's look. "Take the girl out of here and shouuuu!" Sven felt his body jerk and before he realised what was happening, he felt the rope around his waist give away. Miguel watched as Sven fell towards the ground.

"Miguel, look out!" Rheims had taken Sven's momentary distraction to attack. Turning Miguel rolled to avoid the large silver war hammer cutting through the air. Drawing both swords, Miguel knocked away a devastating strike from the hammer. Rheims was unbalanced as Miguel returned his attack, both blades aimed squarely at his upper body. The crowd roared as the clang of metal on metal echoed around the square, both opponents equally matched. Rheims blocked and launched another blow at Miguel, finding his target. The latter felt the full force of the hammer as it lifted him from the ground throwing him into the cathedral.

The Angels of Mercy gave Sven little time to feel the pain of his fall, attacking before he hit the ground. Grabbing a torch from its holder, Sven parried their attack and tossed the flaming torch at them. They recoiled, terrified of the flames, giving Sven a chance to draw his sword. Running to the entrance of the cathedral, Sven saw Miguel locked in a deadly dance of death with Rheims.

Turning to face his own adversaries, he pulled a small silver sphere from his pocket and smashed it on the ground in front of him. Smoke billowed from the sphere, giving Sven a chance to retreat inside and to take Maisie to safety. Pulling the doors closed as he entered the cathedral, Sven saw Maisie running towards the altar, followed closely by Erese. Erese had a golden dagger drawn and had Maisie pinned on the ground in front of the altar. A smile grew upon her face as the first tears broke from Maisie's eyes.

"Now witch where's your coven to save you?" Raising the dagger up over her head, she looked into Maisie's eyes and spoke in a soft voice. "Are you or have you ever practised witchcraft?" Maisie stuttered and choked up on her emotion, answering with one word.

"NO." A look of disgust spread across Erese's face. Miguel was cornered by Rheims as his oversized hammer had smashed one of Miguel's swords, the other lost to a blow from the witch hunter's boot.

"Nowhere to run, it seems and this time I'll finish the job myself!" Miguel watched as the hammer was raised high over both their heads. He kicked out, knocking Rheims back and catching his hammer between two beams of broken wood. Side stepping Rheims, Miguel ran towards the altar, meeting Sven halfway.

"What kept you Gnome?" Miguel smiled as they ran up the isle. Throwing his dagger, Miguel caught the priestesses in the forearm forcing her to drop her own weapon. "No witch today I'm afraid." Miguel grabbed Maisie from the altar and made for a small wooden door to the side. Sven turned in time to see Rheims thundering down through the pews, his hammer at the ready. A sudden burst of sunlight drew his attention to the main doors, two tall figures casting long black shadows into the stream of light, the Angels of Mercy were back to join Rheims in his fight.

"Not this time Witch Hunter, but we'll meet again that I'm sure of. Remember my name Witch Hunter, Sven Thorsen." Sven turned and made his way to the side entrance. Rheims' voice rang through the cathedral, stopping Sven at the door.

"Gnome I already seek you, I've seen your dear wife..." A cold chill ran the length of Sven's body as the name of his wife shot into his ears. "Yes, to see Leona. The goblins want you back, and when I return you I get a new servant, the lovely Leona." Sven forced himself not to return to finish his fight, he knew he must find help and return to rescue Leona and the other gnomes in the goblin mines. Rheims let out a shrill laugh as he saw the look of despair and dread on Sven's face.

"Rheims, I'm on my way back to the mines to liberate my fellow Gnomes from Evermore and those you have taken from other parts of Crintia. Be warned your day will come and along with an end to your one God. Viva la Gnome Resistance... Wahoooo!!!"

A surge of fury ran through Rheims's body as Sven's words rang out in the cathedral. Pulling himself from the doorway, Sven turned to see Miguel beckon him back towards the square and the crowd that was there. Turning to face Rheims would be a mistake and now that three of them stood before him, Sven knew he'd be back in the mines within two days if he did stand and fight. Sven ran down the small alley leading to Miguel and Maisie.

"We can lose them in the square among the crowds and then I'll explain who I am!" Sven followed after Maisie disappearing into the crowd. Sven stopped at a voice calling to him.

"Good show Gnome, when's the rematch?" The tall dwarf clapped as Sven turned to him. Smiling, Sven tossed him a smile and disappeared into the crowd after his new companions.

Sven felt as if they had been running for the rest of that day. It was close to sunset when Miguel stopped and dropped to the ground; gasping for breath he turned to Sven and in between gasps spoke.

"So gnome, what's your name?" Sven had sat down at the first tree trunk he could find, resting his head on the hilt of his sword.

"Sven Thorsen, a free gnome on a quest to free his people from the mines in Stanoss to the north. Who is the brave man to which I owe thanks for helping me save this young girl?" Maisie was lying flat on her back, her body fighting to catch up with her breath.

"Allow me to properly introduce myself. I am Miguel Hernandez Juan Raul Pablo Carlos Alejandro Fernando Pedro De La Cruz, grand Wizard and Keeper of Secrets. But most importantly, uncle to this young maiden, whom you saved today." Miguel pointed at Maisie who was now busy gathering sticks from underneath the tree where Sven was seated. Turning, she smiled at Sven and lipped the words thank you.

"They cut part of her tongue out at the last session of torture and it still hasn't healed. So Sven, where is your next stop?" Miguel looked deep into Sven's eyes wondering at the movements of his thoughts. Sven looked as Maisie moved her lips and then from the air produced a small flame and placed it in the centre of the sticks. As the flames took hold of them, Sven began to speak.

"I need to find some of my people who have escaped the mines of the goblins and try to unite them and free the rest of our people..." Sven was suddenly drawn back to the darkness of the ship's interior and the now familiar voice of Bill.

"Sven, the ship has stopped." Sven listened as the anchor crashed into the sea and down to the darkest depths.

"Listen, sounds as if another ship is along side us, do you hear it?" The small amount of moonlight that had shone in the ship's porthole was now shadowed, leaving Bill and Sven in darkness...

Messengers

"Bill, a griffon has returned with word from Sven on Watu." Sorden burst into the room interrupting Bill and Tilterman. Bill rose to his feet beckoning Tilterman to follow him. "He's in the stable resting, refuses to give the message to anyone but you." They hurried down the dimly light corridor that led to the kitchen, stopping at a picture of an empty room. Bill pulled on a string hanging from the curtains in the picture and watched as it moved up towards the ceiling, revealing a small arch behind it. Walking through the arch, he stepped into a large stable filled with griffons and one large sleeping dragon. Its scales rose and fell in time to Bill's own breathing and as he moved closer, the dragon opened one of its large black eyes.

"Try harder next time Bill, I may be old but my hearing is still good!" Snorting, a cloud of white smoke rolled from his nostrils as he looked at Bill. Patting him on the nose, Bill smiled and hurried to the new griffon. Rising from his food Ergwen turned and upon seeing Bill, bowed low to the stable floor and spoke.

"I am Ergwen of Glen Corrib, friend to the one you know as Sven Thorsen. I have a message for you." Ergwen raised his claw from the floor revealing a small leather roll. Bill bent down and untying the roll asked Ergwen where he had seen Sven last.

"On the hidden lake, where the creature Terock sleeps." Bill turned and walked back towards the entrance to the stable. Unfolding the message from Sven, Bill crossed his fingers in the hope of good news.

"*Terock is awake and I found disturbing evidence that suggests power of a darker nature is among us. Young girl found. Indications lead me to believe that the incantation for flight was used near Terock cave. Proceeding to Watu with utmost urgency.*

Sven.

Bill looked at Tilterman and then at the note he held in his hand. Folding it back to its original shape, he turned to face Tilterman.

"Assemble three of the fastest messengers we have. Tell them they must travel light and with the stealth of Rennick warriors. Hurry, there's no time to waste." Tilterman ran from the stable and up to the common room where the off duty gnomes were resting or playing Slayer. Tilterman approached three young gnomes sitting at a table. As he drew closer, the taller looking of them turned, his face twisted with a disapproving look. Tipping his blue hat, he turned back to the table and grinned.

"Well, that's it lads, our weekend is finished." He pointed at Tilterman and spoke. "The bearer of work and the only gnome who gets unhappy when you're sitting around when off-duty." Laughing, he stood up to let Tilterman closer to the table. Tilterman returned his jest and then broke the bad news.

"Oh you know I like to see you sitting around doing nothing. But today I am the bearer of bad news and you three have a job to do. Come on, Bill wants to see you." Quickly the three gnomes followed after Tilterman, as he led the party into the room where Bill was writing letters. As they entered, he looked up and waved them into the room hurriedly.

"Jay, I'm sending you north to the frozen lands of Stanoss. There you're to look for Zvanick. Give him this and tell him to proceed to Abnos as soon as possible. When you reach the Frozen Toe tavern, ask for Warvanski and ask him to take you to Zvanick. Leave at once and stay in the shadows. Talk to no one!" Jay turned and left the room. Picking up the second of the three letters on his desk, Bill handed it to the next gnome, the smallest of the three.

"Murphy never before have you carried such an important message. It will take all your cunning and skill to get it to the person its destined for, Wang Wu in the forest of Abnos. Tell him to expect the Order within twenty-four hours. Again, keep to the shadows and allow no one to intercept this message." Murphy stared at Bill for a moment and then turned and left the room in silence.

Andy was the last messenger in the room, old and more cunning than any fox in the land. It was said of Andy that he taught the fox how to be cunning and sly. Bill looked at him and handed him the last letter.

"Andy old friend, you have the hardest of all to deliver. You must head to Buttelburg and find the ever-youthful Maisie DuPont. When you hand her this letter, you must stay and accompany her to Abnos." Andy nodded and left the room; Bill turned and stared out the only window in the room, catching a fleeting glimpse of Murphy as he left Dylan Drive.

"Good speed and may the roads be kind." Tilterman wondered at these words but felt it better to let Bill break the silence. Bill surveyed a map of the world hanging on the wall, tracing a line from Dylan Drive to the city of Moucha. Tilterman watched as he stopped in several other cities along the route, Tidalburg, Brenninburg and Patlow, a small city near Moucha.

"Tilterman, pack a bag, we're going to Moucha. I want to know if it is Ehmunnra who is behind this or if there's someone else involved, we...." The doors into the room swung open as Sorden came running in.

"Another message from Sven, Morgab said to bring it to you." Sorden held out the letter while resting his other hand on the door, gasping for breath. Bill unrolled the letter and read its contents.

Island of Watu has been destroyed and the Elders are dead. I've found one alive but died shortly after we found him. This is what he told me: "A demon destroyed the island at the command of Cundra, they were looking for the Book of Demons." This has led me to only one conclusion and that is Ehmunnra is back. Leaving for Abnos and will see you there. In the meantime if you need to contact me, send Morgab. I am travelling with Drego and some of the Forest Elves. They are using the old paths.

See you in Abnos
Sven

Bill pondered the letter and then handed it to Tilterman. Sorden watched as both Bill and Tilterman stood in silence. Bill paced up and down wondering about his next move. If it was Cundra that had destroyed the island and he was indeed looking for the Book of Demons, then it meant only one thing.

"Tilterman, what moons have we?" Bill turned and faced Tilterman.

"It's coming to the third cycle tonight, the new cycle starts on Severn's day, next week." Bill fingered his calendar and began to pace the room again. Tilterman watched wondering what it was that had brought the quizzical look to his face.

"Tilterman, we leave now for Moucha." Tilterman left the room and headed for their bags. "Sorden, send Morgab back to Sven with this note, then gather up the best scouts you have and send them ahead to Abnos without delay." Bill wandered up to the front door and took his long black coat from the dusty rams head, which acted as a coat hanger, thanking it as he did so. Standing in the front door he looked out towards the Castroknoptra Mountains. "Well if it's a fight you want Cundra, then a fight you'll have." With Tilterman close on his heels, they left the familiar surroundings of Dylan Drive.

Murphy set out from Dylan Drive with the minimum of equipment, patting Nugent on the head as he passed him by. Leaving the house behind, Murphy decided to travel courier express to Luthenburg and from there to Abnos on a Grenoc train. The Dead Mans Express Company, as good as any to travel by. Murphy attached a tag to his small rucksack with the address of his destination, Number Twelve, The Spit 'n' Nail Tavern, Top Street, Luthenburg, scrawled across it. He climbed into his rucksack and pulled the zip closed. Murphy waited for a company van to pull up outside the office and collect their deliveries and felt himself being lifted from the floor. Pulling the zip of his bag open a tiny bit he saw the rear door of a white van open and then felt a puff of air escape as he was flung into the van.

"Got a package here for Number Twelve, Spit 'n' Nail tavern, sign here, please." A small sickly looking woman accepted the package and watched as the deliveryman tossed it behind her desk with a loud thud.

"Wart, Wart, where are you boy? If you're asleep you'll feel my boot, boy!" The sickly looking woman screamed and screamed until a scrawny looking child emerged from the kitchen, through a small cat flap in the door. His shirt was black and ripped; his skin covered in mud and dried bits of straw.

"Ere, take this bag to Number Twelve and then finish cleaning out the toilet hole." The boy tried to pick up the bag but failed.

Dragging the bag up to two flights of stairs was no easy task and the young boy sat on the only chair in the room. As he sat staring at the bag, he saw it give a twitch. Jumping to his feet, the boy watched as the bag moved again. Suddenly from the top of the bag, a small hand appeared and began to undo the straps and buckles. The boy let out a high-pitched scream and ran down the stairs, leaving the hand to work on the bag.

Pulling himself from the bag, Murphy found himself in a small damp smelling hallway. A single light illuminated the three doors and the top of the stair well. Folding away the top of the bag, he slung it across his shoulder and opened the door of his room. The shutters on the window were closed and the only light in the room came through a small crack in the shutters. Murphy threw his bag onto the bed and exited the room. At the bottom of the stairs, he found himself in a small common room, where several other guests sat around a small burning fire. As he stepped off the last step, a voice bellowed in his ear.

"You're from Number Twelve then?" Murphy turned to see the old woman peering from behind her desk. "Come 'ere and sign in." Murphy walked over to the desk and signed the tattered book on the desk.

"The bar is there. Breakfast, well git it yerself in the morning. Any questions, no, good." Slamming the book closed, the old woman rose an inch from her seat and walked off muttering something about gnomes not coming like normal folk. Murphy turned and walked toward the bar, looking at his fellow lodgers as he passed. Sitting in a corner where the entire common room was in view, Murphy sat back and relaxed into a doze.

The smell of a freshly cooked rabbit caused Murphy to open his eyes just in time to see his dinner land on the table in front of him. His ale had gone flat and so he called for another jug and tucked into his dinner. The food was about the only thing that wasn't watching him in the tavern but one pair of eyes stood out from the crowd. Murphy had seen the stranger watching him from the darkest corner of the common room. His beady eyes staring from the darkness, occasionally a hand would sneak forward and drag his jug of ale to the shadows. Murphy sank the last of his ale and headed off to his room watching the stranger get up from his table and follow him as he ascended the stairs. Murphy stood on his landing and watched as the stranger proceeded to the next floor, his footsteps grew fainter and the bang of a closing door returned the stairs to silence.

His room was in darkness when he opened the door, only the light from the hallway breaking the blackness of night. Pulling on the chain, the light clicked on, showing the scarcity of his room. The bed was wooden; one of its legs replaced with copies of 'Troll Hunter' and beside it was an old rickety chair, its legs splintered. Murphy closed the door and placed the chair against the handle to slow would be intruders. Lying on the bed, Murphy thought it best to remain awake for the remainder of the night. His eyes were heavy; sleep catching hold at every sign of weakness and eventually getting the upper hand despite Murphy's best efforts to stay awake.

The stranger from the common room peered through a small knothole in the ceiling while Murphy slept. He unwound a small piece of string down towards Murphy's mouth. A small blue bottle sat on the floor of his room; the label on the bottle had only two words upon it, 'Reaper's Poison'. As the string touched Murphy's mouth, the stranger picked up the bottle and poured small drops down along it. As the first drops touched Murphy's mouth, his tongue licked his lips, drawing the poison inside, its recipient unaware of what he had just swallowed...

Jay waited for Murphy to clear the end of Dylan Drive before setting out on his own task. Putting his rucksack on his back, he turned and waved good-bye to Nugent who was sitting on the lawn. His route was to be simple and straight to Stanoss, on the old steamers of the river Logy. He'd take one of the steamers to Stanoss and from there to the Frozen Toe. Walking along the docks in Wobblington could be dangerous for a gnome. Stories of gnomes slipping down to get fresh seafood and not returning for six months were common. Each story was the same, how they had been hit on the head and then woken up on a ship bound for the far reaches of nowhere.

Jay stepped onto the wharf, relieved to see that no tall ships were moored. Two steamers sat tied to the docks, both captains sitting on deck waiting for a new customer. Jay looked at the first steamer and its battered exterior. Its name scrawled across its front, 'The Musty Ghost', paint chipping from its side and floating on a small but noticeable patch of black oil. Jay looked at the other steamer, its new paint shining proudly in the sun and its name standing out in tall bright colours, 'The Golden Rainbow'.

"How much to Stanoss?" Jay looked up at the captain of the Musty Ghost and inquired the price.

"Ha, haaa MacDuff, there yea are wee your new paint and fancy steamer and I'm still getting more passengers. Whoooo hoooo..." Turning back to face Jay, the captain bent down and whispered in Jay's ear, "For you my little friend, half price, I haven't had a passenger in three weeks cause of his painted steamer... It takes two days to get to Stanoss, some of the river is frozen pretty good, so you may have to walk a few miles, you won't mind that will you?" Jay smiled and tossed his bag on board.

"No I won't, but make sure it takes no longer. I'll stay below deck and you can call me when you can't go any further." Jay had noticed a man watching him from the wharf.

"Better get going then, full steam ahead." Jay felt the steamer pull away from the dock, slowly creaking and hissing its way along. Jay watched as the stranger stepped on board the Golden Rainbow and point in their direction. The Rainbow began to pull away from the wharf and slowly make its way along behind them.

"Young gnome, this is as far as I can go." The captain stood at the top of the steps leading below deck. Jay walked slowly up to the deck allowing his eyes to adjust to the daylight.

"The Rainbow where is it?" Jay looked up and down the frozen river but could see no sign of the steamer.

"Old MacDuff pulled into port in Ivanoffski, weather was bad." Jay turned to see where they had landed. He could see smoke rising from a building a short distance from where he was. Climbing off the steamer he turned and tossed the captain payment for his voyage and walked towards the building. A small sign covered in white frost sat on the bank; only part of the towns name was visible. Jay rubbed his sleeve along the length of the sign revealing its name, 'Straffennoss'. Looking around he saw another sign pointing up river, on it his destination, Stanoss, twenty miles.

The Frozen Toe stood at the edge of the little town, its steps white and hard from the winter's frost. Entering after a few minutes, Jay found himself in the warmth of a large open fire. Hanging over it was a deer's head, someone's prize trophy, and its antlers stretching the full width of the tavern. Jay felt his beard begin to thaw in the heat. A tall man dressed in a shirt stood behind the wooden counter situated under the deer's head.

"What will it be, Sir?" Jay looked up at his host.

"Some vodka and a warm room for the night." The man nodded and disappeared under the counter. When he popped back up he was holding a large bottle and a very small glass, half filled with the clear liquid.

"A gnome size room or something bigger? We have rooms for Gnomes to Halflings to Dwarfs and then for the bigger ones that come in here."

"A gnome sized room will do and can you tell Warvanski that I wish to see him." The innkeeper nodded and watched as Jay swallowed the vodka and filled a second for him. The innkeeper placed a metallic key on the counter and replaced the bottle underneath. Jay picked up his key and bid the man good night and left for his room.

"A shekel for an old and very cold beggar Sir?" An old man dressed in rags was standing just inside the tavern door. Jay fumbled in his pocket looking for a single shekel for him, when from the corner of his eye he saw the flash of cold steel. Dropping his bag, he reached for his sword…

Andy watched as Jay pulled the gate closed behind him. Walking along the front of the house he turned and walked through the gates leading to the backyard and the river Logy. Sorden was waiting on the small wharf with a canoe.

"Are you sure this is the best way to get to the train station?" Sorden began to untie the rope as Andy stepped into the small canoe.

"Won't make a difference which way I go. If the house is being watched well, then you can be sure the river being watched also!" Andy pushed away from the wharf and nodded goodbye to Sorden. The train station wasn't far and it wouldn't take long for Andy to find out if he's been followed or not.

The whistle of a train blasted into the morning sky, shattering the bit of peace on the river. Andy watched the banks, checking to see if he was being followed. Turning for the bank at the rear of the train station, Andy saw three other gnomes walking towards the station. Casting a small enchantment, Andy watched as the canoe returned back up the river towards Ten Dylan Drive. The Wobblington Express left in a few minutes just giving Andy time to get his ticket and slip on board.

Sitting by the platform was the Wobblington Express, a soft plume of steam drifting from its stack. Its chrome engine shining from beneath its black body. Seventeen carriages sat behind patiently waiting to start their journey each one shining blue with chrome handles glistening in the sun. Andy scanned the platform for the other gnomes he had seen on the way into the station. Deciding it was time for lunch, Andy walked along the platform looking for the dining car.

"Andy Rentford, how are you my young fellow?" Andy turned around to find a member of the Gnome High Council staring into his face. Bowing his head, Andy stepped back to allow him enter the train first.

"Fine, thank you for asking, and how does this most excellent of days find you?" Andy gave an insincere smile. Paddy Rinehart was a long time member of the Council and good friend to Bill. Andy always thought that he was sneaky and untrustworthy. Watching as Paddy stepped onto the train; Andy turned and held out his hand to the gnomes with Paddy indicating that they should enter the train. Andy smiled as his offer was declined. Nodding to them, Andy stepped onto the train and followed Paddy to his seat in the dining car.

"So Andy, how is Bill and all at Number Ten? I hope we find them all well." Paddy looked up from his menu waiting for Andy's answer. Before Andy had the chance to speak, Paddy had begun again. "I heard he had trouble with a dragon a few days ago, everything ok with that, not too much of a problem was it?"

"No, no problems at all, it was belong to some of the Swaylian Royal Family. They helped to capture it and took it back with them." Before Andy could continue, Paddy stopped him.

"And Bill was ok, nothing different or unusual about him?" Andy watched as Paddy questioned him about Bill's health and began to wonder what lay behind it. "When he came back he didn't seem different or he hadn't changed in any way?"

"No, Bill left as Bill and returned as Bill. Why do you ask?" Paddy's mood quickly changed, cutting into Andy's very soul with a scornful look.

"There is no reason other than I am concerned, a lot of rumours are going around about people returning differently and the Chimera being awake, that is my only concern and you should not question a member of the High Council." Andy bowed his head and waited for Paddy to continue his scorning. "Now, now there is no need to look for pardon. Times are tense; one can be forgiven for being suspicious. Now lets order some ale and lots of food. Waiter."

The Express wound its way deep into the darkening countryside. Andy sat looking out the window at the country passing by. It would take another few hours to reach Buttelburg and the home of Maisie DuPont.

"So, you and the other gnomes are out to find Zvanick, Wang Wu and you're going to Buttelburg to find the charming Maisie DuPont. Bill must be worried about something?" Andy was now even more suspicious of Paddy, no one outside Dylan Drive knew of his mission or that of the other messengers that had left.

"It's true I'm off to Buttelburg to see my good friend Maisie, but that's only because I have a few days off. Bill is at Dylan Drive but I haven't heard of anyone going to gather the Order together. Where did you get that information from?" Andy watched as Paddy struggled to come up with a proper answer.

"It's just rumours then, nothing to it. So Bill is satisfied that everything is ok?"

"Yes, is there a reason to be worried? After all rumours are just rumours!" Andy watched as Paddy called to one of the other gnomes sitting close by. A whispered conversation followed and then the gnome left the carriage.

"Now Andy, you can tell me what's really going on. I know Bill has left for Moucha and Sven is travelling with Drego." Paddy leaned across the table and whispered to Andy. "And the book is missing or is that just a rumour as well?" Andy looked at him in amazement and wondered where he obtained this knowledge.

"How do you know this?" Andy watched as Paddy checked the carriage for unwanted ears.

"Look, Andy I'm a member of the High Council. There is no reason for you to be suspicious of me, what goes on with the Keeper is well known to the Council. You can share your information with me and it shall remain safe." Andy decided it was time to make his excuses and return to his compartment.

"If you will excuse me I need to get some rest, I've had a long day and tomorrow will be much longer. Good afternoon Paddy and I'm sure I'll see you in the morning." Bowing, Andy headed towards the sleeping compartments. How did Paddy know so much about the goings on in Dylan Drive? Andy lay on the bed in the compartment running over the conversation he had had with Paddy, and what was his interest in the information he had in his letter for Maisie? Andy looked up as the sound of a knock came upon his door.

"Yes, who is it?" No answer came. Andy stood up and approached the sliding door, pushing it to one side. When he had opened it fully, he could see no one in the passageway or near his door. As he turned, he felt a hand grab him from behind.

"No, point in struggling little fellow." Andy struggled but found it to be of no use against the strength of his would be attacker. "Now listen, all I want is the letter you're carrying, give me that and you won't be hurt." Andy reached into his pocket and pulled out a slip of folded paper.

"Here take it." Dropping it to the ground, Andy waited for the grip on his neck to loosen.

"Now, you didn't think I was going to let go once I had what I wanted, did you?" The silence of the passageway was broken by the noise of the trees passing outside the carriage as Andy's attacker opened the carriage door. The rocking of the carriages on the tracks made a tramping noise as the metal wheels passed over the joining. Andy found himself staring out the carriage door.

"Last stop, little gnome, and say hello to the trees for me." Andy felt himself being thrown from the train, watching as the trees sailed past. The thud of his body hitting the ground was drowned out as the train rolled passed in the darkness. Andy was rolling head first down the embankment that ran along the trackside. Looking up he watched as the train disappeared into the darkness and the blackness of unconsciousness took hold....

Zarrif Industries

Sven sat and watched as the plumes of white smoke rose higher and higher into the darkening afternoon sky. His search of the island had uncovered nothing, leading him to believe that whatever Cundra had been looking for, he had found and taken it with him. The fires had destroyed all of the buildings, leaving nothing only burnt shells, blackened and grey from the unrelenting flames. Drego and the other Elves were still searching through the rubble and smouldering wooden huts scattered about the island. Sven watched as Drego turned up bits of blackened wood and stone hoping to reveal any clues. The temple on the island was still burning as Sven walked back towards its arched entrance, the only bit still intact.

Sven saw a small white piece of parchment, its edges scorched from the heat of its burning surroundings. Bending down, Sven picked it up and looked in amazement at the symbol on the top of it. It was a symbol he had seen several times in his life and one that he lived by. The symbol was made up of two crossed spanners on a red pointed hat with the words 'Gnomes Forever'. But why would a symbol of the High Council of Gnomes be here? Sven looked at it, turning it over to look at the back. He could just make out some writing on it:

"Flight and the everlasting life,
Power to create life from death
And to"

He pulled the parchment he had found at the lake from his pocket and held them close together, making an almost full sentence.

"Ascend from the depths of hell,
And give the power of flight and
The everlasting life, power to create life.
From death and to..."

He stared at the parchment in his hands wondering what it all meant, was this what Cundra had sought?

"Sven, its Morgab, he's back from his errand." Sven's thoughts were interrupted by Drego's voice and then by the beating of Morgab's wings. Sven looked up as Morgab hovered overhead and then touched down gently beside him. Folding up the pieces of parchment, Sven moved towards Morgab.

"Have you word from Bill?" Morgab held out his foot and his message from Bill. Sven untied the leather tube and emptied its contents into his hand and then unfolding it to reveal its contents.

Sven, I am proceeding to Moucha to see Zen Zarrif. You are to go to Ingles. Bring Ingles and Red Raven to Abnos without delay. Have sent messengers out to find remaining members of the Order. Time must not be wasted, will explain when we all arrive in Abnos.

Bill

Bill and Tilterman arrived in Moucha as the sun sank into the horizon. Tilterman felt the first drops of the approaching rain and the dark grey clouds they had seen on their way into the city of

Moucha. As Bill and Tilterman travelled deep into the city, its high rise buildings blocked out the night sky, giving increasing shelter from the rain. It was the first city in the world and the largest not only in size, but also in height. The tallest buildings reached high into the clouds with some finding themselves beyond the clouds. Bill had never liked the cramped lifestyles of the citizens in Moucha preferring to live in the small town of Wobblington. Zen Zarrif's building was visible from almost every point in the city; it's black exterior shining on the smaller buildings near it.

"Are we staying in the 'Sleepy Dwarf' or somewhere else?" Tilterman broke the dull sound of the city's traffic and brought Bill back to the task at hand.

"Yes, if we're being watched and I suspect we are, then there's no point in changing our routine. The 'Sleepy Dwarf' it is." Bill turned down a small narrow lane followed closely by Tilterman. The 'Sleepy Dwarf' rose out of the pavement, its red exterior breaking the dull surroundings of its otherwise mundane appearance. Three grey steps climbed to meet a splintered purple door, two myrtle silver door handles hanging on it. Tilterman pushed the doors inwards revealing a candlelit reception area.

"I'm sorry but the bell boy has killed my electricity and we'll be in the dark till morning, I do apologise." A squeaky voice broke the inner peace of the hotel, its owner a small bent dwarf, greed hanging in every wrinkle on his face.

"Will you be wanting your usual room Master Brickton?" Bill nodded and followed the dwarf to the third floor and to the last room on the left, room Number Ten. Tilterman gave the dwarf some money for his insincere kindness and closed the door behind him. The room had not been touched since Bill was in Moucha two years earlier. The curtains were half drawn and the bed covers still pulled back. Bill had left the room before he had time to settle in on that day, Zen Zarrif had phoned just as Bill got into his room. The tomb of Scaripdemus had been broken into and his sword was gone. Neither Bill nor Zen Zarrif had seen the sword since that day and had no idea of what use it could be to anyone.

"Tilterman, its time I paid Zen Zarrif a visit and more importantly, to check on the book. Search for any indication that his followers are meeting and where if possible. I'll be back as soon I can." Bill dropped his bag and left the room.

Bill stood in the rain watching people entering and leaving Zarrif Industries. As people emerged they unfolded black umbrellas, giving them protection from the driving rain. Taxis drove puddles from the ground forcing them to find their way back to the potholes. The Zarrif Industries building rose into the grey clouds, its shadow falling out across Moucha. Its name stood in gold letters over the double doors leading into its darkened interior, the dark windows preventing spying eyes from catching glimpses of the activities inside. Bill walked slowly across the road avoiding the traffic, stopping at the footpath. He let his eyes climb the outside of the building, remembering how it looked two hundred years ago. It had grown over that time and now stood as the largest building in Moucha.

Bill stood waiting for the double doors to open and reveal its interior and its workings. As Bill stepped inside a warm blast of air hit his face. The lobby was dimly lit, with only the reception desk standing brightly in the centre of the lobby. A young girl stood in front of three glowing orbs entering information into their memory. As Bill came closer to the desk, she stopped and looked up, waiting to help the approaching gentleman. Bill saw a large muscular security guard in a dark blue uniform watching him from near the elevators that stood open near a large waterfall situated just behind the reception desk. His beady eyes followed Bill as he walked towards the desk. Bill caught his own reflection in the badge on the security guards hat. He checked the guard's belt for any weapons or spray canisters. A long black torch hung down his leg beside an empty radio holder.

Bill walked closer to the reception desk ignoring the attentions of the security guard. The young girl behind the desk flicked the pages in her diary, only looking up as Bill came closer to her. He watched as she turned her attention to him and had the look of confusion as he walked straight by her and the reception desk. Bill watched as the security guard drew his radio up towards his mouth and muttered silent words into it. A brown door opened on the left side and two more security guards entered the lobby. A silent conversation took place between them and then the smallest guard left.

Bill continued his short walk to the elevators, watching the security guards watching him. Something about them didn't feel right to Bill. As he got closer to the elevator, he saw one of them place his hand in his pocket, the outline of his fingers moving along the pockets lining. Bill stopped at the elevator and pushed the button to open the doors all the time watching the guard's hands. As the doors pulled to the side revealing the red interior of the elevator, Bill saw one of the guards step back through the side door and disappear from sight. The sound of elevator music slowly filled Bill's ears as the doors closed leaving the security guards behind in the lobby.

Zen Zarrif had his office located at the top of the Zarrif Industries building; the only access was gained by using a private elevator located on the floor below. The security on this floor was in the form of 'Black Dog'. Black Dog was a member of the Raven Clan of the frozen wastelands of Stanoss. The only member to survive the great blizzard of 1567, Black Dog was the last of his people. Skilled in the art of assassination and stealth, no one could hope to get past him alive or in one piece and this was why Zen Zarrif used him as his bodyguard. Bill was a life long friend of Black Dog, and looked forward to seeing him again.

Bill stood back as the doors of the elevator slid open revealing a long corridor. At the end of the corridor the doors of another elevator and a chair, where Black Dog would sit. The corridor was bare, its emptiness caused it to appear cold and unwelcoming to those who were not wanted there. Bill stepped out of the lift expecting Black Dog to appear. The elevator door slid gently closed behind him and cast a silence the length of the dimly light corridor. He stood motionless, waiting for any sign of life. The corridor stood in an eerie silence, its blue colour casting shadows into the corners.

The sudden movement of the elevator Bill had just stepped off corrupted the silence. Bill watched as the indicator light illuminated each floor it passed and eventually stopping at the lobby. Then it began to rise slowly up through the floors it had just descended from. As he walked slowly towards the elevator that led to Zen Zarrif's office he saw the familiar shape of Black Dog lying on the floor, his large body motionless. Bill bent over his massive body to see if anything could save him but Black Dog was already gone to his ancestors. Only someone of great stealth could have surprised Black Dog.

Drawing his sword from under his long coat, Bill pressed the small green button to call the office elevator. He held his blade along his forearm, prepared for combat. The elevator stopped and Bill watched as the doors slowly opened revealing its blue interior. Slowly stepping inside, he pressed the solitary red button and waited in silence as the doors closed. Feeling his body sink as the elevator began to move up towards its final destination, Bill raised his sword. The blade pushed into his forearm as he waited to swing it in defence of any oncoming attack. The lift jerked to a stand still, leaving Bill to wait for the doors to open.

Tilterman watched as the lights came on through the city of Moucha. Its streets had been dark most of the day due to the rain clouds sitting over the buildings. The sun peeped through once or twice but only for a short while. Tilterman had searched cyberspace all day for any indication of a gathering of Scaripdemus' followers, but his search had found nothing. He found his eyes getting heavier as the day had worn on but he refused to give into tiredness. Pushing his chair back from the desk, Tilterman jumped down from it and walked to the window and jumped up onto the sill.

The street outside was empty except for a small blue van with yellow writing on its side. Tilterman read the words out loud breaking the monotone silence in the room.

"Merton Breads, mmmm wonder what they do?" He gave a small chuckle at his own humour. "That's a bad thing Tilterman, laughing at your own jokes. Maybe its time you go for a walk." Nodding to himself, Tilterman picked up his jacket and climbed through the window of his room. Drops of rain sprinkled his face as he stepped onto the tiled roof outside his window. The once black tiles were now covered in a green moss with their blackness fading to a dark green colour. Tilterman slowly walked to the edge of the roof and peered onto the street below. The blue van was sitting quietly on the edge of the street but now it had a companion in the form of a hooded stranger.

Tilterman watched as the stranger pointed towards his room and then turned back to the van's window. As Tilterman watched, he saw another emerge from the opposite side of the van. Both men had black hoods drawn over their faces and their dark coats brushed the street as they walked towards the entrance of the 'Sleepy Dwarf'. Once they had disappeared out of view, Tilterman turned his attention back to the city lights and the fading sun.

The night sky was dark and filled with falling rain. Tilterman's thoughts drifted back to Dylan Drive and to his friends, wondering what was on the menu tonight. He was drawn back to the rainy rooftop by a sudden banging on his room door. Dropping back in through the window, Tilterman saw a small white envelope pushed halfway under his door. Picking up the envelope, he pulled on the door forcing it to open. As he looked up and down the hall, he peeled the envelope open. A small piece of brown parchment slowly drifted to the floor. Tilterman picked it up and slowly read the words on it:

'Scaripdemus is not the person you seek, look closer to your own and find them you shall'.

A Friend.
P.S. Get out now

Bill watched as the doors slowly opened to reveal Zen Zarrif's office. Sparks jumped from a wall lamp hanging from its fixture, showering the floor with yellow dancing lights. Papers had been thrown all over the floor, filing cabinets dragged to the carpeted floors spilling their contents. Stepping from the lift as the doors began to close, Bill saw a window was open behind the large oak desk. Its drawers had been pulled open and their contents thrown across the floor. Bill walked slowly across the room his sword held stiffly along his forearm.

He tried to piece together what had happened in the office and to Zen Zarrif. Zarrif's scimitar was lying on the carpet beside his desk, its blade stained from a recent fight. Walking around the desk, Bill found the sleeve of a blue shirt like that of the security guards from the lobby. A small black radio lay on the ground, cleaved in half, its circuits scattered across the ground.

Bill suddenly became aware of another presence in the office. Turning just in time to see the glint of blue steel, he ducked underneath the swinging blade of the muscular security guard. A second swing of the guards blade, shaved the buttons from Bill's coat as he bent backwards to avoid the sharp edge of the blade. As he did so, he brought his foot up catching his attacker under the chin, knocking him backwards. Bill followed with a blow from his own blade. His assailant parried the strike and lunged forward with a smaller dagger that had been concealed in his belt buckle.

Bill felt the cold steel rip into his shirt cutting across his stomach. Pain shot through him almost doubling him over. Bringing his sword in an arching blow, Bill forced his attacker's sword high over his head, giving him the chance to drive his foot deep into his assailant's stomach. The security guard stumbled back and fell through the window, leaving Bill to hold his stomach in agonising pain. The blade was razor sharp and had sliced deep into his stomach, blood spilled from the wound. Bill took a small sliver box from his pocket and placed it on Zarrif's desk. Inside was a small amount of black powder and a curved metal plate. Taking the plate from the box Bill pressed it into the bottom of the cut. He then placed some of the black powder on the plate and pressed it into the cut. At first nothing happened and then after a moment a sizzling sound, then the smell of the cut being burned closed.

Stepping to the window, he found the security guard hanging from a flagpole several floors below. Bill turned and sat on the window ledge his eyes scanning the room for anything he had missed or that had become uncovered in the fight. A small disc caught his eye, its metallic surface reflecting the sparking lights in the office. Reaching out with the tip of his sword, Bill moved papers back revealing the entire disc, he recognised it instantly.

Picking up the disc, Bill ran his finger over the surface. The intricate design caused his finger to rise and fall on the tribal marks. At the end of the tribal marks, his fingers ran across a snake's head, small eyes made from red gems. Pressing down on the eyes, Bill released the snakes tongue from it mouth, the key still worked but where was the book and for whom was the security guard working? Bill walked back to the window and sat on the ledge. Looking out he saw the security guard swinging from the flagpole.

"Who do you work for?" Bill watched as the security guard

looked up. "Tell me and I'll help you. Now, who sent you for the Book of Demons and why didn't you take the key as well?" The security guard stared up at Bill and said nothing. Bill stood up and disappeared from the edge of the window only stopping when a voice called to him.

"Pull me up and I'll tell you everything." Bill reappeared at the window and looked down waiting for more information. "Ok, we couldn't find the key and the people who are following you work for the same people I do, now pull me up and I'll tell you the rest." Bill pulled on his belt buckle releasing it from the belt. As he pulled on it, it revealed a long back slender rope. Lowering it down to the level of the security guard, he tied it off on some pipes at the base of the window. Watching as the guard pulled himself up the rope and drop inside the window, Bill quickly held his sword against the guard's chest holding him on the ground.

"Every time you tell me something I like, I'll let you move a little, so start by telling me who hired you to steal the book and why you have people following me?" Bill waited to see if the security guard would attack him or co-operate with him. Settling himself on the ground, the security guard began to speak.

"We were hired by a gnome, he didn't give his name but he did pay well. He told us to come from Wobblington to Moucha and steal the book from Zarrif Industries." Bill pulled the sword back allowing the guard to rise to his feet. He thrust his sword back into the guard's chest urging him to speak some more.

"We were told you were travelling here to Moucha and we were instructed to locate and follow you. We were to prevent you from leaving the city if you got close to the identity of our employer." Bill stopped the guard by pressing his sword a little harder.

"What happened to Zen Zarrif and the book?" Bill watched as the guard opened his mouth to speak. A look of pain spread across his face as he stumbled forward and fell at Bill's feet. Bill saw a small red arrow in his back. Running to the window, Bill saw a man scrambling across the roof of the building across the street, his cloak blowing in the wind. Bill replaced his sword into its scabbard and leaped from the window spreading his coat to either side causing him to float across the sky towards the building across the street.

Bill glided towards the gritted rooftop and the assassin's escape route. Skidding to a stop, he looked around the roof for possible hiding spots and a surprise attack. Only a closing door stood between Bill and his would be assassin. Running across the roof, Bill slowly opened the door and stepped into the darkness of the stair well. Listing for sounds he waited for his eyes to adjust to the darkness. The faint sounds of footsteps on the cement stairs alerted him to the location of his assailant. Bill hurled himself over the support rail, his coat slowing his decent as he fell. The sound of the fleeing footsteps grew louder and louder as Bill drifted towards the ground floor. Spotting his fleeing assailant, Bill reached out for the handrail, slowing himself down by stretching his coat out almost to the stair's edge.

As he pulled himself onto the stairs, he saw a brown fire door close, the emergency light dying in a flicker of sparks. Bill read the red and white sign beside the door, 'Thirteenth floor', and the tall red numbers standing out in the dim light. As he reached to pull open the door, it came crashing into him, forced open by a kick. He stumbled back on the steps leading to the floor below. Looking up he saw the red cloak disappear back through the brown door. Bill stepped cautiously towards the door and pulled it open. The corridor beyond it was empty. Looking both ways for any sign of his attacker, he saw no trace of him. The only escape from the corridor was a dusty old window, and as Bill eased his way down the corridor towards it he noticed a shadow moving just beyond it.

"Bill, over here." A familiar voice called out to him from the fire escape located outside the corridor window. Peering through the window was the friendly face of Tilterman. Bill smiled as he forced the window open, wondering how Tilterman had found him. As the crack at the bottom of the window grew larger, Tilterman pushed a brown piece of parchment into Bill's hand.

"Where did you get this?" Bill pushed the window open to its full height allowing him to step out onto the fire escape. Drops of water fell onto his face from the railing above them.

"It was shoved under our door in the 'Sleepy Dwarf'. I didn't see who pushed it in but a few moments earlier I saw some men in long black coats enter the Tavern and then a few minutes after that it was pushed under." Tilterman watched Bill's eyes move over the lines on the parchment, reading it again and again.

"Come on, I'll explain what happened here on the way." He grabbed the edges of the fire escape ladder and slid down the thirteen floors to the ground, Tilterman sliding after him.

"We have to contact Wang Wu and let him know what's happening, and I need to find out what's happened to Zen Zarrif and the Book of Demons!"

Sven's Truth

The top of the Gordic Mountains began to show over the horizon as Sven and his party soared through the grey clouds. Their shadows darkened the green forests that lay in the valley at the foot of Duranic Peak, home to the Dwarf Lord Ingles. A small stream wound its way down the mountain side, flowing into the larger river Logy and disappearing over the world's edge and out of sight. The treetops swayed to and fro in the gentle wind, allowing glimpses of the forest floor far below. Sven caught the sight of a hunting party chasing down a deer, two hounds nipping at its heels.

Mordell turned and began to drop down towards Duranic peak. Sven watched as one of the dwarf guards disappeared into the bowels of the mountain keep. Mordell began to hover just above the guard's head waiting for the signal to touch down. The dwarf's belly far outstretched any other part of his body, his chain mail shirt hanging over its edge. His hand held a long wooden pike, its blade covered in dwarfish runes. Sven watched the entrance for the return of the second dwarf and their permission to touch down inside Duranic.

Duranic was the mountain fortress of the Dwarf Lord Ingles. Hidden from prying eyes of the mere mortal folk who used these woods for pastimes and exercise, by dwarf runes placed there by the dwarf wizards of bygone years. Its five towers rose far from the ground, built by the goblin slaves taken during the great war of 1012 when Beric Iron Foot took lands from the Goblin Prince, Jeranic the Slob. When Beric Iron Foot had won the war he captured all the remaining goblins in the Gordic Mountains and forced them to build his fortress. Nothing on such a grand scale had ever been built by dwarfs above ground before this and it placed Beric Iron Foot in grand favour with the King of Dwarfs, Thorin of the Stone Hand.

Moments later the second dwarf returned, his face red from the run up the steps. His chain mail clinking as he tried to catch up with his breathe. His red beard dancing on the growing wind, only to be calmed by his leather clad hand pushing it back to rest. A muted conversation took place beneath Sven and his party as the waited for their permission to enter.

Sven looked back as Mordell took to the air again and drifted silently down towards the stables to a waiting feed of hay and water. He followed the red bearded dwarf down the twisting stairs, his eyes sailing on the rolling dwarf's belly as it tilted with every movement of his short stocky legs. The stairway soon opened up into a large banqueting hall filled with tables and people of all races. Sven's attention was drawn to a group of gnomes sitting at the head table.

Sven watched as the Dwarf Lord Ingles was carried down the hall on his shield. His cloak of the finest silk flowed out behind him, carpeting the floor in waves of purple shimmering silk. Sitting on his head was the famous crown of Gvenoc, stolen from the depths of hell by his father Wernock of Duranic. Ingle's beard tipped over the edge of the shield and drifted from side to side, its blonde colour matching the shield's golden edges. His forearms tattooed in mystic dwarf runes and the side of his neck covered in old writing of another nobler time long forgotten.

"Welcome to my castle good friends. Word has already reached me of the tragic events on Watu. As you can see a member from the Gnome High Council is here, Paddy Reinhart." Sven looked down along the table to see the face of the High Councillor staring back up at him, nodding his head by way of a greeting. Sven turned to see if any other members of the High Council were present but only Rinehart was present.

"The High Councillor came in earlier today with the tragic words from the Keeper. He told me that you would be arriving and that the Order's presence is required in Abnos." Sven's mind raced, a hundred questions crowded his mouth, all trying to escape together. The most confusing thing of all was how did Paddy find out about Watu?

"Sven, I've not seen you since 1812 or has it been longer than that my old friend?" The insincerity of Paddy's voice sickened Sven to the pit of his stomach. Sven never liked him and the fact that he was a member of the High Council only added to Sven's hatred. Paddy had run for the Council against Sven and had gained the seat by using trickery and lies to win the single vote that separated them in the final count.

"Terrible news about the Elders on Watu, did you find anything of use in the ruins or did the fire destroy everything?" Paddy smirked at Sven, watching his reaction.

"No, the fires destroyed everything. Only the shells of the temples are left standing. How, if I may be so bold as to ask, did you hear about Watu so quickly?" Sven studied Paddy's face, watching for any indication of a lie or mistruth in his movements or his voice.

"Bill contacted me during the night and we discussed the possibility of another war between us and Cundra. If Scaripdemus is alive, then we must act quickly. When Bill told me that he was contacting the remaining members of the Order, I knew that the Council must be summoned and our plan of action be put into motion at once." Paddy looked at Ingles and Drego, looking for nods of approval. Paddy turned to Sven awaiting his nod of acceptance of his answer. Sven slowly smiled and bowed down.

"As always you prove your experience is invaluable on the Council and to the nation of gnomes under the Council's protection." Paddy bowed in acceptance of Sven's compliment and reached out his hand in a gesture of friendship, Sven accepted it half-heartedly.

"Ingles, I have word from Bill. Both you and Red Raven are to leave for Abnos. There the Order shall assemble under their banner again and if need be, they shall face together that which threatens our peace and anything that may attempt to unleash the Book of Demon's powers upon us." Sven paused and bowed to the Dwarf Lord.

"That my Lord is the message given to me for you." Sven watched as Ingles sent two dwarves to the head table, where they began to prepare seats for the newly arrived guests.

"First, you shall drink my ale and eat my game. Then you shall rest in my finest sheep skin beds and at first light we shall leave for Abnos." Holding out his hand, Ingles led Sven and the others to the head table where they were seated and food was placed in front of them. Sven looked around the room for the one known as Red Raven but could not find him anywhere in the crowd.

"Red Raven is hunting in the forest, I have riders out looking for him now. Our Indian friend will not keep us waiting for long, now eat, drink and rest your weary bones." Ingles clapped his hands summoning three dwarfish ladies from the edge of the hall. As they stepped onto the floor, musicians burst into old dwarfish songs and melodies, their instruments were set ablaze with their passion. Sven had always found it hard to distinguish between Dwarfish men and women as both had long beards and the women were every bit as muscular and every bit as ugly as the men.

The sweet scent of fresh cut flowers filled Andy's nostrils, the feeling of soft sheets and the warmth of his sheepskin blanket touched against his skin. He opened his eyes expecting to find himself in the sleeping quarters of his train, but it was the sight of a tall, slender woman that met his eyes. She was standing across the unfamiliar room stirring a clear liquid in a small glass bowl. Andy watched as her light red hair reflected the sunlight, its fiery sheen brightening her surroundings.

"Your drink will be ready in a moment, Andrew. You had quiet a nasty fall from that train, I was meant to be on the train also but unforeseen circumstances prevented me from being there, at the time I thought the were unforeseen but now I know it was to keep me from receiving word from Bill." Turning around Andy saw his hostess's face, its warmth casting a radiant glow across the sheepskin blanket. Her face was pale like that of snow, her eyes blue like the morning sky and her smile warm like the midday sun. Andy recognised her face and her kindness. Maisie DuPont, one of Bill's oldest friends and long time member of the Order of the Dragon.

"Its time I had a fire burning in this room." Andy watched as Maisie turned and walked towards the open fireplace, her flowing blue dress trailing the ground. A great ball of fire rose from the palm of her hand and drifted slowly towards the heart of the fireplace, igniting the coals in a loud crack. Andy propped himself upon the edge of the bed, pain coursing through his weak body. His head felt light as he moved from the edge of the bed, grabbing a wooden chair to hold himself up, his legs buckling under his own weight.

"Not yet little one, you are still far too weak to be out of bed." Maisie grabbed Andy's arm and helped him back into the warmth of the bed. "You will remain here until I return from Moucha. Now drink this, it will make you stronger." As the warm liquid flowed down towards his stomach, Andy felt his veins and skin beginning to warm gently. Maisie sat down on the edge of the bed and helped him to feed himself; his body still very weak from the fall.

"My daughter, Ra-Mada will look after you while I'm away. I found the note Bill gave you for me and I now have to believe that Bill and Tilterman are walking into a trap in Moucha!" Maisie ran a silk handkerchief across Andy's lips taking the last of the liquid from them. "I'm leaving for Moucha in the hope of warning Bill and Tilterman of the danger that awaits them in the city." Andy watched as Maisie swung a long black cape over her shoulders and turned to walk from the room.

"When you're feeling up to it Andy, leave for Dylan Drive and act as if nothing happened to you. When you arrive at Dylan Drive, you'll find members of the High Council there with word of Bill's death but remember this, unless you have word from me, don't believe anything you hear." Maisie turned and left the room, leaving Andy to ponder on her words.

Sven sat watching the three dwarfish maidens dance, but all the time his mind was on the question of how did Paddy Reinhart know so much about Watu? Sven watched Paddy as he left the great dining hall.

"My Lord Ingles, if you could excuse me for a moment?" Sven started to get up from his seat but was stopped halfway by the strong arm of his host.

"My young friend, please sit for a moment for the best of the entertainment is about to start. I have fire eaters from the furthest reach of the Dwarf Realm, please sit and enjoy my hospitality!" Ingles watched as Sven bowed and sat back down at the table waiting for his opportunity to follow Paddy, hoping it wouldn't be too late. Watching the flames as they rose high into the raised ceiling of Ingles' castle, Sven didn't see Paddy return with a taller gnome walking closely behind him. Long silver robes trailed the ground as Paddy and his new companion walked towards the head table and Sven.

"Mallard, so good of you to join us, I hope your trip was a pleasant one?" Ingles rose to greet the tall slender gnome, holding his hand out in friendship. A long pallid, bony hand reached out from beneath the sleeve of the silver robe.

"It is good to see you, I hope everything went to plan?" Mallard smiled and turned to Sven absorbing the look on his face. "Sven, I have word from Bill concerning Watu and our arrival in Abnos, if you could follow us into the courtyard we will explain all." Mallard placed his hand on Sven's shoulder coaxing him forward toward the courtyard.

"Ingles, is everything prepared as I have asked?" Mallard turned his attention to Ingles, a sly smile on his face. Ingles smiled and nodded towards a staircase leading down into the famous pits of darkness in Duranic. Sven followed Mallard and Paddy out into the courtyard followed closely by Drego, his fingers caressing the hilt of his sword.

Torches were being lit on the edge of the courtyard as Sven followed Mallard and Paddy. The statue at the centre of the courtyard stood tall showing three dwarfs carrying a fourth on a shield, his sword held high over his stone head. Gvenoc stood proudly on his shield watching over his descendants and their loyal subjects. His stone beard fell all the way to the green grass flattening it. Sven searched the ramparts for any hidden archers and passed a glance to Drego to keep an eye on the surroundings just in case. Drego stood in the archway watching as Mallard turned to Sven, a sly look in his eyes.

"Bill wants you to return to Dylan Drive and await his return there. He's travelling to Abnos as we speak, to send the Order home, as their services are no longer needed. It has come to the attention of the High Council that Scaripdemus has not returned." Mallard paced the green lawns of the courtyard and was about to speak when Sven interrupted him.

"I have only spoken to Bill less than a day ago, his orders were to meet him in Abnos and not to go anywhere else. When did you receive these instructions?" Sven withdrew a few paces opening up his distance between the necromancer and himself. Mallard flicked his cloak around as he turned and walked straight up to Sven. Before Mallard could snap at Sven, Paddy stepped forward and took Sven by the arm leading him away from his escape route.

"Sven, you know who Mallard is and how powerful he is. He speaks the truth; Bill has sent word for you. The paper you found outside the cave of Terock and the other piece on Watu were part of an old book of poetry by Meisser." Sven looked at Paddy as he spoke; how did he know about the parchment?

"Just one question." Sven ran his hand towards the hilt of his sword, sliding his fingers along it. "How do you know what's on the parchment that I found, I have not shown it to anyone?" Paddy's face drew blank wondering if Sven had kept the parchment from Bill or if he had even told him! Sven drew his sword halfway from the scabbard waiting for Paddy to answer his question.

"Seize them, they must not be allowed to escape from the citadel!" Drego quickly drew his sword and ran towards Sven. As he reached him, several dwarf guards ran from the castle into the courtyard surrounding the two lone warriors standing on the grass. Sven and Drego watched as the prospect of a fight glinted in the eyes of the dwarf guards.

"Lay down your weapons and no harm shall come to you on that I give my word. Come now, enough is enough." Ingles stepped forward. Hesitating, Sven dropped his sword and watched as Drego slowly placed his along side it.

"Take them to the dungeons and separate them, we shall be along shortly to explain all to you Sven." Paddy and Mallard watched as the guards led the two companions away to the wet cells in the depths of Duranic.

134

Maisie closed the large wooden doors that lead into the bedroom where the injured Andy lay. She fastened her cloak securely around her neck before stepping onto the street outside her house in Buttelburg. The street was almost empty, only a solitary black cat sat licking herself at the bottom of Maisie's steps. Maisie checked the street once more before setting out for Moucha. Light winds whisked up her cloak from around her ankles as she walked along the edge of the footpath.

"Maisie DuPont?" The silence in the street was shattered by the gruff voice of Erasmus Reich. Maisie recognised his weak attempt at a Buttelburg accent. Turning slowly to face the owner of the voice, Maisie found herself looking at the bent shape of an old man but not the figure of Erasmus.

"Maisie don't let your eyes deceive you. It is me Erasmus, but as you know my head is worth too much to those who would think themselves more powerful than I." Maisie scanned the street for anyone that would help Erasmus or had he come as a friend?

"What do you want Erasmus? Why are you in Buttelburg?" Maisie shifted her cloak to one side and slid her hand into a small leather bag hanging over her shoulder. Her fingers soon found the small ball she was looking for.

"I've come to tell you of Bill Brickton's treachery and of his lies to the Order of the Dragon." Erasmus slowly hobbled towards Maisie, his body bent over clutching a red-crooked stick. As he walked, Maisie saw a movement in the stairwell near where she was standing. Shifting her eyes, she saw two Rennick warriors watching her movements from the shadows.

"Brickton is trying to bring Scaripdemus back, he is using the Book of the Demons for his own ambitions. He has killed Wang Wu and Zen Zarrif is in great danger. You know that he has sent out his so-called 'Messengers' with instructions to meet in Abnos. Is that not where you are now planning to travel to?" Maisie watched as Erasmus moved up the footpath towards her.

"What are you up to, Erasmus?" Maisie watched as the shadowed figures began to climb the stairs towards the street. "Come on Erasmus, what's your game?" Maisie released the clear glass ball from between her fingers smashing it on the ground. Grey smoke filled the street around her, choking the words of Erasmus.

"Get her she must not escape!" Black shadows ran about in the smoke rising from the footpath. As it cleared, the figures became Erasmus and the two Rennick warriors. "Where is she? Find her!"

Maisie slipped down the stairwell across the street from where the commotion was taking place. She watched as Erasmus took on his more familiar shape and left the Rennick warriors to search for her. Standing much taller than any other person Maisie had ever met, Erasmus was a formidable opponent to the best of men with or without magic. His red stick had grown into a long steel staff, a red ruby sitting on top of it. The Eye of Gordanna, Goddess of the Under Realm and the Dark Arts, it was the source of his magical powers.

Maisie watched as the two Rennick warriors left the street and followed a dark alley away from her hiding place. Slowly emerging, from the stairwell Maisie checked the street for any other would be followers. Once she knew it was safe to proceed, Maisie stepped on to the street and quickly disappeared from view.

Sven sat in the corner of the wet cell, his elbow grazed and bleeding from the bang it had received at the hands of the dwarf guards. Struggle as he might he had been no match for their brutish arms and their forceful grip. Drego seemed less eager to escape or maybe he was part of the plan formed by Mallard and Paddy. Sitting in the corner opposite Sven was a large brown rat, its fur eaten down to its pink skin by fleas and tics. Sven watched it staring at him; it had an almost sinister look in its eyes. Perhaps it was eyeing up Sven as a potential next meal.

The smell in the dungeon was enough to turn anyone off food, a pungent stale smell of rotten carrion and clotted blood stains. The sudden sound of dead steps alerted Sven to the arrival of Paddy and Mallard. Muffled voices and then the sound of the locks arrested the last of the eerie silence in Sven's cell. A shaft of light rushed into the dark cell, hurting Sven's eyes.

"Sven, its time you heard the truth behind our plans to use the Book of Demons!" Mallard broke the clean shaft of light, his figure casting a black shadow across the cell. Sven looked up at his captor waiting for the rest of the lies and deceitful words that would follow.

"When Bill went to deal with that dragon in Surbia, he didn't know at the time that there was no dragon." A smile set itself upon Mallard's face as he saw Sven sit up and take notice of his words. "I set the trap for him using the young foolish Prince Vladimir as bait. When Bill arrived in Surbia he found the nest mound of a Swaylian dragon and believed it had escaped from someone's stables, and then when Prince Vlad appeared and told him that it was his Cynthia, my plan was set for Bill's capture." Sven stood to his full height staring the necromancer in the face.

"For my plan to be effective I had to make sure that Bill returned to Dylan Drive and that you and the others suspected nothing. I had Bill send you to Watu where Erasmus was ready to destroy the island when you arrived." Sven stepped away, letting everything sink into his mind. Thoughts ran around in his head and turning around, he saw Paddy and Mallard looking at him.

"Once Bill was replaced by a shifter, it would make things easier for us to deal with the rest of the Order and for us to use the Book uninterrupted. Now that you and Drego are in these dungeons we can proceed to Abnos and take care of Wang Wu without anyone stopping us." Sven ran to attack Mallard but found his way blocked by two large dwarfs.

"Mallard I promise you'll not get away with this. I'll see you're dealt with by the High Council..." Sven found himself talking to the back of the studded cell door and the fading laughter of Mallard and Paddy. Sven called out to see if Drego was nearby and if he had heard what had been said?

"Drego can you hear me?" Sven waited for an answer. "Drego can you hear me?" Again Sven sat in silence waiting for his answer. "Drego can you..."

An Evil Plan

"I want that door guarded until you are told otherwise." Mallard barked at the two dwarf guards as they shut the cell door. "If he escapes it will mean your heads on pikes outside of the citadels gates!" The dwarf guards nodded at Mallard and Paddy as they turned and walked down the dimly light passage leading back to Mallard's lab. As they walked, Paddy found the passage growing smaller and more to their height, its musty smell filling his nostrils. The light from the torches had faded sometime ago and Paddy found himself following the dark outline of Mallard in front of him. The passage ended in a small round room with only one point of entry and exit. Paddy watched as Mallard stepped up to a featureless wall opposite them.

"Ocarnon." Mallard spoke in a low commanding tone. Paddy watched as the wall in front of Mallard began to move. The sound of stone scraping on stone filled the chamber as the first rays of light filled Paddy's eyes allowing him to see the dwarfish runes on the chamber walls. As his eyes adjusted to the light, he saw a room beyond the moving wall filled with paraphernalia of foreign lands and times long past. Mallard stepped forward, his hand preventing Paddy from entering the room.

"Perventus subtractus." A green glow filled the room and the sound of sizzling filled Paddy's ears. Mallard summoned Paddy into the room. As he entered, Paddy felt his body fill with cold air and then moments later a warm breeze stopped him shivering. "Spells of protection to prevent the dwarf necromancers entering my domain and stealing my powers." Mallard grinned as he watched Paddy stare at the walls and benches in his lab.

A black raven flew in through a small hole in the roof above them. Paddy watched as it landed on the bony shoulder of the necromancer and dropped a small brown parchment into his claw like hand. As Mallard opened it, Paddy watched the raven take flight and land on a nearby perch, biting at a black rat dangling from it. Paddy's attention was soon drawn back to Mallard and his screams of anger.

"Idiots, I have idiots chasing their own tails..." A bolt of bright blue light streaked across the room striking the raven and knocking him from his perch. Paddy dived behind a bench as two more flashes of light traversed the room towards him. It struck the bench causing it to smash into splinters around Paddy. Mallard screamed again.

"Tomeba, get down here now!" The black raven glided down from the rafters of the lab where it had sought refuge from Mallard's fury.

"Tomeba go and bring me word from the other scouts following the remaining members of the Order." Tomeba dipped his head in respect and flew from the laboratory. Mallard sat at the large metal table in the centre of his lab, his eyes reading the parchment Tomeba had brought him.

"It's word from Moucha, Zen Zarrif has escaped with the book and Brickton showed up while the Rennick warriors were searching for the key." Mallard looked up from the parchment and glancing back at it one last time, then rolled it in his fingers. Paddy watched as Mallard stood up from the table and tossed the parchment into the bin in the corner of the room.

"We have to raise Du'Ard Duchan, without him our task will be futile. Scaripdemus will have no chance of using the gate to get back to the future. Are the preparations complete?" Mallard focused his attention on an old manuscript that lay spread out on a reading table. Its tattered edges held in place by gold pins. Paddy stepped forward and pulled a chair from beneath the metal table and sat down on it.

"Everything shall be ready in time to raise this, Du'Ard. Why is it so important to have him raised before we bring Scaripdemus back to us?" Paddy watched as Mallard sat back on the table's edge and pulled a small ball from a wooden chest and placed it on the table between them. Paddy watched as the green smoke in the ball began to swirl, forming images on the inside.

"You want to know why it's so important that we have Du'Ard back before we perform the ritual to bring Scaripdemus from the past? Watch the ball and it shall reveal all." Paddy stared into the depths of the green smoke and watched as a picture formed.

The green smoke soon dissipated into the dark interior of a cave. Light cut through the darkness allowing Paddy to see further into the belly of the cave. Standing in the darkness, Paddy saw a silhouetted figure at the edge of a small fire. Sitting at the centre of stalagmites forming a raised circle around him, Paddy watched as the darkened figure walked towards a small cascading waterfall, its black liquid disappearing underground. Paddy's thoughts were interrupted by the voice of Mallard.

"The person is Du'Ard and the black liquid is the flowing blood of the world upon where you stand. After Du'Ard gave his soul to the dark God Kriyo, he was given the location of the Everlasting Blood of Life. Once he had this, he could create the ritual that we are about to use to open the portal that will bring back Scaripdemus." Paddy turned back to watch Du'Ard as he gathered the blood from the pool at the bottom of the falls. His crimson cloak hung loosely on his shoulders and flowed across the dirt floor. As he rose from the pool's edge Paddy heard the faint sounds of his chanting, a language strange to his ears. As they watched Du'Ard, a strange orb of light emerged from the black pool.

"This is it, this is when you see the power bestowed on Du'Ard by Kriyo." Paddy moved closer to the ball and watched. He became suddenly aware of a chill in his bones and as he watched the orb of light in front of Du'Ard. He felt that the scene in the light was familiar. His thoughts were brought to an abrupt end as two Rennick warriors burst into the room.

"What is the meaning of this intrusion?" Mallard cloaked the orb hiding it from the view of these unwanted eyes. As he did so, he turned and stared at the warriors waiting for their explanation.

"Maisie DuPont has eluded us, we were unable to capture her as you requested. Ragmar has returned from his mission..." Mallard's face gave way to a blank expression, one Paddy could only assume was fury.

"Take Ragmar to the pit of fire, failure can no longer be tolerated. Our plans must not fail." Bowing to Paddy and Mallard, the Rennick warriors left the lab. Pacing up and down, Mallard wrung his hands running his plan through his evil twisted mind. Paddy watched as the images in the ball dissipated into the green smoke.

"We have to kill Wang Wu before Bill or any of the other members get to him. Zvanick is already in my power and can help no one not even himself. Come, we must leave." Paddy followed Mallard back along the dark corridors to the damp and dark dungeons of the dwarf stronghold. "We have three days before conditions are right to raise Du'Ard. You, you and you come with us." Mallard pointed too three burly dwarfs all holding axes with dwarfish runes engraved into their blades. Picking themselves from the wall they had been leaning against they followed Mallard out into the courtyard of the citadel. "We leave for Abnos and the destruction of Wang Wu."

Tilterman and Bill ran from the fire escape of the Zarrif industries building and back in the direction of The Sleepy Dwarf. Bill's thoughts drew him back to the dragon in Surbia and to Ivor Jones.

A black twisted, shadowed hand crept towards Bill's sleeping face unaware that his every movement was being watched. The small bottle of poison hissed as the top was twisted open. Bill stirred, stopping the assassin from moving. Bill's eyes were open staring into the eyes of his attacker, his silver dagger pressing into his side.

"Back up slowly, keep your hands where I can see them. Ivor turn on the lamp." Ivor stepped from the shadows, a small lamp hidden under his long brown leather coat. As the light filled Bill's tent, the assassin saw four hefty gnomes standing in the corners all armed with swords and nets. "So, who sent you shape shifter?" Ivor stepped forward and began to tie the assassin's hands.

"We've seen his contact outside the camp, he sits on the far side of the dragon's nest. Do you want us to take him as well?" Ivor watched as Bill paced the tent floor, a curious look on his face.

"No, lets see what their plan for me is?" Bill picked up a small black book; its spine tattered from years of use and mishandling. Flicking through the pages Bill began to read:

> "Show your shape, the shape of those you'd trick
> And deceive. Change and be held there till released."

A scream of pain filled the tented room as the shape shifter was forced to take on the form of his prey. Bill watched as he transformed into another Bill. Ivor stepped forward and pushed the tip of his sword to the shape shifters neck.

"What is your name and the name of your contact?" Ivor placed a little more pressure on the blade, forcing the assassin to speak.

"Ragmar and my contact is Surnam. I don't know what my mission is, I was told to kill Brickton and wait to be contacted." Ragmar tilted his hip towards Bill. "In my pocket there's a double sided silver coin of Ronin, Son of Thorin." Bill flicked his sword against the cloth of Ragmar's trouser and watched as the coin twisted down to the ground.

"When Surnam contacts you, you must toss this coin to him. If he catches it, you will be safe, but if he drops it, then your deception has not worked." Bill picked up the coin and turned to Ivor, indicating with a nod to keep a watchful eye on him. Bill stepped out of the tent leaving the light cloaked in its interior. Walking towards the dragon's nest he saw the shape of a man walking slowly towards him. His fingers gently played with the doubled sided coin and as casual as he could be, Bill flipped the coin towards the shadowed figure. As it spun towards him, Bill caught the glint of its silver edges reflecting the pale moonlight. The stranger plucked the coin from the night air and as he walked by Bill, he spoke in a cloaked voice.

"Return to Dylan Drive as if nothing has happened and then proceed to Moucha. You'll receive further instructions once you arrive there." Before Bill could respond, the shadowed figure transformed into a black raven and disappeared into the night sky. His deception had been successful. Bill walked back to the tent and as he entered, he met a gnome bursting through the canvas door. Entering he found the shape shifter, Ragmar, fighting with Ivor. Bill grabbed Ragmar from behind and pulled him to the ground. As they struggled, Ragmar transformed into a coiling snaking, striking out at Bill.

Ivor quickly pulled a flaming torch from its steel holder and thrust it into Ragmar's serpent face. Hissing and spiting, Ragmar recoiled and slithered back into the shadows of the tent and before either Bill or Ivor could grab him he disappeared under the canvas. Running from the tent, Bill and Ivor came face to face with the dragon they had come to recapture. Its golden scales reflected the early morning sun like stacks of clean banker's coins. Its tail whipping the sand into dark beige clouds, stones flying high into the air and crashing down on the camp. Bill and his companion struggled with the dragon until they captured it. But Bill was not concerned with the captured dragon; his thoughts were on Ragmar and the persons behind his attempted switch. Bill's thoughts were interrupted by Tilterman's voice.

"Bill, behind you!" As Bill turned he saw two Rennick warriors running towards them, swords drawn. Drawing his sword, Bill turned to where Tilterman was standing. Flashes of bright yellow sparks flew from Tilterman's sword as he fought with a Rennick warrior much larger than he. Bill turned and charged down the street at his own opponents, meeting his sword in mid flight. The sound of steel on steel echoed out in the streets of Moucha as they fought.

Having managed to lose the Rennick warriors, Maisie made her way swiftly to the old stockyards of Buttelburg. It had been a long time since traders had dealt in dragons or cattle for that matter in the old yards. The metal stocks and pens were showing their age, rust eating away at their once vibrant exterior. Maisie followed the winding maze of steel and emerged in front of a tall warehouse. Its exterior looked old and weather beaten from years of neglect.

Swinging merrily on the rooftop, an old weather vane greeted her with a slight squeak as it twisted in the gentle breeze. Its windows were blackened out with dirt and dust. Maisie slowly made her way to the only entrance, a small wooden grey door in the centre of the warehouse front. As she pulled it open to reveal the interior a figure ran from the shadows.

"Ra-Mada, what is it?" The young girl grabbed Maisie's arm and dragged her into the warehouse. The clanking of her blackened armour echoed in the darkness.

"It's Reginald, I've had it with him and his antics. No more, I've had it." Her voice drowned out the noise of her armour. "Juvenile dragons are more trouble than they're worth. Reginald is the worst, constant pranks..." As she breathed her voice returned to a quiet relaxed and calm tone.

"Reginald has tossed water down on Theo and now he can't breathe fire to heat the furnace to warm Nancy and Lizzie. Words cannot describe their temper and we know how Griffons like their comfort." Ra-Mada pulled her helmet off revealing a head of flowing blonde hair and a partly blackened face. Maisie began to smile as a grin slowly crept across her Dragon Keeper's face. "Its not funny Maisie..." Her laughter escaping before she could control it.

"Reginald and the Griffons will have to wait till I return from Moucha. I have to find Bill and warn him." Ra-Mada nodded and set her problems aside.

"The Gyrocopter is ready." Ra-Mada flicked a switch on the wall next to her. Lights began to flicker into life revealing a small launch pad in the centre of the warehouse. On it sat a small green suitcase, its silver handle sparkling in the flickering lights. Maisie walked to the centre of the pad and pushed firmly down on the handle. The sound of hissing filled the warehouse as steam flowed from the sides of the case. Maisie and Ra-Mada stood back and watched as the case unfolded itself.

Its sides fell to the ground and a large green skin rolled across the floor. Slow rising rods began to emerge from inside the case, rising several feet into the air and then collapsing to the ground, forming a cross as they hit the green skin. Picking itself up, the skin folded back over the poles and tied off with golden string form-ing the wings. The base of the case began to lift from the ground, dropping its sides underneath the newly formed wings. The handle pushed itself away from the case and followed the centre pole to its end and formed a small upright triangle. More green skin snaked its way down the centre pole and onto the triangle concealing the pole and forming another wing.

The case rotated ninety degrees and formed a seat at the mid point of the cross. Several other poles emerged and formed a cockpit around it. A long silver pole, much thicker than the others, pushed itself towards the warehouse roof. Reaching six feet over the top of the cockpit, it began to divide into three smaller silver rods. Each of these rods rotated to push away from the centre rod and formed the blades of the gyrocopter. As the hissing noise died away, Maisie approached the copter and placed her sword in the cockpit.

"I shall return in three days and if I do not then you know what to do." Ra-Mada nodded and watched as Maisie and the gyrocopter slowly rose into the rafters of the warehouse.

Bill twisted the end of the sword hilt in his hand releasing a cloud of black smoke onto the street. Tilterman had already made his escape down a small sewer inlet and disappeared into the darkness under Moucha. Bill turned and fled the street leaving his attackers coughing in the smoke. Replacing his sword in its scabbard, Bill slowed his pace to a walk once he was convinced that he had lost the Rennick warriors. The streets of Moucha had come alive with the sound of traders and the citizens going about their daily business. The Sleepy Dwarf soon came into view but Bill had decided that rushing in could land him in more trouble and he wasn't sure if Tilterman had returned.

Across the street from the Sleepy Dwarf stood a small bar, its marine blue exterior dull and in need of a paint job. The Blind Eye, a foul and dark haven where the scum of the sea and the underworld of Moucha drank and dealt their dark trades. Bill carefully scanned the street for any sign of Rennick warriors or anyone else that would pose a problem. A vid-link stood on the street outside the bar and was unoccupied. Bill dialled in the number for Maisie DuPont and waited for the small black screen to display the interior of Maisie's answering service. Nothing happened so Bill dialled again and waited. This time the familiar voice of Andy came across the round speaker.

"Hello, who is it? I can't stand up my leg is badly hurt and I can't see you." Andy's voice fell silent.

"Its Bill, is Maisie there Andy, its important that I talk with her!" Bill checked over his shoulder and then turned his attention too the grunts of discomfort from the speakers on the vid-phone. As he watched he saw the top of Andy's brow come into view on the screen in front of him. "Is she there, Andy?"

"Bill, Maisie is on the way to Moucha to find you, she has word from me of what happened. Where are you? Are you still in Moucha? Paddy, from the High Council is involved in everything that has been happening. He had meeeeeeee...." Bill watched as the vid-link between him and Andy failed. What had Andy been talking about and how was the High Council involved?

"Andy, can you hear me? You need to get back to Dylan Drive and prepare for trouble, can you hear me?" Bill hit the off button on the vid-link and then hit the redial button and waited for the link to be re-established with Buttelburg. A red warning flashed up on the screen in front of Bill.

"No such number, please dial again using correct number." Bill hit the off button and then the redial button for a second time, only to have the same message flash at him again. Bill turned from the vid link and entered The Blind Eye. His eyes were drawn to a movement in the corner as he entered and then the familiar voice of Tilterman spoke to him.

"So you made it back then?" Tilterman smiled up at Bill from underneath a picture of an old woman. Her beady eyes watching his every move, Tilterman ran his eyes over the small golden plaque underneath her, reading her name as he did so.

"The honourable Lady Periwinkle of Ducksburg."

Bill sat in the seat beside Tilterman with a thud of exhaustion.

His black coat flapped outwards from the gust of wind from the cushion.

"I've been in contact with Buttelburg and it would appear that Maisie is travelling to Moucha even now as we speak." Bill glanced around the bar to see who was sitting in the shadows.

"There's no one here, I've checked. The rooms up above are empty and the barkeeper has told me that today is always quiet in here. What of the messengers you sent out, any word from Andy on their situation?"

"I'm not sure, Andy was telling me something about Paddy from the High Council and then we lost the link. We'll have to wait for Maisie and then leave for Abnos at once." Bill had a second glance around, his gut was telling him they were being watched by someone or something.

"We'll have to stay somewhere else. I saw two Rennick warriors leaving the Sleepy Dwarf as I returned." Tilterman moved forwards because from the shadows his eyes were drawn to a picture hanging behind Bill. The face of the old woman in the picture seemed to move closer.

"Bill, look out!" Diving across the table Tilterman rammed his sword through the picture. The old woman fell from the picture and transformed into Surnam, his stomach oozing black liquid. "Quickly Bill, let's get out of here. Where there's one shifter there'll be others." Bill and Tilterman ran from the Blind Eye and headed towards the cathedral at the centre of Moucha.

"Hello, Bill Hello..." Andy hit the on/off button on the vid-link.

"Andy you need too...." Static filled the line between Andy and Bill. 'Dylan Drive' the broken words from Bill slowly filtered through to Andy. "Expect trouble." Again static interrupted Bills voice.

"Bill are you there?" No answer came, leaving Andy to wonder if Bill had got what he said about Paddy and the High Council. Andy could only guess at Bill's broken sentence and decided it was time to get back to Dylan Drive and relay the broken message from Bill to the other gnomes. Andy gathered up his sword and placed his boots on his feet. He would head for Maisie's warehouse and travel from there on Torch, one of her smaller dragons, to Dylan Drive. Before he stepped out from Maisie's house, he looked up and down the street to make sure it was safe to leave. Andy made good time to the stockyards.

"Ra-Mada are you in here old friend?" The small burnt figure of Ra-Mada came walking up from the stalls, her armour smouldering from the latest burst of flames from Reginald. "Looks as if you're having one of those days!" Andy chuckled as Ra-Mada scoffed at his remarks.

"How can I help you Andy or did you just come down here to poke fun at me?" Ra-Mada flicked the visor on her helmet revealing her blue eyes to Andy.

"Can I have Torch, I need to get to Dylan Drive in a hurry and contact Maisie and tell her I've spoken to Bill..." Andy relayed his conversation with Bill to Ra-Mada. Once he had finished he saddled Torch and set out for Dylan Drive. Ra-Mada watched as Andy and the coppered body of Torch disappeared into the setting sun. Turning, she headed back in the direction of Reginald and his antics.

Revelations

Sven and Bill made their way to the small ship's porthole. As they watched the other ship pull up along side the Lucipher, they felt it rock in the waves caused by the dropping of the larger ship's anchor. Sven climbed through the ship's porthole to get a better look at the ship. As Sven looked up at the side of the ship, he saw it was twice the size of the Lucipher, with twice as many masts and portholes. Its hull and sails were as black as night. Sven saw the deck was in darkness and only the moonlight illuminated it, but a yellow glow came from inside the ship.

"Bill, grab that rope and tie it on me, I want to know what's in that other ship." Bill grabbed a long yellow rope from the top of the boxes and tied it around Sven's waist. Bill barely had time to take the other end in his hand when Sven launched himself towards the ship. Bill watched as his companion grabbed onto the first open ship's porthole that came into reach and pulled himself up and peered into the ship.

Several thousand candles and a few oil lamps swayed on rusty hooks illuminating the ship's vast interior. The light cast shadows across the galley revealing some of its contents. Lying at one end of the galley were armour racks, empty of their weapons and shields. The sudden screech of a dragon pulled Sven's eyes skywards, his heart racing at the prospect of been plucked from the side of the ship and swallowed. Sven searched the night sky for the dragon's black shadow and for the oncoming attack. He felt a hot blast of air rush from the window. Sven slowly turned to look for the source of the warm blast, his eyes widened as he saw where it had come from. At the far end of the galley were the largest black dragons he had ever laid eyes on.

Sven watched as a man clad in blackened armour dressed the black dragons in silver and red armour. Their black scales gave off a blue hue in the burning light of the candles and shimmered in the glare of their armour. As each dragon was dressed in their armour, they flapped their wings in expectation of flight. A yellow shine caught Sven's eye and drew it behind the dragons. Hanging from the ceiling of the ship were large golden spikes each one fitted with a harness of brown leather. Sven had never seen weapons like these before. A short lever sat at the end of the spike just below the harness.

A loud bang echoed between the ships's causing Sven and Bill to look up in the direction of the deck. A gangplank had been dropped to join the two ships together and as they watched, the sound of a horn blasted from the Lucipher. Sven watched as the red cloak of Scaripdemus crossed from the Lucipher and disappeared into the shaft of light from the doorway of the ship. The gangplank was slowly pulled back towards the Lucipher and as Sven watched it disappear onto the deck, a loud cheer erupted inside the larger ship.

"Bill, pull me back." Bill tugged on the rope as Sven jumped from the ship's porthole in the Lucipher. "I have to get on board the other ship." Sven pulled his hood over his face.

"Why, what's going happening on the other ship?" Bill looked at Sven and waited for his answer.

"It looks like there could be an entire army over there. I have seen dragons being dressed for battle and that cheer we just heard sounds like Scaripdemus has his army on that monster and more on this ship. I need to be sure so whatever happens don't move from here, if we're separated stay here. The ships are going to the same place." With those words Sven disappeared through the door and up towards the deck of the Lucipher, leaving Bill in the dark galley. More cheering erupted in the larger ship drawing Bill back to the window.

A dark veil lay on the deck of the Lucipher allowing Sven to move in the shadows and away from the unwanted eyes of the night watch. Sven saw the wheelman slumped over the wheel and an empty bottle of ale held loosely in his hand. Slowly moving across the deck, Sven picked up a length of discarded rope and moved to the edge of the ship. Keeping a watchful eye on the snoring wheelman, he tied the rope on the gunnels of the ship. Sven picked up an old wooden bucket and tied it to the rope. Looking across at the larger ship, Sven realised that there was nowhere to secure the bucket. His only way on to the ship was to drop into the water below and climb the anchor chain. The water below looked cold and unappealing to Sven and caused his mind to go back to the sewer he had waded in to escape Theobald Rheims earlier and to the docks when he had slipped onto the Lucipher. Looking over the side, Sven climbed through the miniature pillars of the railing.

"Well here goes nothing, time to get wet!" He dropped over the side and fell silently towards the waves below, the bucket held tightly in his hand as he fell. His body stiffened up as he hit the icy surface of the sea, his ears and nose quickly filling with water, his body jerking to catch air. Pulling his arms to his side and kicking his legs downwards, Sven forced his body back to the surface. Rubbing the water from his face, he quickly located the Lucipher and then with all the strength in his body pushed off the hull towards the other ship, a mere arm's length for a bigger person but a good swim for a gnome.

The anchor chain of the larger ship was like a grand staircase and allowed Sven to walk up it with no problem. As he ascended the chain, he saw the ship's name in gold lettering. As he spelled it out, he realised that this was the ship that sailors and ports feared. It had a reputation for destroying fleets of ships and cities of vast proportions. The ship was The Nannreb.

The God of the Under World once owned the ship, according to legend. It would carry Nannreb and his Seven Dragon Slayers all over the nine seas of Niemad. No ship had ever survived an assault from the ship and no city ever stood after it came into port. Those who had seen and survived the Nannreb, only ever told their tale after going crazy. Sven feared that Scaripdemus had raised Nannreb and his Seven Dragon Slayers. He would have to search the ship from top to bottom and hope that he wouldn't find Nannreb or worst still the Seven Dragon Slayers.

Sven peeped through the chain hole in the side of the ship expecting to see an army of dragons and men but when he looked all he saw were four guards. He pulled himself through the hole and darted behind some ale barrels that were stacked on the otherwise empty deck of the Nannreb. The wheelman stood staring into the darkness suggesting to Sven that he was in a trance. Either way if he saw the gnome sneaking about on his ship, Sven would be tossed to the sharks. Another of the guards stood at the opposite end of the ship staring in the other direction. Two more were marching up and down each side of the ship. Sven looked for his next hiding place but he couldn't see any where on the featureless deck.

The deck's sides were filled with cannons in every possible place and more mounted on the side railings. The cannons on the railings were smaller in size than those on the deck floor itself. The small cannons were on pivots and could swing to fire anywhere they were being attacked from. Sven counted one hundred small rail cannons on each side, each one reflecting the moonlight on its pearly black surface and sixty bigger cannons on the deck floor. He saw two large canopies at either end of the deck and wondered what was under them. As he watched the patrolling guards turn and walk towards the opposite end of the ship, Sven rolled under the canopy.

He had heard stories about the breath of Nannreb and how it would engulf any size ship in flames and here was the source of his breath. A cannon in the shape of a devil's head was what he saw and on further investigation Sven found the mechanism from which the flames came from. A large metal pipe carried a black liquid know as the Blood of Rou, God of the Sun, to the mouth of the cannon. As the cannon shot its missile forward, it was carried into the liquid and then passed through flames on the other side causing it to ignite. Sven decided it was time to search below deck and see what other secrets the Nannreb held in the pits of its belly but first he'd leave a little surprise for the users of the cannon.

Poking his head from underneath the canopy, Sven located the stairwell leading below. Once he had the all clear Sven ran for the stairwell and disappeared below decks taking cover under some sheepskins. Breathing as softly as he could, he listened for any sign that he had been seen descending the stairs. Once he was sure the coast was clear, Sven peered slowly from behind the sheepskins, searching the darkness for any patrolling guards. Lying on the ground beside him was one such guard; asleep his jowls rattling as he snored. A small slice of bacon was drifting in and out of his mouth but never making its way onto his tongue. Sven looked into the darkness of the galley and discovered that the guard was not alone in his snoring. The outlines of several hundred other soldiers came into view. How many decks contained soldiers and how many contained dragons? Sven moved slowly through the snoring soldiers not daring to stop until he reached his exit to the next level.

"Mammy, stop I'm want my cuddles back, give em' ere?" Sven froze as a large and very hairy soldier grabbed onto his leg and pulled it close to him. "Ah, Cuddles Tiny loves you, yes he do..." Sven couldn't afford to be Cuddles too long. The faint sound of voices drifted up the stairs leading from the deck below. He needed to move quickly or run the risk of being captured. Sven recognised one of the voices, its sly harsh tone. He pulled his leg free and slipped behind a bale of straw, hiding himself in the shadows.

Maisie had watched the sun travel through the sky from the time it rose to now when it had begun to set behind her. Moucha began to climb over the horizon, the Zarrif industries building rising high into the starry sky. The cities old gothic shapes silhouetted against the newer more modern buildings. She guided her gyrocopter towards the glassed building of Zen Zarrif and his helipad on the roof. The large red G indicated where Maisie should touch down her flying machine. She touched down dead centre blocking out most of the G. As she stepped from the gyrocopter she tapped a small green button marked 'Fold'. Stepping back she watched as her copter folded itself away into the small green suitcase it had evolved from back in Buttelburg. Picking it up Maisie sought out the fire escape door and followed the steel staircase down to Zarrif's office.

As she stepped from the door leading to the corridor outside Zen Zarrif's, she saw Black Dog slumped on the floor and the crumpled body of a security guard next to him. Walking slowly towards the door of the office she cast a charm of protection. A blue aura surrounded her, flowing around every move she made. Slowly pushing on the door Maisie entered, checking the room for any threats. The room had been searched and nothing had been done to conceal it. The skies around Moucha had also darkened considerably in the short period of time that Maisie had spent in the office.

As she re-emerged onto the roof, her eyes were slowly drawn to a bright light rising from the sea. She pressed on the handle of her suitcase and stepped back as her gyrocopter unfolded in front of her. Maisie followed the light's path to the cathedral in the centre of Moucha, where she lost it. She sat on the edge of the cockpit of the gyrocopter and picked up a small black box marked 'transmitter.'

"Gyro One to Bill, do you receive, over?" The radio just hissed and scratched noisily in Maisie's hand. "This is Maisie calling Bill, do you receive Bill?" Again the radio gave no answer. Maisie placed the radio back on its holder and stared out over the city, watching the neon signs come to life. The Sleepy Dwarf would have to be Maisie's next stop. The gyrocopter chucked to life as Maisie pressed the start button, its very skeleton rattling as it took to the air. She pulled on the brown stick beside her knee, urging the copter to the left and in the direction of the Sleepy Dwarf.

The Sleepy Dwarf soon came into view, its neon dwarf snorting blue 'Z's' into the night sky. The building was too small for Maisie and her gyrocopter, but the large black building beside it was perfect for a landing. The copter touched down gently like only Maisie could do. As she stepped from the cockpit, she saw the spire of the cathedral light up as if a million fireflies had landed on top of it. Taking a black pouch belt from the copter, Maisie set off for the Sleepy Dwarf. Walking to the edge of the building, Maisie leaned over to see how far down it was to the roof of the inn.

"Fifty floors, dear. Hmmm, not bad!" Maisie had jumped from higher buildings, but not too much higher. The offices at the Premier's building in Buttelburg were only five floors higher than this and there was the added discomfort of landing on a spiked railing if you miss your landing.

"Well, Maisie here it goes...." She moved back, gauging the amount of run up she would need to clear the safety railings on the roof's edge. Taking in a deep breath Maisie ran and launched herself over the edge of the building. As she cleared the railing, she turned her face back towards the building and arched her back to form the perfect swan dive. Floor after floor passed in front of Maisie each one becoming a number bringing her closer to her landing.

"Five, Four, Three, Two and now..." Maisie pulled her feet down towards the ground and spread her coat out to each side forming wings. As the air trapped itself in Maisie's coat it slowed her down to a floating motion. As she felt the solid ground touch her feet she rolled across the balcony, stopping at the door's edge. "Perfect as always Maisie..." She spoke softly to herself and stood up brushing herself down.

Pushing the door open, Maisie found herself in the lobby of the Sleepy Dwarf, its desk unattended and dusty. The bar was empty, the hall was empty and the stairs leading to the rooms was dark and silent. Walking towards the desk, Maisie saw a small bell and a sign with the words 'Ring For Assistance'. So Maisie pressed down on the top of the bell, its jingle bringing momentary life to the empty inn. No one answered the bell so Maisie rang a second and a third and a fourth time but still no one came to assist her. She looked at the bell with the intention of ringing it a fifth time but decided the information she wanted was right in front of her. A small book filled with names sat on the desk, wide open, just begging for someone to read it.

"Bill Brickton room 312." There he was in bold and very black ink. Maisie looked at the floor directory, lying beside the resident book. Once she found the room clearly marked on the third floor. She turned and walked up the wooden staircase. Maisie followed the staircase until she reached the door leading onto the third floor. As she opened the door, the sound of two people fighting slowly drifted into her ears. The language was a familiar one, one she had heard and fought against many times, Rennick warriors. She drew her sword from beneath her coat and stepped into the hallway. Slowly making her way to the door marked 312, Maisie listened to the argument inside, trying to catch any words that made sense. Drawing herself along the wall outside the door, Maisie glanced in and saw the warriors trashing the room.

She found herself looking at the usual pairing of Rennick warriors, one tall and burly for high attacks. The other one small and well built, sturdy for lower attacks. Maisie would have to outsmart them and do her best to capture one them for questioning prefer- ably the smaller of the two. She wondered if Bill had succeeded in finding the Book of Demons and the key or had Zen Zarrif safely taken the book to Abnos. As Maisie watched the warriors search the room, she heard another set of voices just outside the window.

"Durac, come on we've been called back by Mallard, he's cap- tured Sven and Drego and he knows the location of the key." Maisie watched as Durac and the smaller warrior exited through the win- dow, transforming into black ravens and flying off to meet Mallard. She entered the room in the hope that there was some clue as to the whereabouts of Bill and Tilterman. Staring out over Moucha, her eyes were drawn back towards the cathedral and the bright light that had captured her attention earlier. "Maybe its time I investi- gated that light!" The spire had grown brighter and she watched as the light drifted down towards the lower levels of the cathedral.

Sven lay as still as possible behind the bale of straw. Listening to the voices, as they got closer and closer, he watched as the figure of Scaripdemus came into view and Cundra following in his shadow.

"Our preparations are almost complete, once we capture the town of Moucha, we can travel forward and join forces with Erasmus and the Gnome Necromancer Mallard in the future. The head is in place and soon Brickton will be on board and then every- thing will be set." Sven watched as Scaripdemus faded from view and his voice disappeared into the sounds of the sea. Once they had passed from Sven's view he proceeded to the steps from where they had come.

Sven made sure that no other guards were on watch and then slipped down the steps. It was dark and he could only see a few feet in front of him, the silhouetted shape of an oil lamp swing- ing from the rafters of the galley. He reached out and slowly pulled the lamp from the wooden beam and as he did so he uttered some magic, "Infernus" and the lamp's oil slowly formed a small yellow flame. Sven watched as the galley grew brighter its interior becoming more visible. In the centre of the galley, Sven saw the head that Scaripdemus had referred to standing alone in the darkness.

It was the Dragon of Nannreb, recognisable from the large curved horns pointing at the Underworld. The light from the lamp was reflected off its black armour, overlapping like an archer's mail. Black ring hiding black ring, all set against one another to protect the soft skin of the once magnificent beast. Long white teeth hung sharply from the burning red mouth, the dragon's tongue was missing a large wedge shape from its centre. Sven ran his hand along the scaling skin, it roughness a sign of long years of life and the many battle scars testimony to its great prowess in battle. Stepping back from the head, Sven stared at its eyes. To his amazement, in the eyes of the dragon were the crown jewels that Bill had set out to recover from the thief.

The jewels were set in the deep black pits that were the dragon's eyes. He caught the reflection of the lamp in the jewels and was drawn into their deep red colour. As he stared at his own reflection he saw the scene around him change. His reflection stood in a large chapel, candles and burning lamps set around the dragon's head. Sven watched his reflection walk between the burning candles, his eyes searching for anything he might recognise.

Walking around the dragon, Sven found himself watching a woman shrouded in a blue mist performing spells. Her lips franticly moving, blue arrows shooting from inside the mist and travelling deep into the dragon's head, causing the chapel, around the woman, to rock in its foundations. His eyes locked on her features, Sven felt that this woman in the mist was somehow familiar but where had he seen her before?

Sven was drawn back to the creaking interior of the ship, voices breaking his concentration. Cundra and Scaripdemus were coming down the stairs from the upper levels, their voices cutting the air like a cold winters frost. He had little time to react and only managed to hide himself in the dragon's mouth.

Falling across the edge of the top step Sven saw Scaripdemus's red cloak, its edges sniffing at the air like a serpents tongues. Watching as the two figures grew into the full forms of Cundra and Scaripdemus, he listened to their conversation.

"It's time to activate the gateway to its full potential and see if Erasmus is as powerful as he claims." Sven slipped from the dragon's mouth, deciding that this might be a bad place to hide. Sliding around the edge of the darkened galley, Sven slipped behind some straw bales. Peering over the top he watched as Cundra splashed a smoking liquid into the mouth of the dragon and saw his lips speak a silent incantation. The dragon's mouth began to glow a brilliant white causing Sven to cover his eyes.

"Damn it, why does it not work?" Cundra began to speak in a strange tongue, words which Sven could only guess to be curses on his failure to open the gateway. "Its Brickton, he must be the key to operating the gate!!!!" Turning on his heels Cundra stormed back up the stairway, Scaripdemus following. Sven waited till he was sure the coast was clear and slowly emerged from his hiding place. Looking for the nearest ship's porthole, Sven decided it was time to return to Bill on the Lucipher.

Maisie brought the gyrocopter to life and motioned it towards the cathedral and the mysterious light. Flying over Moucha was hazardous at the best of times. Its skies were notorious for the heavy volumes of blimp barges; they floated across the sky like super clouds slowing other traffic down to a virtual snail's pace. Maisie guided the gyrocopter in and out of the traffic, dodging the larger slower moving vehicles. The cathedral grew in size as she swiftly moved towards it; its gothic shapes becoming more and more detailed in the setting sun. Two large gargoyles sat watching her approach, their expressions set in deep grey stone. Setting the gyrocopter down in their vast shadows, Maisie looked up at the giant talons of the gargoyles and in a mocking voice spoke to them.

"Don't scratch her boys, be gentle and you can wash her as well..." The stairs leading down to the centre of the cathedral was dark and smelled of old socks. The cobwebs were big enough to catch the brown rats that scurried around busily under Maisie's feet as she descended the stairs. The stairs spiralled its way down through the darkness to the brighter lower levels of the cathedral. At each level a small brown door stood greeting all those who came close.

Hanging upon the door was a sign indicating what floor had been reached. Maisie read each sign as she descended towards the main praying area of the cathedral. The first sign she met was written in faded gold letters, *'Storeroom'*. Maisie continued down into the lower levels of the cathedral until she came to the brown door she wanted to pass through, *'Praying area, Quiet Please'*. Maisie pushed down gently on the brass handle until she heard the latch click open; slowly pushing the door forward Maisie took a few silent moments to check the large room beyond the door.

The cathedral's pews had all been pushed up against the walls clearing the central area. The stained glass windows had been covered in black cloth, but Maisie couldn't help notice that the room was as bright as if the sun was shining through the windows. The details of the large stone pillars were clearly visible, each crack appearing to be illuminated by a light hidden inside their stone bodies. All the statues in the cathedral had been covered in red covers hiding their features to curious eyes. It wasn't long before Maisie found the source of the cathedral's light. In the very centre of the cathedral was the ball of light Maisie had seen from the top of the Zarrif industries building.

She watched as the ball floated several feet from the ground, its light penetrating every darkened feature of the cathedral. She stepped between the large stone pillars and watched to see if the ball followed her movements. As she moved in and out of the pillars, the ball began to spin ever so slowly at first, then faster and faster causing the dust beneath it to rise up into a mini tornado, Maisie moved out from behind the pillars and began to chant a spell of protection around her. Her words filled the cathedral, echoing off every wall and pillar.

"PROTECTUS TOTALUS." Maisie repeated the words over and over again. Slowly a mist grew up around her, its blue hue reflecting the light from the spinning ball casting shafts of blue into the cathedral. As Maisie got closer to the ball she stopped and held her hands out in front of her with a small amulet and its chain intertwined in her slender white fingers. A blue dragon began to move in the amulet, circling the moon and as it did it began to grow in size and the moon along with it. The mist began to cover Maisie. Her body began to jerk and shake, as the circling dragon grew bigger, lifting her from the floor. Maisie floated above the cathedral floor at the same level as the ball of light.

"Forward." Maisie spoke softly. As the words landed on the mist a black shadow began to move around Maisie causing her to float gently across the distance between her and the ball. "Enough." The black shadow halted keeping Maisie floating at the same level as the light.

"Penetras, reveal to me the source of this light." A flaming blue arrow shot from her fingertips causing the ball of light to shake and rumble. Again Maisie spoke the spell and again a flaming arrow shot from the tips of her finger and pierced deep into the ball of white light. Maisie felt the cathedral shiver around her its very foundations rocking beneath the blue mist. The black shadow began to steadily grow larger in size with each arrow of blue flame. She watched as a picture began to form in the white light, silhouetted shapes slowly stepping into the white light. The interior of a ship became visible, a solitary figure watching her from beyond. A face that Maisie had stared into many times, a face that came to her rescue in her most desperate times of need.

"Sven, can you hear me?" Maisie watched as he stared back into her eyes. Did he not recognise the face of the girl he had saved so many centuries ago? "Sven, where are you, what is the ship's name?" Maisie slowly began to understand, she was staring into the past. It was a portal in time. Maisie watched as two men walked in front of the gateway, her eyes widening as she recognised their faces. Maisie watched as Cundra stepped closer to the portal and cast a liquid into it.

The ball of light began to spin frantically and Maisie watched as the picture grew in size. Her lips moved frantically casting spells, waves of blue light travelling into the portal blocking it from opening and causing the cathedral to shake violently. The picture began to fade in front of her, leaving only the bright orb of light floating in front of her. Sweat and tears ran the length of her pale face, the blue mist fading back into the amulet as Maisie let it fall from her fingers. The last rays of light from the orb faded as her eyes closed, releasing her from her exertion.

Dragon Droppings

"Bong, Bong, Bong." The sound of the cathedral's bells stirred Maisie. Her eyes felt heavy and her head even more so. Slowly she forced her eyes open, the light caused her to blink repeatedly. The orb was still floating in the centre of the cathedral and slowly Maisie remembered what had happened. As she raised herself from the ground, she thought of her protection spell and how it had not been strong enough to withstand the power contained within the orb. She had never failed before at protecting herself with that particular spell and wondered why it had not worked on this occasion. Forcing her hand from the floor, Maisie took hold of the nearest pew. Her grip felt weak on the hardened wooden seat, her arm aching and her fingers numb.

She pulled herself off the ground, her legs felt weak beneath her. Her stance was unsteady and her head began to spin. Her hands shook as she gripped the seat to keep her balance. Slowly she pushed her left leg forward, urging her body to make the first steps towards contacting Bill and Tilterman. The stairs seemed twice as long and twice as steep as when she had descended them earlier.

"How long have I been unconscious?" Maisie's own words rang out in her head, sounding much louder than the cathedral bells. Would she be too late in contacting Bill? *"Storeroom."* A few more steps and Maisie would be on the roof and then she could contact Bill. She pushed the door open revealing the pale moonlight reflecting from a solitary puddle beyond the door. The gargoyles sat still on their pedestals, watching all who moved on the streets of Moucha far below. Maisie sat into the cockpit of the gyrocopter and picked up her radio transceiver.

"Bill, are you receiving, over?" Maisie waited for the familiar voice of Bill to filter over the airwaves. Several minutes passed without any reply. "Bill are you receiving?" Again the airwaves were silent. She stared out over the city and wondered if Bill was still somewhere within its ancient streets or had he left to find the other members of the Order. The Zarrif industries building loomed in the distance its tall dark shadow falling over Moucha. Maisie started to think about the possible places Bill could be. He had already left the Sleepy Dwarf, perhaps he was on the way back to find Zen Zarrif or a clue to his whereabouts, or had he travelled further perhaps to Abnos to find Wang Wu?

The blades of the gyrocopter slowly came to life as Maisie laid her finger on the red start button. She eased back on the control stick and rotated the lever at her side to motion the copter into action. As it slowly lifted itself from the cathedral's roof, she pushed the control stick forward and the copter took flight in the direction of the Zarrif industries building. The city streets below were full of people busily going about their nightly activities. The city skies were quiet now with only cabs and emergency services flying low over the rooftops. The city lights drowned out the starry sky allowing only an orange hue for company.

"WHOOOOOSSOOOOSSSSSS." Maisie's attention was drawn away from the Zarrif industries building and the streets below by an unfriendly but recognisable sound. Her head turned frantically as she searched the night sky for the source of the sound. "WHOOOOOSSOOOOSSSSSS." This time she saw the stream of white smoke coming from the rear of a rocket, as it propelled towards her. Maisie jammed the control stick to the right, forcing the copter to turn onto its side and fall towards the streets of Moucha far below. She watched as the rocket passed within inches of the tail of her copter and then she heard the 'WHOOOOOSSSOOO' of a second and a third rocket being launched. She quickly located them as they came close, she jammed her knee against a small blue button marked 'Dispersal'.

A small door on the underside of the copter fell open and re-leased several bright flares. Two of the rockets raced after the flares and exploded as they made contact. The last rocket had turned and was chasing after Maisie with increased speed. The copter turned. Twisting to check over her shoulder, Maisie found herself along side the cathedral. Its gargoyles watching, their laughter frozen in time as they waited for Maisie's doom. The rocket was closing in, giving Maisie only seconds to react and avoid becoming dust.

Forcing the copter into a straight dive Maisie hoped she could gain enough speed to out run the rocket. As the streets began to close in, Maisie pulled as hard as she could on the control stick forcing the copter to level out just above the street. She guided the copter through the neon signs of Moucha, glancing over her shoulder to see if the rocket was still chasing her down. The people on the streets and walkways watched as the green copter flew past. When the rocket came screaming shortly after her, people ran into doorways and dived under dumpsters where they could find pro-tection. One old man dived behind a grey metal bench while his dog chased after the rocket until he lost it.

Every move the copter made, the rocket mimicked, ducking and diving as it did. The copter gave a cough alerting Maisie that her fuel was almost spent and soon not only would the rocket be a problem but also, the sudden impact of the street below. Pulling with all of her might, Maisie forced the copter back towards the sky and the tallest spire of the cathedral. As the copter climbed it began to cough and splutter more violently its red fuel light flashing franticly. It was now or never for Maisie!

She had only just cleared the spire when the copter gave up and its engines died. Maisie turned the copter back towards the ground; the rocket closer than ever before. Aiming the copter for a space between the two gargoyles, Maisie closed her eyes and turned the copter at the very last second. The copter bounced off the stone wing of one of the gargoyles causing it to spin onto the flat cathedral roof.

Maisie opened her eyes and saw the rocket crash into the cathedral wall and explode. She covered her eyes as the bright yellow flash gave way to grey falling rubble and roof tiles. The copter skidded and stopped beside a door. Dizzily Maisie stepped from the cockpit and fell to the ground. Dragging herself to the small guard wall around the edge of the roof, she placed her back against it and stared at the copter. It had been damaged and would need to be repaired before she could reach Bill. Its tail wing was bent and the green skin on it was torn, an easy task for Maisie as soon as she regained her strength.

Sven pulled himself up to the ship's porthole and checked above it. Once he was sure no one was looking over the edge, he pulled himself out and dropped down into the water below. He slowly swam back towards the Lucipher, running the events on the ship through his mind. The lady in the dragon's mouth was somehow familiar but how, he wasn't sure. The chain of the Lucipher was cold and hard when Sven reached it, the green discolouration just visible under the moonlight. He climbed up the slippery surface of the chain, watching the decks of both ships as he did so.

As the first ship's porthole came into reach, Sven heard the sound of someone moving inside. Slowly moving towards the darkened ship's porthole, he saw the dark shape of two hands reaching out from just inside. Sven soon made out the familiar features of the young Bill Brickton. The inside of the galley was brighter than when Sven left earlier. Bill had obtained a small oil lamp and it was burning slowly.

"So, is it them on the ship?" Bill watched as Sven paced the galley, his hand on his chin. "Sven, what is it, what have you seen on the other ship?" Sven looked up at Bill and relayed everything he had witnessed on the Nannreb and how he had seen the lady on the other side of the Dragon's mouth.

"It's a time portal, I'm sure of it but I don't know where it leads to and there was something about the woman. I've seen her before, I just can't remember where." Sven sat back on a brown bag of grain, the top of his hat just reaching Bill's chin. Bill stared out of the ship's porthole and watched the two ships as they began to sail, the Nannreb taking the lead, its massive sails blocking the moonlight.

"Sven, if it is a portal then why did they need the crown jewels?" Bill turned and stared into Sven's face waiting for his reply. He remained silent leaving Bill to wonder if his uncle was the reason, or had the jewels been used to lure him into the hands of Scaripdemus? Bill sat down beside Sven and drifted off to sleep.

"Bill, Bill wake up, we're here." Bill opened one eye hoping to find himself back in his warm bed. As he looked up he saw Sven looking out through the ship's porthole. "I had a feeling this was where we would end up." Sven stuck out his hand, beckoning Bill to join him at the ship's porthole. "The city of Moucha." Bill stared out the ship's porthole and was greeted by a picture he had only ever seen through the eyes of his father, in his stories and tales.

The Nannreb and the Lucipher had docked in the shadow of a large grey city, the biggest Bill had ever seen. The buildings seemed to disappear at the other side of the world; perhaps even some had fallen off the world's edge. In the centre of the city stood a large gothic cathedral, its pointed arches standing out in the sun. The large spire at the centre of the massive building watched the activities that unfolded in the city. In its shadows sat two grey gargoyles, their menacing gaze watching the city, their wings wrapped around their bodies adding to their colossal size and threatening pose. Angels sat on other spires, swords and shields at the ready for the defence of the cathedral.

"Bill, out the ship's porthole before they come for us." Sven pulled at Bill's sleeve urging him out the window and into the cold water below. Bill climbed up on the edge of the ship's porthole. No one was watching and Bill tumbled out and down towards the water. Sven checked the decks and dropped towards the water. As they hit the water its cold touch caused them to shake and gasp for breath. Bill raised himself out of the water, wiping it from his eyes and nose. Turning he searched the water's surface for Sven. He found Sven sitting on a small slipway, his socks in his hand.

"What are you waiting for Bill?" Sven twisted his sock and watched the water run out of them. "Come on, there's something happening. We must hurry, we have to know where they're going in the city." Sven was already putting his socks back on by the time Bill had gotten out from the water.

Sven positioned himself behind three wooden crates filled with a strange yellow fruit. Bill sat next to him and pulled one of the small oval fruits from the crate and offered it to Sven. Sven shook his head. Bill opened his mouth and bit down firmly on the fruit. Sven turned just in time to see Bill's face grimace in disgust. Laughing, Sven pointed to the sign above the crates. Bill lurched as he read it.

'DRAGON DROPPINGS ONLY'.

The sound of drums drew Bill and Sven back to the activity on the Nannreb. As they watched the ship they saw the bow begin to split into two, revealing the large hold Sven had been in earlier. Soldiers began to emerge in lines of five, their armour reflecting the sun into the water. Bill counted eighty-seven lines of warriors, and then rolling slowly from the darkness came the Dragon's head.

Its large curved horns pointing at the Underworld, the sunlight was reflected by its black armour.

Long white teeth hung sharply from its burning red mouth and its dead jewelled eyes stared into the souls of every man, woman and child. Bill watched as its thunderous rolling brought the city of Moucha to a stand still. Sven moved slowly through the streets, being careful not to be seen by any of Scaripdemus' men. Bill followed closely behind him concealing his face with a crate of dragon droppings.

As the dragon was rolled through the streets of the great city of Moucha, Sven saw two of Scaripdemus' men drift away from the main body of troops and decided to follow them. Bill watched as the two soldiers slipped down an alley near the cathedral, discarding their armour as they went. Sven drew his sword and called after them.

"FRIEND OR FOE OF THE ORDER." The two stopped and drew their curved swords and slowly turned, their matt black helmets concealing their faces. Bill pulled his sword from its scabbard and stood along side Sven.

"In your case gnome, I'll choose friend as I can't afford to fall in our time of need." Bill eased his grip on his sword and waited for the next move. Sven moved forward, replacing his sword as he moved towards the soldiers.

"You truly are a sight for sore and weary eyes my old friend." The stockier of the two stepped forward and removed his helmet to reveal darkly tanned skin. His eyes were wild with the fires of freedom and his smile warm in the greeting of an old friend.

"It was true then you were on the Lucipher and young Bill was with you, excellent. Come, we are camped on the outskirts of the city." Sven beckoned Bill to follow them and he found himself been ushered into yet another sewer.

Sven and the strangers were out of earshot and Bill could only catch every other word of their conversation. He heard the words dragon, which he was used to hearing, but the words 'time por-tal' and 'time travel' meant little to him. Bill became aware of his surroundings as Sven stopped to watch the stranger untie a small boat. The sewer wasn't like what he had waded and fought his way through in Wolfenbuttel. The main cavern in which they stood had large stone archways leading into the darkness of the vast sewer system. The walls were decorated with murals of battle scenes from legends about great warriors such as Thorsic Iron Butt and Sylvia Gold Mane. Great lanterns hung burning brightly in the claws of enormous stone eagles.

A short distance from where they stood, Bill saw a maze of metal walkways and passages leading away from them into the darkness. Standing on the nearest walkway was a tall man, a sword hanging loosely by his side. Sitting on his head was a small and battered hel-met, a red plume lilting on the breeze blowing through the sewers.

"Step into the boat young Bill." The stranger was now standing in front of Bill. "The man you're watching is our guide, he knows these sewers like the back of his hand so don't worry about meeting any unwanted swimmers down here..." The stranger winked at Bill as he stepped into the boat. Bill felt it rock gently in the water and then settle as he sat on the cold damp wooden seat. The stranger pushed away from the sewer's dock with a large wooden pole, a green mist curling its way up the pole as the water-rippled outwards. His eyes grew heavy as the green mist drifted up around his face and as Bill watched the other boats he saw their occupants drift away into a deep sleep and soon afterwards he was sleeping soundly.

The Gnome Express

The large wooden door leading into the cathedral moaned as Bill pushed it open, letting the sun's light rush into the darkness. Tilterman followed close at Bill's heels, his sword drawn and his eyes searching every shadow for the presence of Rennick warriors or any other danger. Walking slowly inside Bill noticed movement just beyond the lines of brown pews. Tapping Tilterman on the shoulder, he pointed to where he had seen the flash of something move. There lurking among the shadows was a gnome, his armour just visible in the darkness. Tilterman called out to him but the gnome paid him no attention and moved further into the shadows, his armour sparkling in the dim candlelight of the cathedral. Tilterman and Bill followed him and they saw him descend a wooden staircase leading to the catacombs beneath the cathedral.

The stairwell fell sharply into the catacombs and stopped in front of an arch leading to large circular room. Several arches stood on the outside of the room leading into darkness. Tall-cloaked priests were carved into the archways, their hands grasping large swords and each one prepared to defend the catacombs against unwanted visitors. The grey stones in the arches were fading from the sunlight and small patches of mould were flourishing at their bases.

Tilterman spotted the gnome slipping into the darkness of the tombs. Bill moved around the room surveying each inhabited shelf. Dusty skulls and bones stared back at Bill, a thousand stories all held in the silence of death. Tilterman moved around the edge of the room, slowly moving towards where he had seen the gnome disappear. Staring into the darkness, Tilterman saw a glimmer of reflected light, straining his eyes he stared into the darkness and watched, as the glimmer grew stronger and brighter.

Bill stared in the direction of the light and soon became aware of the true source. Emerging from the shadowed depths of the catacombs a white demon approached them. The tunnel around him began to turn to frosted white and as he came closer, Bill and Tilterman felt the cold lashing of his breath against their bodies. The demon towered over them, his ice blue talons extended for the kill. His breath had frozen Bill's sword into its scabbard refusing to let it be drawn.

"Ternack the Enforcer, loyal servant to Erasmus Reich. I am here to destroy Bill Brickton, Keeper of Secrets. Whom do I face?" The demon spoke, his booming voice shaking the catacombs and the insides of the tiny individuals standing before his mighty mass. Bill turned and looked down on Tilterman, who had begun to pull on his trouser leg.

"What now?" Bill shrugged his shoulders and stared back at the demon in front of him. It stood three times the height of Bill its head tipping the inside of the catacombs ceiling. Bill watched as the mass of blue ice stared down on them its eyes dead and cold.

"You face the one you have been sent to destroy..." Before Bill could finish his sentence, the demon lunged forward; its icy talons piercing the ground where Bill and Tilterman stood. Bill had anticipated the attack and rolled swiftly to the side, forcing his sword from its scabbard. As Bill regained his feet his sword found one of the demons fingers, melting it away from the ice blue hand. As it hit the ground it melted and ran back into the foot of demon.

Tilterman dived to the centre of the room, his sword at the ready for the oncoming attack. The demon struck out again at Bill, this time his talons found their mark. Tilterman cried out and jumped onto the demon's back the ice burning his hands as he gripped the spikes running its length. The demon's hand reached round and flung him to the ground, where its foot crashed down towards his defenceless body.

Bill picked himself up just in time to see Tilterman roll from beneath the icy foot. He felt a surge of cold pain race through his body. Blood flowed freely from his arm, freezing as it came into contact with his skin. His arm began to feel numb and the blood in his vessels cold and hard. How could he destroy a demon of ice?

Tilterman rolled just narrowly missing the demon's cold foot. His sword dug deep into the icy skin of Ternack causing no reaction from him. He saw Bill struggle to his feet and attack the demon with all his might. Tilterman jumped onto the demon's back striking it again and again but having little effect. As he held onto the demon, his eyes were drawn to a movement in the shadows just beyond the room. It was a man standing concealed in the darkness, the outline of his body visible in the flashes from Bills sword as it attacked the demon.

"Bill its Erasmus, he's controlling the demon. Its not real it's a puppet demon." Bill turned to where Tilterman was pointing and there in the shadows was Erasmus Reich. Bill saw a puppet in the shape of Ternack in his hand. "Destroy the puppet and we can vanquish the demon!" Bill pulled a small a dagger from his belt and released it in the direction of Erasmus, which struck the puppet squarely in the abdomen. The demon Ternack screamed out in pain and dropped to its knees. Tilterman saw the decaying look in the demons eyes and sank his sword deep into its chest, melting it back into the clear water from where it was created.

Bill ran towards Erasmus but in the flash of blinding light, he found only the wall of the catacomb knocking him onto his back. Tilterman sank onto the wet floor and stared into the darkness. His body ached from the exertion of the battle and his chest rose and fell rapidly as he tried to catch up with his own breath. Bill lay motionless on the ground his arm pounding with the pain.

"Tilterman quickly you must get a fire burning before the ice takes over my body and I become consumed with frozen madness." Tilterman climbed to his feet and began to gather the unlit torches scattered around the walls in the catacombs. Piling them beside Bill, Tilterman whispered a short incantation and finished with words of magic. As he uttered the final word a flame leaped from his hands onto the torches.

A shimmer caught Tilterman's eyes causing him to leap to his feet and draw his sword once more. The shimmer was moving away from them and down one of the tunnels leading deep into the catacombs. Running down the tunnel, Tilterman saw the shimmering mail of the gnome from earlier. Calling after him, Tilterman again got no answer. The tunnel grew darker and darker and the footsteps of the strange gnome soon faded. After several minutes, Tilterman gave up and returned to Bill. Walking back into the chamber where Bill lay Tilterman saw splinters of ice emerging from under Bill's skin and falling to he ground. Bill's face was filled with pain as the last of the ice spilled from his eyes, melting as it touched the warm air.

"Did you catch him?" Tilterman shook his head. "He has something to do with Erasmus and this whole sorrowful affair but for now we must hurry to Abnos and find Wang Wu before Mallard gets to him!" Bill was searching the area where Erasmus had stood and was now holding the burnt puppet remains of the demon. Upon the puppet's handle was a half moon encircled by two ravens, Bill knew this to be the mark of Mallard.

The sight of an orange setting sun greeted Bill and Tilterman as they emerged from the dark interior of St. Stanosnos's cathedral. The streets were busy and businesses were staring to finish up their trading for that day. Abnos lay several days to the south of Moucha and the quickest way to travel to Abnos was by 'Gnome Express'.

Tilterman led Bill along a narrow and dark street named 'Blind Lane'. At the end of the street stood a small shop, its dark exterior blending with the dirt and bleak surroundings making it almost invisible to the eye. Bill looked up at the small sign swinging merrily from an old hag's hand and on the sign was a scribble, what Bill made out to be 'The Windy Nag'. Tilterman pushed the door open and disappeared inside leaving Bill outside staring at the sign.

"Bill, today, inside man." Tilterman stuck his head out the door and looked up at Bill. Promptly obeying, Bill followed him inside. As he stepped through the door he saw a black phone on a table.

The room was almost empty, its windows blacked out. The dappled light fractured the darkness, allowing Bill to watch as Tilterman picked up the receiver. His stomach twitched at the prospect of travelling by the Gnome Express. He heard Tilterman say 'Abnos' and before he knew what was happening, he felt the tingling sensation of been sucked into the telephone receiver in Tilterman's hand. Tilterman laughed, as Bill screamed and disappeared into the phone receiver. Placing the receiver on the table, Tilterman repeated the word and disappeared down the telephone line after Bill, leaving a blue trail of dying sparks dancing across the table.

"I hate that feeling." Bill shook himself clean, ripples of electricity wriggling across the ground as he did so. "It's the sizzling in your ears that gets me and why can't you see anything? All I ever hear are voices filling out conversations that make no sense whatsoever. The conversation I heard was, 'My dog told you that the mattress would probably fly off with the duck soup yesterday and Miss McGrath was in the pharaohs tomb left of yellow and blue socks'. See, no sense whatsoever! Why can't you gnomes invent a better way of travelling?" Tilterman was still laughing at Bill and his dislike of the Gnome Express.

"With all the inventive ways of Gnomes you'd think that a more comfortable way of travelling you would up with come." Tilterman fell about laughing as Bill fell over his words. It was an after effect that humans suffered from after travelling via the telephone. Shaking himself, Bill followed Tilterman from the large dead tree in the centre of Abnos. The trunk creaked an eerie sound as Bill pushed the wooden entrance closed.

The wind whistled through the treetops and rustled the fallen leaves on the forest floor. 'The Hang Man's Tree' stood in a large clearing in the centre of Abnos, its dead exterior hiding the Gnome's creation. Bill looked to the treetops to see what direction they would have to travel to find Wang Wu's home. Two crows circled high above and when Bill called out they soared down to the ground in decreasing circles. The lead crow sat on a branch just over Bill's head and began to groom himself as he spoke.

"Who isssss it you look for, caw?" Bill pulled the amulet of the Order from his pocket and held it out for the crow to see. The crow's eyes widened and he took flight, hovering just above their heads. "This way master, I will take you there myself. Your friends have arrived and are at present with the one called Wang Wu." The crow flew out from the clearing and headed into the sun, Bill and Tilterman following at a slow trot.

"Who has arrived to see Wang Wu?" Bill shouted up to the crow, his pace quickening along with the beating of his heart as he anticipated the crows answer.

"Two Gnomes and some dwarves came not more than two minutes before you stepped from the Hang Man's tree." The crow looked back at Bill, a cunning look in his eye. "Paid me ten sssshinning sssshekels to take them to him without any noise and once we were close they dismissed me..." Bill and Tilterman drew their swords and continued to follow the crows to Wang Wu's. Stopping short of where Wang Wu's house was, Bill dismissed the crow and called

Tilterman to his side.

"If it is Paddy and Mallard that have arrived in the forest it could only mean one of two things." Bill paused and after a few minutes broke the silence. "Tilterman, Wang Wu is in danger and I fear we may be too late. We'll split up and cover his house from both sides. I'll take the front and you the back. Once you enter, whistle." Tilterman nodded and disappeared into the undergrowth of the forest. Bill stood for a moment and thought about how he would play out the events to his advantage, knowing full well that Wang Wu could have already been killed or worst still, tricked into siding with Mallard. He dropped to his belly and crawled along the forest floor. Standing out in front of Wang Wu's house was Mallard, Paddy and three dwarfs standing guard in the yard. Wang Wu stood on the steps leading up to his humble dwelling, his hands gripping his walking stick.

"Mallard these lies you bring before me are ridiculous, Bill would never threaten the Order with such recklessness. Where did you obtain your information from?" Mallard looked at the old and withered man standing in front of him. His long grey beard lilted on the whispering wind. Two old and wrinkled hands sitting on the top of a crooked black ivory stick their skin withered and weak.

"Why would I lie about something so serious? Wang Wu you have known me for three centuries now and have I never let the Order down?" Mallard smirked at the old man as he moved across the courtyard of Wang Wu's house. Wang Wu stood silent and listening to the unfamiliar song of a Blue Jay. It had been two years since the last blue jay sang in the woods, since the crows had started to multiply most of the other birds had left or been killed by them.

"I've known of your plans to bring back Scaripdemus and the five Generals for sometime now, Mallard, will you deny that you're trying to bring back Du'Ard Duchan for that very purpose!" Wang Wu

179

watched as one of the dwarf warriors moved towards the front of the house and entered it.

"It would seem old friend that you do indeed have your ear to the moss on the trees and your eyes on the waters of time. Your information is correct old friend. So now you understand why you must either join me or be against me. The choice is yours!" Mallard stopped as a commotion erupted in the house behind Wang Wu.

"I found this one hiding inside, says he's alone. Should I carry out a search of the forest?" Tonark The Iron Foot reappeared in the small bent door of the house, Tilterman held upside down by one ankle, kicking and squirming to free himself. Mallard turned and faced the trees behind where he stood.

"Bill you can come out now, I know you are here..." A deadly silence fell on the forest as Mallard's voice echoed through the trees. Paddy and Mallard watched as the shadowed figure of Bill appeared in the trees not far from where they stood. The two remaining dwarfs rushed, axes raised and ready to attack. Bill walked halfway across the courtyard and stopped, his hand gripping the hilt of his sword.

"Mallard, tell your men to back down and I will not harm them." The two dwarfs' stepped closer to Bill, their grip tightening on the handles of their axes. "I will only ask once Mallard, don't make me repeat myself." Bill drew his sword halfway letting its blade reflect the freckled sun.

"Drop your weapons!" Mallard shouted at the two dwarves to comply but both stood firm, their axes raised and ready for the fight.

"Arrrrrrgggggghhhhhhhh!" The flash of blue steel raced at Bill as the two dwarfs attacked with every bit of their strength. Bill sidestepped, striking him on the back of his helmet and knocking him to the ground. The second brought his axe down, aiming it for Bill's bandaged arm. Bill grabbed the dwarf's hands and pushed him back towards Mallard and the third dwarf standing on Wang Wu's doorstep. The third dwarf dropped Tilterman and charged at Bill, his axe and shield ready for the fight.

"Stop, drop your weapons and I will let you fools live..." Mallard screamed out, his voice sending the fear of Crom into the heart of the dwarf. Bill stopped short of his attack and watched as the dwarf stopped dead in his tracks, looking at Mallard.

"You can have your way later but for now I need to talk to him while he's still able too. Stand down." A look of dread fell across the dwarf's face at the sight of blue energy fizzling around Mallards hands. Dropping his axe he helped both his fellow warriors to their feet. Bill replaced his sword in its scabbard and walked to Wang Wu's side. Mallard began to pace back and forth as he watched Bill and Wang Wu whisper, he mockingly spoke.

"Don't you know its not polite to talk about people when they stand near you and even less polite to whisper while in their company!" Bill looked at Mallard, a smirk running across his face.

"So Mallard, what have you told Wang Wu. Have you told him that I was replaced when I was dealing with the dragon or that I've lost my mind and have become consumed by a lust for power? Well, what have you told him?" Bill left Wang Wu's side and walked around Mallard and Paddy waiting for his answer, eyes firmly fixed on the dwarfs. Mallard followed Bill's movements and stepped forward towards Wang Wu. Bill drew his sword and placed it on his shoulder awaiting Mallards next move.

"My good friend, I will prove it to you that the Bill here is not the real Bill." Mallard turned and faced the trees from where Bill had emerged. "Bill come forward and tell Wang Wu who you are!" Bill turned and watched as a figure emerged from the trees. Tilterman looked up from the ground his mouth hanging open in disbelief. Wang Wu watched as the figure crossed his courtyard his features becoming clearer with each step.

"What trickery is this Mallard? You know you can't fool me; I raised Bill from a child. Your deception will not work here." Wang

Wu pointed his black stick at Mallard, sparks leaping from the end. Bill stared into his own face standing mere inches from his own; his amulet hung from his neck and his sword was identical to his own. His long black hair sat on his shoulder and his blue eyes the same as his own.

"So we meet again shape shifter or are you another of the Clan Tannernockai?" Bill stared at himself, watching to see if he could spot any differences in their appearances. Mallard had been watching the reaction on Wang Wu's face to see if he had any doubts about which one was Bill.

"So Wang Wu, do you now believe me? We replaced Bill several months ago when we discovered what was happening. It was while he was in Titeldorf searching for Erasmus Reich that he discovered our plan to bring back Du'Ard and replace the Order." Mallard signalled to the dwarf warriors to start encircling Bill and Wang Wu.

"Now that you and Bill are here we can continue with our plan, we already have Ingles and Zvanick on our side and as we speak Sven is sitting in his dungeon, and I have a report that Maisie was shot out of the sky in Moucha. We tried to bring her on board but she wouldn't join us either, so we had to dispose of her. So again I'll ask you Wang Wu, will you join us?" Mallard began to rub his hands together creating a blue glow within them. Wang Wu had his stick pointed in Mallard's direction but before he could say 'no', a shot of blue lightning struck him in the chest.

Bill drew his sword and cut down the shape shifter with a clean blow, turning him to a wriggling mass of black jelly. Tilterman rolled down the steps to where Wang Wu had moments before been standing, pulling his sword as he did so. Two black boots now stood on the ground, their toes blown clear off them. Tilterman shook his head and uttered the words 'we'll miss you old friend'.

Tilterman had little time to think of his friend as his dwarf captor sent his axe cutting through the air and crashing into the ground with tremendous force. Tilterman narrowly avoided being cleaved in two and managed to dig his sword into the dwarf's foot causing him to roll on the ground calling for his mother. Tilterman looked up to see Paddy Reinhart sneaking into the trees, well if he thought he was going to get away so easy then he was wrong. Picking himself up from the ground Tilterman prepared himself for a quick run through the forest and should he catch a gnome on the way well all the better.

Mallard shot bolt after bolt at Bill as they duelled in the courtyard, Bill had to fend off the attacks from the two remaining dwarfs as well. Taking a moment to see where Tilterman was, Bill saw him disappear into the forest: maybe now would be a good time to run and fight another day. He threw a pile of clay into Mallards eyes causing him to lose sight of him. Now he could disarm the dwarfs and make his way after Tilterman. Turning, Bill tossed two silver balls into the air and then dropped them to the ground. When the dwarfs saw what Bill had done they stopped and began to laugh at him.

A sudden blinding flash of light caused the dwarfs to drop to the ground holding their faces in their hands. Bill ran in the direction he had seen Tilterman run. Not far into the trees he heard the sound of a sword fight ahead. Tilterman was in trouble. Running towards the sounds, Bill soon found Tilterman locked in a deadly struggle with Paddy Reinhart and the shape shifter Bill had knocked with his sword earlier. He had taken on the form of a larger fire breathing demon know as Dagnarassic, whom Bill had destroyed years before in Cape Wilts. Mallard and the two dwarfs soon arrived on the scene, axes drawn ready for the fight.

The Hangman's Tree stood just behind Mallard, its entrance open and ready for use. Tilterman was locked head on with Paddy, swords sending sparks high into the sky and the sound of steel on steel ringing out in the green forest of Abnos. Bill had grabbed Tonark The Iron Foot by the wrist and was pushing him in front of the other two dwarfs, one of them taking a bolt of blue lightning from Mallards hands. As the lightning sizzled through his body, his legs went numb causing him to slump to the ground. Mallard watched as Bill gained the upper hand against the two remaining dwarfs, disposing of them with ease. Turning his attention to Tilterman and his struggle with Paddy, Mallard decided it was time they left Abnos and got back to Moucha to help Erasmus prepare for Du'Ard's return. He entered the Hangman's Tree and dialled the entry code for Moucha.

"Paddy, leave, we'll deal with them later but now we need to return to Moucha, come on." As Paddy ran towards the tree, Tilterman disabled Mynoki and went after Paddy, but Mallard closed the door leaving Tilterman banging on it. He heard the clanking of the Gnome Express move into place and then the wires in the trees began to glow bright yellow indicating that transportation was happening. With only seconds to act, Tilterman pulled a small disc from his belt and threw it at the wires. As it flew through the air it opened to reveal three shining blades. 'Twang'. The sound of snapping wires echoed in the forest. The two Dwarfs retreated, disappearing into the darkness of the trees.

"They're gone, Paddy and Mallard, they managed to use the Hangman's Tree." Tilterman sat down on a stump beside Bill who had fallen to the ground from exhaustion. "I cut the wire as the transportation started that should have stopped them somewhere between here and Moucha. But that leaves us with another problem, we're stuck here until we find another mode of transport, any ideas?" Bill remained silent and motionless on the ground, his arm bleeding from the wound received from Ternack the Enforcer. Tilterman picked some white flowers and began to mash them together forming a paste.

"Don't move, this will heal your wound, stay still." Tilterman rubbed the white paste onto the gaping wound and as he did so Bill squirmed in pain as it began to smoke and seal his wound. Within a minute the wound was fully healed and only a small scar

184

remained.

"Yea." Bill started to get up from the ground. "Yea, I have an idea but it depends on Snuggles." Tilterman looked at Bill and scratched his head. "Who or what is Snuggles?" Bill looked down at Tilterman and smiled. Tilterman however didn't smile but wondered about this Snuggles! Bill walked back towards Wang Wu's house. The green forest of Abnos was now silent with only echoes of the battle rustling the trees.

The two crows were still hovering overhead watching Bill and Tilterman as they walked through the forest. Tilterman was aware of their unwanted guides and their spying eyes and wondered if they were some how linked to Erasmus and Mallard. Were they bringing information of their own movements back to them? Tilterman cast an eye back to where the crows had been hovering and found that now they were gone.

"Here is our transportation back to Moucha..." Tilterman returned his attention to Bill and as he did so, he saw what Bill was referring to. Standing in a large fenced paddock was a dragon of colossal size, the biggest Tilterman had ever seen. "He only lets Wang Wu travel on him, but I know something that only Wang Wu knew about him. Come we leave." Tilterman stared in amazement at Bill and his planned mode of transport.

"And how pray tell do you plan on riding him back to Moucha?" Tilterman raised an eyebrow as he threw glances from Bill and then to the massive 'Snuggles'.

Dragon Lancers, Fly!

The sound of flowing water soon drew Bill from his sleep, the boat had stopped and Zen Zarrif was looking down from a small wooden dock. Bill raised his head from the hard wooden seat; his neck was stiff and ached from the uncomfortable position he had slept in. As he rubbed his neck he saw four soldiers in red and white armour come out of the darkness behind Zen Zarrif, their plumes bobbed as they bowed and greeted him. Bill watched as a silent conversation took place between them. After a few moments Zarrif turned back to the boat.

"Bill, we have arrived and it's safe to emerge from the sewers. I have something to show you on the surface, something you will be amazed by." Bill climbed from the boat and walked after Zarrif and the rest of the party. The four soldiers stopped underneath a ladder rising toward the surface. The soldiers lined up on either side of the ladder and watched as Bill and Sven climbed to the top and opened the brass cover to the outside world.

A shaft of light penetrated the darkness causing Bill to cover his eyes. Sven tapped his leg and pointed towards the ladder, the party that had travelled through the sewer with them were now awaiting Bill and Sven to move on. Bill stopped to allow his eyes to adjust to the glaring sunlight. As the dark shapes and shadows took form he found himself staring out over a vast sea of sand, rising and falling in beige waves. Bill stared into the featureless landscape that spread out before him, following it until it disappeared over the horizon. Sven pushed at Bill to move as both the smell of the underground and his curiosity getting the better of his patience. Bill lifted himself and strolled across to a sand dune nearby, climbing slowly to the top of the dune, he was amazed by the sight that met him.

"Well, Bill what do you think of my army?" Asked Zarrif as he placed his hand on Bill's shoulder while he pointed to a vast army of men and beasts. Never before had Bill seen such a sight, thousands of men carpeted the desert floor, their tents adding colour to the otherwise featureless landscape. A scream rang out overhead piercing Bill's ears. Looking up into the glare of the sun, Bill could just make out shadows moving towards them. As they came closer, Bill felt his heart starting to race, almost bursting out with excitement and fear. As he watched, dragon after dragon passed overhead the beating of their wings; a thunderous boom. Each dragon wore dull silver breastplates and their claws were capped by shining silver gauntlets. Riders dressed in light blue sat upon their backs, each one carrying long red lances with their helmets' blue plumage waving in the breezes of flight.

"My Dragon lancers, Bill." Zarrif looked down on Bill, the fires of respect burning in his eyes. "These are the bravest of all my warriors and each one will defend their dragon as if it was their kin and their dragons defend them as if they were fellow dragons. There are a family each a brother and each a close ally in battle. Their motto is a simple one 'Everyone comes home or we all die together'". Bill watched as the last of the Dragon Lancers flew overhead, the thunderous noise fading into the distance.

Bill's heart was still racing from the sights and sounds of the dragons and his hands trembling at the thought of them riding into battle. What fear and panic they must send into the hearts and minds of all who were brave enough to stand before them.

187

"Come, we'll have much to talk about and much to plan for the events of the coming days." Bill turned and walked after Zarrif down into the heart of his camp. As they walked among the soldiers, each stopped and greeted Zarrif, bowing low and wishing long life. Banners flew over tents each one with different colours and pictures. A red and white flag flew near Zarrif's red tent, an emblazed golden dragon upon it, fire reaching up around its body. Behind a light blue flag flapped in the desert breeze: two dragons stood on their hind legs locked in deadly battle with a fiery demon, flames issuing from their mouths as they fought.

Next to it flew a black and white banner with black and white arrows crossed upon it. Sitting beneath it were men dressed in black tunics and white pants, Bill watched as the waxed bow strings and sharpen arrows. One of the men nodded and winked at Bill, his face was somehow familiar to him but from where, Bill couldn't remember.

Zarrif's tent stood tall amongst the others in the camp, its flags flying higher than the others around it. Two guards stood at the entrance dressed in red and white, each one carried a sword by their side and each held a long gold trident. As Zarrif stepped up to the front of the tent, the tridents fell across blocking his path. Without turning to look at the person standing in front of them one of the guards spoke.

"Halt, who goes there and what is your business within?" Zarrif stepped closer and in a commanding tone replied.

"Tonarkum sen torack narsec tonak." Bill suppressed his laughter at the strange words but as Zarrif finished, the two guards retracted their tridents and pulled back the flap. Zarrif held out his hand and allowed Bill and Sven to enter the tent before him. Bill was amazed at the size and coolness of the tents interior. Its walls were covered with strange weapons and tapestries. He walked around looking at all the stories that were held on the woven cloths.

"Who is this here?" Bill pointed to a tall man standing before a bright orb of light, his hands held forth. Zarrif traversed the room and looked at the man.

"That Bill was the founder and creator of the Order of The Dragon, Du'Ard Duchan. He was at one time the most powerful of all Keepers and wizards that ever lived." Bill looked back at Sven and shrugged his shoulders. "Du'Ard was banished from the Order and cast into the waste lands of Werdnad. His body and mind separated so he could no longer be a threat to the people of the world. His power became stronger than him and began to control him. To be a great person you must have self-control and act for the good of all and not just yourself. That was Du'Ard's downfall, his quest for absolute power took control of him and eventually would have destroyed him and the world." Bill stared into the eyes in the tapestry and wondered what they saw in the orb of light.

"Now, tell all that has happened since last we spoke Sven." Bill turned and followed Zarrif and Sven to a rug in the centre of the tent's floor. It was filled with all kinds of food and drink; Bill sat and listened to every word that was being spoken. Sven spoke of everything that had happened since Argyle took Bill from his home and up until they had left him in Lichberg castle.

"We've been following Chaykin's trail ever since he took the jewels here to Moucha." Bill stared in amazement at Zarrif's words. "Chaykin was asked to steal them and sell them to the King of the Orcs to lure Scaripdemus out into the open." As Zarrif spoke Bill suddenly realised that the archer who had winked at him on the way to Zarrif's tent, had been Chaykin. Sven stared at Zarrif in disbelief.

"So, while I was tracking Chaykin your men were the ones who had stopped me from capturing him whenever I got close?" Zarrif smiled at Sven, almost laughing at the expression on his face.

"It was necessary to stop you from catching him for our plan to succeed and bring Scaripdemus out into the open and discover his plan." Bill's thoughts had returned to his uncle on the Lucipher and to his safety. "Your uncle Bill is not the man you saw being dragged onto the Lucipher." Zarrif clapped his hands and as he did so a man came into the tent. The tall shadow stood in front of Bill and as Bill's eyes focused on him, he realised who he was.

"Have you not got a hug for your uncle Bill, or would you prefer to give it to the shifter?" Bill jumped to his feet and wrapped his arms around his uncle. His unkempt hair was a replica of the shifters; his dirty brown leather tunic had the same old and sweaty smell. "What is it boy?" Bill blinked back a tear in his eye.

"My Dad is he here?" Argyle shook his head and sat Bill back down. He explained that his father had set sail for Linksburg and pirates had overrun his ship in the far north.

"The entire crew were taken as prisoners and sold to the goblins and set to work in their mines alongside Sven's people. We don't know where exactly but we have scouts out searching for the mines." Bill began to think of his father's fate at the hands of the goblins but felt reassured by the escape of his new friend, Sven, from the mines.

"Bill do not worry about your Dad, he'll be fine and once we've dealt with Scaripdemus we'll leave to find him." Bill smiled at Zarrif and knew he would have the help of the Order to rescue his father. "Come and see what surprises we have for our unwanted visitors down in the harbour!"

Zarrif led the way back out into the heat of the desert sun. As they walked through the tented city, Sven began to speak of the blue mist that surrounded the lady in the dragon's head.

"She was somehow familiar to me but I can not place her face to someone I know. She is definitely a sorceress but not of this time, her clothes were strange to me and she stood in the cathedral in Moucha but it too was different. Is she trying too help us or is she with Scaripdemus? I wish I knew." Zarrif looked down at Sven and nodded in agreement. At the edge of the camp a puff of black smoke rose up over the tents closely followed by a small white cloud of smoke. Bill drew his sword and started to run in their direction but was stopped by Zarrif.

"Bill it's not a fight, its just Steve and his contraptions..." Bill replaced his sword and walked past the last tent into a small opening between two large sand dunes. A small man stood staring at a pile of smouldering armour. A pair of wire frame glasses sat on the end of his long bent nose, his hands were poking about in the armour, and as he saw the party arrive he scratched his head.

"Just won't do Zarrif, if they have anything like my fire powder, our troops are in trouble. Any word of Torenta and Divine?" The small man looked at Zarrif.

"No, nothing so far. Our lookouts saw them climb onto the ships and they haven't seen them since! So Steve, what new surprises have you for our foes today?" Zarrif rubbed his hands in anticipation and watched as Steve disappeared into a large brown box. Muttering and grumbling could be heard and when Steve remerged he was holding a large arrow.

"Right gnome, run towards the dune and when you get hit don't wriggle too much, ok?" Sven began to run towards the sand dune. As he neared the bottom, he felt a sudden thud and fell face first into the sand. Bill watched in amazement as the arrow opened up and engulfed Sven in its shaft, completely immobilizing him on the ground. Zarrif clapped and patted Steve on the back while telling him he had 'out done yourself once again', Sven wriggled about trying to free himself from his worm like prison.

"Steve, I'd like you to meet the youngest member of the Order, Bill." Bill stuck out his hand to greet Steve who turned and climbed back into the box. As Bill watched Steve's legs wriggle about furiously in the box, a glove shot into the air and landed on Bill's hand followed closely by a second, which landed perfectly on his other hand. Steve remerged and held Bill's hands.

"Ah, a perfect fit." He looked Bill right in the eye. "These along with your sword and shield will come in very useful in..." Before

Steve could finish his sentence a soldier came running up towards them and interrupted him.

"They are moving the dragon's head off the ship and wheeling it towards the cathedral and two more ships have arrived in the harbour all of them are flying the flag of Scaripdemus. What should we do?" The soldier stopped and waited for his orders.

"Send out the lancers and stop the head from reaching the cathedral. Don't worry about the other ships for now; we have to prevent the head from reaching the cathedral." The soldier ran towards the camp and shortly after the sound of a horn rang out in the dunes. Bill saw the first of the lancers rise from the camp and fly towards Moucha. Soon after him another dragon rose up and soon the sky was filled with the black shapes of dragons flying towards the city.

"Come on we can see what's happening from the dunes." Zarrif pointed to the dune standing beside the camp's edge. As they reached the top of the dune, Bill saw the lancer's swoop down over the soldiers leaving the ship. The dragon's head was being pulled along the streets of Moucha, protected by the army Scaripdemus had brought to the city.

"Dragons coming from the desert. Assume attack formation. The head must be protected at all costs..." Mucktaba's cries rang out over the trundling noise of the wheels of the dragon's carriage. Mucktaba watched as the lancers began to drop from their high altitude and launch their lances at them. "Come on just a bit closer and then you're mine!" Rubbing his hands together, Mucktaba waited for their approach.

"Ready the bow." The creaking of the bow's rope being stretched to its limit came from behind the dragon's head. Two soldiers wearing silver chain mail loaded a long black arrow into the jaws of the metal bow. Its wheels pressed against the huge blocks that prevented it from moving back with the soldiers as they pulled on the rope.

The lancers passed over Muctaba's head and as the first three dragons cleared the carriage, his voice rang out again, almost drowned out by the thunderous beating of the dragon's wings.

"Fire!" A fat green goblin kicked a bronze lever and released the arrow into full and unhindered flight.

The black arrow cut through the air, racing towards its final destination with lethal accuracy.

"Clang." The arrow found its mark, ripping cleanly through the breastplate of the lead lancer's dragon. The animal screeched as the black arrowhead tore into his soft under belly exposing his tender insides to the world. Stopping in mid flight, the dragon unseated his rider and sent him crashing towards the ground, his own body failing to support his weight in flight he plummeted towards a spiked rooftop. A second lancer saw his companion fall and dropped into a steep dive and managed to catch him before he fell to the street below. Mucktaba and his soldiers' let out a triumphant cheer as the dragon crashed.

"Again fire and don't stop till you have 'em all on their backs." Mucktaba ran towards the front of the carriage and ordered his men to start moving it on towards the cathedral before the lancers could regroup and attack them again. The lancers renewed their attack, fired up from the loss of their dragon and the near loss of a comrade. The lancers dived with renewed hatred, weapons at the ready. Again the bow creaked as it was drawn and its arrow nocked. The goblin smiled as he saw a young lancer take the lead followed by two others, their breastplates in full view. Lining the bow up with the dragons heart the goblin began picking at his yellow teeth, foot ready on the trigger.

The lead dragon screeched and belched out red flames, at the same time the goblin released his arrow. The flames destroyed the arrow before it found purchase in the dragon chest. Again the goblin gave the order for his bow to be stretched and loaded. The second dragon reared up and released a black noxious gas; screams of pain gave way to choking gasps for breathable air. The third dragon swooped in and grabbed the bow in its claws and climbed high into the sky over the city. As he reached his zenith he let go his grip and watched as the bow crashed down upon Scaripdemus's troops. An ear splitting roar erupted from the company of lancers and they watched the panic-stricken troops flea in terror. Slowly Mucktaba reached the safety of the cathedral, his troops struggling to haul the now wheel-less carriage up the steps and inside.

"Shoot the dragons, protect the head." Mucktaba's men crouched in the door of the cathedral, firing shot after shot at the now re-treating lancers. Once the lancers were gone from sight, Mucktaba and his men placed the dragon's head in the centre of the main praying area, splitting pews with axes and large board swords.

"Now we defend the cathedral and wait for Scaripdemus to do his thing. Right lads, get into place or I'll splice yer livers. Move!" Pews were placed up against the stained glass windows blocking the light from entering. Sentries were posted throughout the gothic building and as day ended things were set in place and ready to activate the head.

Two clouds drifted slowly overhead as Maisie opened her eyes. She began to get up but her legs felt weak and unsteady. Her head be-gan spinning frantically, her stomach lurching. As she found her feet, she stumbled towards the door leading back into the cathe-dral and down to the main praying area. The main body of the ca-thedral was now dimly lit as Maisie entered from the stairwell, her eyes slowly adjusted to the dim light and she was able to make out the outline of a small water fount. The water was cold but refresh-ing as she splashed it across her face. It trickled down her face and back into the font causing ripples to lap against the fount's edge. Maisie watched as a single drop fell from the edge of her chin and splashed into the fount. As the drop hit the water she saw a blue reflection ripple upon its surface. She wiped the remaining water from her face and turned to the face the blue light.

In the centre of the cathedral stood Erasmus Reich and the orb of light that Maisie had witnessed earlier hovering in front of him. Maisie watched as Erasmus held out his long steel staff, its red ruby glowing on top of it. The Eye of Gordanna, Goddess of the Under Realm and the Dark Arts, the source of his magical powers was now getting ready to destroy. The orb started to increase in size, a picture forming at its centre. Erasmus had a sinister blue glow around him as his black cloak reflected the orb's light, his evil black soulless eyes cold and dead in their sockets. Maisie moved slowly through the pews trying to get a better look at the orb and Erasmus before she made her move.

"Maisie don't be shy, come from the shadows and see what I have created from nothing, come!" Erasmus turned and looked directly at Maisie, his eyes burning into her soul. Walking towards Erasmus, her lips moving as she cast a protection spell about herself. "Oh my dear, dear little Maisie." Erasmus said in a condescending voice as she came closer.

"Don't waste your time with silly and inferior protection spells. They won't help you against me. Why you should know that I, Erasmus Reich, am the greatest Necromancer ever!" His voice echoed through the bowels of the cathedral causing glass to shatter in the highest windows. "Oh, did I break those windows, oh I am sorry." Erasmus held his finger to his mouth in an apologetic way and stared innocently at Maisie.

"Repairus!" Erasmus pointed his staff at the broken glass and if felt as if time reversed as the glass picked itself back up and travelled backwards to the windows from where it had fallen. "Did you see that Maisie? I now control time itself. Yes time is mine to control." Erasmus held his hands as if a crowd had begun to clap in appreciation of his power.

"I am now stronger than Du'Ard Duchan ever was. Think of what we could achieve, together Maisie, think of the kingdom we could have among these pitiful fools, who we protect and get no thanks from." Maisie watched a glint of madness spark in Erasmus's eye. Her attention left Erasmus and his ramblings as she saw upon the table the thing she most wanted to obtain and return to Zen Zarrif: the brown leather-bound book with gold writing on its edge. The Book of Demons, with this Erasmus would be unstoppable. Edging closer to Erasmus and the Book of Demons, Maisie asked how Mallard and Paddy fitted into his plans. Erasmus laughed and rubbed his withered hands together.

"Pawns, pitiful pawns. I had to distract young Bill and his foolish companions in G.I.U. I don't need them, the same as I don't need Du'Ard. I will bring back the five Generals of Gordanna and the blood thirsty Dragon Slayers of Nannreb. Together we will be invincible." Maisie had watched Paddy and Mallard step into the shadows on the edge of the cathedral floor, unnoticed by Erasmus.

"So how do you plan to dispose of Mallard and Paddy?" Maisie moved closer her eyes on the book and glancing to see what Mallard and Paddy were doing. Erasmus continued to tell Maisie of his plans and as he did so he watched as the orb grew bigger the picture becoming clearer.

"Its easy, once I have the Generals on my side I will just dispose of them in the old fashioned way, the same way I'm about to dispose of you if you don't join me. So Maisie what is your decision?" Erasmus was fully aware of Maisie's path towards the book and had allowed her to get within reach of her desires.

"My answer is a simple one." Maisie pulled her hand from her pocket and fired a silver ball at Erasmus, as she shouted 'NO'. Erasmus reacted quickly and grabbed the book before Maisie could reach it. Realising that he had been quicker than she was, Maisie waited for the smoke to clear. She had taken a small clear glass bottle from her bag and stood ready for Erasmus to launch his counter attack. As the smoke cleared from around her, she found herself alone.

"Quick but not quick enough Maisie DuPont. Would you like another try?" Erasmus's voice echoed in the cathedral. She walked slowly through the upturned pews aware that Paddy and Mallard were waiting to attack her as well.

"Paddy, Mallard join the lady, please don't leave her standing on her own, come join us!" She watched as they stepped from behind a large pillar at the far side of the cathedral, Paddy's sword drawn and Mallard's staff at the ready. "Step towards the centre of the altar, all together now." Maisie drew another bottle from her bag as she walked towards the altar. Paddy and Mallard were on her side all watching for Erasmus. As the orb grew bigger the light in the cathedral also grew making Maisie to search harder for the elusive Erasmus.

"Here, above you." Maisie and the two gnomes looked above their heads to see Erasmus floating above them, his cloak spread like a great pair of black and evil wings. "You see how powerful I have become, no one has ever obtained the power of flight." Mallard stepped forward and shot a bolt of purple light from the end of his staff and watched as Erasmus deflected it with his hand. "Puny weak gnome you think you can hurt me with such simple spells. Hahaha!" Erasmus let his laughter ring out through the cathedral, his hands spread to each side of him.

"Watch as I show you truly powerful magic." A blinding flash left the end of Erasmus's staff, striking Mallard in the chest, throwing him back across the altar, his body limp and helpless against the bolt of light. Paddy dived among the pews, scuttling away from Erasmus and his madness. Maisie dived beneath the benches just short of the glowing orb and now could see all the way into the light. A picture of a much newer cathedral flickered in the shimmering blue light, two men staring into the orb from the other side. Maisie quickly recognised one of the figures as Scaripdemus. She now realised what the orb was, a gateway to another time.

Back To The Sewers

Bill walked nervously towards Snuggles who lay on a large bed of hay. Vents of hot air rushed over him as it began to sniff. As he got closer the red scales of the dragon stretched out adding to his already colossal size. Raising himself up from the ground, Snuggles walked away, his tail whipping at the blackened dust. The cloud of black dust covered Bill and half the buildings that stood in Wang Wu's courtyard. He continued to walk towards the dragon and now that his back was turned, he could walk that little bit faster.

Snuggles lay back down and began to roll about in the dust and dirt of his pen, flicking his tail at the wisps of dirt that rose up around him. He waited for Snuggles to stop playing and sit up. Suddenly without warning the red dragon turned and stared down on Bill, his snout rippled as a rumble of anger rose up from the pits of his stomach. Bill stood his ground and waited for the dragon's next move. Hot air rushed around him as the dragon shoved his nose right up to his face and sniffed him again. White teeth filled Bill's eyes as Snuggles opened his mouth; his red tongue slid out slowly and coiled itself around Bill's body.

Bill's body stiffened with fear, his hand frozen on the hilt of his sword. His heart had moved to his throat and his knees had given way to jelly. He could feel the coarseness of the dragon's tongue through his long coat, drool dripped down his face covering him in a fowl smelling white slime. As quickly as Snuggles had grabbed Bill, he let go and returned to his rolling, completely ignoring Bill and Tilterman. Snuggles stopped rolling and began to chew on some food that had been left out in his pen. Bill moved towards him and this time managed to put his hand on the ruby red scales of Snuggle's hind leg. Moving slowly up towards the dragon's head he signalled to Tilterman to start moving forward.

Tilterman stepped into the pen and began walking towards Bill; Snuggle's turned his head and stared at Tilterman who stopped as soon as the dragon's head moved. Turning away again, Snuggles began to chew on more of his food allowing Bill and Tilterman to move right up to the side of his head. A great shadow fell over Bill and Tilterman causing them to look towards the sky. Snuggles had stretched out his massive red wings. A worried look fell over the two companions as the dragon began to beat his wings in preparation for flight, sending dust and wood high into the air. Bill turned to Tilterman and shouted.

"Now, get on. This is it..." Tilterman grabbed Bill's jacket as he jumped onto the dragon's side and climbed up the rough scales till they reached a small hollow between Snuggle's shoulders. Snuggles felt the two unwanted passengers on his scales and turned his head around and plucked Bill off, dropping him on the ground. Turning again Snuggle's gave what Tilterman though looked like a grin as they climbed higher into the sky.

Bill picked himself up from the ground and as he brushed himself off he watched Tilterman holding onto the rippling red scales of the dragons back as they flew through the clouds. Tilterman's knuckles were white as he gripped furiously to Snuggle's back. His hands were becoming numb from the cold and his hat had been blown off leaving his hair wind swept and frozen. Snuggles suddenly stopped in mid flight, his wings stationary. Tilterman looked down to see how high he was from the ground, as he peered over the side the colour faded from his face at the sight below him. Three white clouds drifted lazily by covering the black specs that made up Wang Wu's courtyard.

"Snuggles, do you think you could get Bill and I to Moucha, please?" Tilterman was terrified and hoped that Snuggles understood him. Turning his head, Snuggle's stared at Tilterman, hot vents of air coming from his nostrils warming Tilterman.

"Ok." The thunderous boom of Snuggles voice rattled every bone in Tilterman's body. "Why didn't you ask instead of trying to trick me?" Tilterman shrugged his shoulders and smiled apologetically at the massive eyes staring at him. Snuggles dropped into a steep dive, the wind cut through Tilterman chilling him, as they dropped to the ground. Tilterman slid from his back and ran for the main house to warm himself. Bill followed closely behind him as Snuggles dropped down and began rolling in his dirt once again.

"Are you ok?" Tilterman nodded at Bill as he shuffled closer to the fire to warm himself. "What happened up there in the clouds?" Tilterman turned to face Bill, his teeth chattering in his mouth.

"Next time just assssk hhhhim..." Tilterman rubbed his shoulders trying to draw heat back into his once warm body. "He'll take us if you ask him nicely, now make me some tea, please!" Tilterman began to pace up and down in front of the fire as Bill started to make warm tea for him. A blast of hot air filled the little room where Bill and Tilterman stood. As they turned they found two large nostrils filling the front of the house.

"Ready when you are." A whisper filtered through the room, knocking Bill and Tilterman off their feet. Standing up, Bill and Tilterman walked outside and mounted Snuggles. "Moucha here we come!" Snuggles rose up into the sky and before either Bill or Tilterman could respond, they flew off higher than any eagle could soar and faster than anything else that could take to wings.

The lancers retreated from the battle as arrow after arrow streamed past them in the air. The red lances hung dully by their sides as defeat ate away at their moral. Dragons wept for the loss of their friend. Zarrif's camp came back into view and as the lancers touched down, the white coloured medics ran from the hospital tent to tend to the cuts and bruises from the battle. Zarrif counted the dragons as the landed and soon discovered his numbers down by one. A tall soldier ran forward and addressed Zarrif in the most formal of ways.

"Commander, we have lost one of our dragons." Prince Weldermere stood as tall as Zarrif his long blonde hair plaited and tied with the colours of the Dragon Lancers. His silver chain mail reflected the sun, a blue cross sat in the middle of the chain vest refusing to reflect all the sun's light.

"They have a new weapon, an arrow that rips into our armour and then spreads out to cause maximum pain to our good friends." Zarrif was grief stricken at these words and the prospect of loosing his Lancers to a new and evil weapon.

"I grieve our loss but for now we must not mourn our friend in sadness. Come let us defend the lives of our friends who will suffer at the hands of Scaripdemus if we do not succeed in defeating him and stopping his plan for world domination." Zarrif turned and walked towards the centre of his camp. "Alert the captains to muster their men and to report to the command tent." Two small messengers dressed in blue separated and ran for the different banners signalling to the men to rally and gather arms for it was time to face Scaripdemus and his armies.

Horn after horn sounded in the camp as men ran to and fro gathering their belongings and standing behind their banners. Large wheels began turning as the black flag of the artillery moved to the front of the ranks. The three red hammers upon it formed a triangle and men cheered as the large crossbows and trebuchets rolled forward. At its head was a small man with thick black-rimmed glasses sitting on the end of his nose.

"You there, yes you. Out of the way man, unless you want to be squashed." MacGarrif of Loch Lyman roared. His mouth made up for the lack of size and his eyes were better than any mans, some said as good as a dragon's eye for spotting a target, no matter how small it was. Leaving the head of his column he headed straight for the command tent and his orders. Zarrif stood at the top of the tent, a model of Moucha City on a table before him. As the last of his captains entered, he called Bill to his side.

"This is Bill Brickton, the newest member of the Order of the Dragon. Our entire victory depends on Bill's success in the cathedral today." A lump swelled up in Bill's throat. "Bill will enter the cathedral via the sewers and emerge at the back of the altar with a band of volunteers. Now I know that more of you would have liked to accompany Bill on this daring quest but I can't afford to let you all go." Bill watched Zarrif as he explained to his men what was going to take place.

Standing at the rear of the command tent were two skinny men know only as Tank and Cannon. They listened to every word that Zarrif was saying and when they received their orders, they left to join their friends under the red and white flag of Zarrif's men.

"Now is the time for us to leave..." Tank whispered into the ear of his friend Cannon. The two men slipped into a nearby tent closing the flaps as they entered.

"Give us yer knife Tank so we can git outta this foul smellin' place." Cannon pushed the blade of the knife through the canvass of the tent and cut a long slit from top to bottom. Slowly pulling the slit apart, Cannon used his knife like a mirror to check if anyone was watching. "Coast is clear, lets go!" Cannon stepped into the open and watched as the skinny form of Tank emerged shortly after him. The edge of Moucha and the sight of guards patrolling the city soon greeted the two spies.

"Halt, who goes there?" A guard ran across the sand towards them. On identifying themselves, they were lead straight to Scaripdemus on board the Lucipher.

"Zarrif has sounded the advance on Moucha, Oh Great One and is preparing to march on the city. The one you asked about is travelling in the sewers and will arrive in the cathedral." With a wave of his hand Scaripdemus dismissed the two spies.

"See these men are rewarded and summon Guts. Go, what are you waiting for?" A messenger ran from the room where Scaripdemus stood, the sound of his footsteps disappearing in the ships interior. "So Zarrif, you think that Brickton is strong enough to defeat me. How foolish you are?" Scaripdemus turned to greet Guts as he entered the room. "Dock all ships and give the order to disembark. Zarrif's army is on the way, they must not be allowed to enter the city, GO!" Guts bowed and retreated from the room.

Guts licked his lips and pressed them against the ram's horn on the bow of the ship and blew a single note. It was soon answered by the two ships in the harbour as they drew up to the docks and opened the hulls of their ships. The wood creaked as it moved to the side allowing several gangplanks to be pushed forward onto the wooden dockside. From within the darkness, shapes began to move. Emerging from the darkness, row after row of soldiers moved onto the gangplanks and then onto the dockside.

The Lucipher's hull opened wider than any of the other ships and flying from the inside came five large black dragons. Their breastplates shone black in the high sun as they flew out across the city, screaming across the skyline. The Nannreb remained lifeless and still in the water. Scaripdemus stood with Cundra on the deck of the Lucipher watching as Guts McCracken led the army out of the city and onto the desert plains on the outskirts of the city. As the army formed into defensive lines on the edge of the city, Scaripdemus and Cundra left the deck of the Lucipher and proceeded to the cathedral. As they entered the cathedral, Mucktaba

203

issued the order for his men to barricade the doors and prepare to defend at all costs.

"Mucktaba, I want you to take some of the men and remain concealed at the back of the altar. Brickton and some men are travelling in the sewer. When they arrive I want a nasty surprise waiting for them. The rest of your men can report to Guts at the front line to meet Zarrif." Mucktaba nodded and split his men up and hid from view. Scaripdemus stood in front of the dragons head and watched as the blue light in it mouth started to grow bigger revealing Erasmus and their future empire, five hundred years from now.

As Zarrif finished laying out the plan of attack to his captains, he turned to Bill. "You have the hardest task of all our men Bill. You must defeat Scaripdemus and Cundra but most importantly, you must destroy the dragon's head. Two of my men are in the city and if they can they will help you. We strike at first light, which should give you enough time to get in place. Good luck and remember the Order is on the way to you." Zarrif placed his hand on Bill's shoulder and wished him a final good luck. Bill turned and left the tent with Sven at his side. The sun had begun to set over the sandy plains as they headed to meet their band of men.

"Back to the sewers Sven, so what is it with you lot and sewers?" Bill smirked at Sven as they joined the five men in front of the entrance to the sewers, each one carrying a sword and wearing a blue helmet. A small man stepped forward, his shoulders almost as wide as he was tall, his voice was gruff and jagged as he introduced his men to Bill.

"Corporal Keg Materson of the Lancers, Sir. This is Kreig." A tall skinny man stepped forward and held out his hand for Bill to shake it, his grip was strong and hard, leaving Bill's hand wrinkled. "This is Manfred." A man of Bill's own height stepped forward and bowed, his right hand swinging outwards in a wide ark as he did so. Bill bowed and held his hand out to shake but Manfred stepped back into line.

"Manfred won't shake hands, he can tell the future when he touches you and it causes him great pain when he does so." Bill nodded his head and waited for the next man to be introduced. "These two are Smith and Jones, Sir both of them are shifters. Come in very useful when times call for it." Bill suddenly found himself looking at himself and Sven standing in front of him.

"At your service Sir, anytime you need to get away just call on Smith and Jones's Sir. Glad to lend a hand or four." Bill smirked as the two shifters sounded off together their words echoing around the sewer entrance. Kegs stepped forward and pulled the cover from the entrance to the sewer and lead the way into the darkness.

The sewer was foul smelling, green slimy water running down the brick walls. A small stream flowed down the centre of the tunnel and disappeared behind them. The faint scream of a Gundarc could be heard far off in the dark distance, as could the squealing of rats as they ran about Bill's feet. They had been walking for hours and finally found Jones sitting in a wide cavern, several tunnels leading away from the stagnant green lake in its centre. Pulling his pack from his shoulder, Bill fell to the wet ground his hands covering his face. The smell had grown steadily worse as they ventured further into the sewers.

"What's the smell?" Bill placed his hands to his nose and waved the air with the other hand. Kreig began to laugh as Bill waved more and more frantically.

"It's a Gundarc. Do you not know of the legendary smell of the Gundarc?" Kreig smiled at Bill and offered him some currant bread. Lurching, Bill held out his hand and took the bread; he knew he'd have to keep his strength up for what lay ahead. Kreig stood up and began to sniff the air in the sewer.

"Quickly, hide, someone is coming..." One by one Bill and the others slipped into the shadows of the sewer.

"I'm telling you he has it out for us, why would he leave the rest of them in the cathedral and send us down to the sewers to follow them, well?" Two guards stepped into the cavern where Bill and the others had been eating moments before. The black jaw line of Volk's helmet reflected the green water as he spoke. His armour was black and dirty from the sewer, his red plume hung limp and stiff with dirt.

"It's your mouth and the way you talk to Mucktaba." Yarik started to laugh and then stopped abruptly. "What's that?" Pushing his visor from his face he revealed a small bent and blackened nose. His eyes squinted as he looked into the darkness. "I heard something, I'm sure of it." Drawing his sword he walked slowly into the vast openness of the cavern, his blade sparkled in the dim light from the water. Bill watched as Smith and Jones transformed and stepped from the shadows.

"Hey, did you hear that?" Volks and Yarik stood in disbelief as they stared into their own faces. "See I told you I heard something, there!" Yarik stood pointing at himself. Volks walked around the man standing in front of him.

"Shifters!" At this, the two Yariks and the two Volks locked into battle, flashes of steel filling the carven. The echoes of the sword fight travelled deep into the sewers along dark passages and through gridiron gates. Yarik struck hard and fast at the man standing in front of him, his sword was deflected into the brick wall of the sewer where it shattered. Volks saw what had happened and decided two against one was an unfair fight and he dropped his weapon.

Smith and Jones transformed back into their more familiar selves. Bill and Sven stepped from the shadows as Keg and his men bound the two soldiers.

"Kreig, you bring them back to Zarrif's camp and extract whatever information they have." Kreig pushed the two forward with the point of his sword into the dark tunnels of the sewers. Keg gave the command to move on towards the cathedral at double quick time.

Looming in the darkness Bill saw a large wooden door with two large devil heads as handles. Slowly pushing it open Manfred stepped onto the staircase that lay on the other side. All was clear and the staircase was silent in its winding towards the back of the altar. This entrance was used for those who wanted to avoid the long arms of the law and for those who would seek help from the monks of the cathedral. Keg raised his hand stopping Bill and his companions. Manfred had gone ahead touching the wall to see who had passed on the stairs and if any more of Scaripdemus's men had slipped into the sewers.

"It appears that our two shifters got the only two soldiers sent out to find us." Keg nodded and beckoned the others to follow him up the stairs. The back of the altar disappeared into the rafters of the cathedral and the darkness. Bill stepped behind a small spire and looked out across the darkened cathedral and saw the blue glow of the dragon's head. Swirling blue lights left the dragon's eyes and travelled out and around the cathedral, returning to its mouth. Bill saw the flickering images inside the dragon's mouth and summoned Sven to his side.

"Is that what you saw in the ship?" Sven arched his neck to get a better look at the images in the mouth.

"Yes, it's the same. That's the girl I saw earlier staring into the light." Bill stared and watched as Scaripdemus and Cundra stood in silent conversation. Kreig pointed to the main entrances, where Mucktaba and his men stood guarding the doors.

"Ok, lads nice and quietly towards the doors, we'll keep them occupied while Bill and Sven deal with the head. Go!" Kreig watched as one by one his men slipped into the shadows and moved towards the doors, before he himself moved, he turned to Bill.

"Good luck." Bill nodded and watched him disappear after his men. A sudden cold feeling of steel touched Bill's hand and as he turned he found himself looking into the eyes of a soldier.

"Up, now." Poking Bill in the ribs he urged him forward from his hiding place. "You too gnome..." Sven strolled forward hoping for an opportunity to disarm his unwanted guard. The soldiers at the main door turned and drew swords on Keg and his men forcing them to the centre of the cathedral. Cundra and Scaripdemus stood smiling as Bill and Sven were brought forward to where they stood.

"So Bill, you have travelled a long way since I saw you last, how was your journey?" A smiled flickered on Scaripdemus's face as he watched Bill. Sven dropped his hand to the hilt of his sword and waited for Bill to answer.

"Disarm the gnome, I wouldn't like to see him cut himself." Sven began to unbuckle his dark brown leather belt and as the clasp fell open he flung the scabbard at the advancing soldier, striking him in the face. Sven's sword flashed as he swung it for another soldier coming from the side aisle of the cathedral. Bill drew his sword and ran for Scaripdemus, his sword drawn and ready to do battle. Scaripdemus reacted, his sword clashing with Bill's...

Battles Old And New

Snuggles soared higher than the tallest peaks of Surnocktar and twisted and weaved his way through the valleys of Adnama. Tilterman had never seen the flat plains of Tidalbloom from such a great height; their vastness was greater than anything he could have dreamed of. After flying so far, Tilterman was glad to see the first signs of Moucha come into view. The high-rise buildings that made up the slums of the city began to jut from the land and then the great city of Moucha exploded onto the horizon.

The spire of the cathedral sat alone in what was now the only green area of the city and the only safe place on the absolute ground level. The city levels rose far into the sky, city cabs and sky frigates reaching to the top with ease and freedom from security checks. Snuggles wound his way through the levels following Bill's every direction until they reached the green lawns of the cathedral. He dropped from the sky and touched down with the gentleness of a feather on the wind. Bill and Tilterman slid down Snuggle's rough scales and thanked him for his kindness and watched as he rose into the sky and returned to Abnos. The shadow of the cathedral fell over Bill and Tilterman blocking the rising sun from their view.

"This is it, the source of all our problems. Let's go, Tilterman." As they turned to the entrance they became aware of several Rennick warriors sitting on the steps that lead to the large double brown wooden doors of the cathedral. "So much for a quiet entrance..." Bill drew his sword slowly from its scabbard and walked towards the warriors who ignored the advancing Tilterman and Bill. Tilterman held his sword with the usual firm grip that gnomes were famous for but as he climbed the steps, his sword fell from his hand, a look of awe on his face. Bill had stopped beside him, his mouth open as he stared past the Rennick warriors.

Standing larger than life at the entrance of the cathedral were two of the undead, Vampires. Their cloaks floated softly on the wisps of wind. Their skin was pale and rotting, stains of blood covered their pale lips. Tilterman had heard stories of the undead rising from the after life to steal the blood of anyone foolish enough to wander into their domain. Bending down Tilterman picked up his sword and as he straightened up he saw Bill standing face to face with one of the vampires.

"Allow me to introduce myself." His lips puckered as he spoke, his voice full of elegance. "I am Count Endomire and this is my beautiful wife, the Countess Kali. We are so pleased you could meet us here, Mr. Bill." A faint smile rippled across Bill's face, as he looked his new adversaries up and down. The Countess watched from the top of the steps eyes fixed in a piercing stare, Tilterman held firmly in her eye.

"We have old scores to settle with the Order and with your people Tilterman." Gripping his sword, Tilterman stared defiantly at the Count. "Such bravery from such a small mouth full of food." The Count began to laugh as Bill held back Tilterman from attacking him.

"We have no quarrel with you or your kind Endomire allow us to pass and deal with our problems." The Countess was now floating overhead, her hands stretched out each side letting her cloak form red silken wings beneath her small frame. Bill replaced his sword and started to walk. Hissing and spitting at Bill, the Count placed his hand up to Bill's chest.

"Do not defy me mortal, we have business here while my companions complete their work inside." Retreating, the Count hissed at Bill who drew his sword and turned a small dial on its hilt. A small glass bottle fell from inside the hilt, landing in Bill's hand.

"We shall pass in peace and you shall return to Carantia in peace and not show your vile features here again. Be gone!" Bill splashed the clear contents of the bottle into the Count's face and watched as Tilterman turned and ran for the Countess. Endomire screamed as the clear liquid burned into his pale, rotting skin. Tilterman dodged the Countess as she swooped in for the attack, cutting her on the back as she flew past. Her scream echoed through the streets and walkways in Moucha, pedestrians stopped in terror as it reached their ears. Tilterman watched as the Countess turned and dropped back to the ground, her hand clutching at the wound, but the cut began to heal itself before his very eyes.

"You are very quick little one but watch." Tilterman watched as the Countess disappeared and reappeared beside him. "And see now how quickly I can move..." Her mouth opened wide as she moved to sink her teeth into his neck, her sharp claw like nails cutting deep into his arm. "Sssssshhhhhhh, my child it won't hurt... too much!" Tilterman struggled as her cold icy lips touched his neck, her stale venomous breath stinging his nose. Count Endomire flashed from view as Bill lashed out with his sword; it cut the air and missed his target. Turning frantically around Bill saw Endomire rubbing his eyes and skin furiously. His holy water had touched and burned true evil. Three wooden crosses stood on the centre of the lawns marking the places where Calinoff and his two loyal servants lay in peace. Bill grabbed up the wooden cross and broke it in two.

"Kali, help me, it hurts and I'm blind." Kali turned as she heard the mournful cry of her beloved Endomire. His skin had started to break away from his hands where the holy water had burned and Bill was walking towards him with a sharpened stake in his hand. Dropping Tilterman to the ground she rushed to Endomire's side, hissing at Bill as she picked Endomire from the ground. Bill could only watch as the two vampires drifted from sight. Tilterman sat dazed on the grass where the Countess Kali had dropped him. His head was spinning and his body felt weak. Slowly picking himself up from the ground Tilterman walked to Bill's side, his neck was stiff and ached from the Countess's attack.

"Are you ok, Tilterman?" Nodding his head Tilterman followed Bill up the cathedral steps to where the Rennick warriors had been sitting. The steps were empty and the way was clear. As they entered the cathedral they saw the glowing orb of light.

Standing in the centre was Erasmus, a surprised look on his face. When Paddy saw Bill running up the centre of the cathedral he decided now would be a good time to slip from view leaving Mallard to deal with Tilterman. Maisie ran to Bill's side. Tilterman had spotted Paddy's sly exit and followed him into the shadows, his sword at the ready. Bill confronted Erasmus.

"You'll not succeed while I have breath in my lungs Reich, your evil plan has been discovered." Bill circled Erasmus, waiting for him to make a move. "Your companions, Mallard and Paddy, have already met their doom in Abnos." Maisie looked at Bill shaking her head.

"They're here!" Maisie whispered into Bill's ear and pointed to Mallard who lay stiffly on the ground near Erasmus. Bill saw the lifeless body of Mallard and looked back at Erasmus.

"It appears you have dealt your twisted punishment out on Mallard!" Bill shifted his stare from Erasmus as Mallard slid awkwardly off the altar's edge and dropped into the pews. Erasmus began to laugh as Bill climbed the few sacred steps leading to the alter.

"You are as foolish as ever, now feel my power and let it be known that I, Erasmus Reich, rules all of this world!" Erasmus charged at Bill, his staff above his head and as he lowered it to attack, the flashing of purple light lit the cathedral. Tilterman edged his way through the darkness, sword raised and ready for his defence. Step by step he edged deeper into the blackness, his eyes could see the outlined shadow of Paddy. Tilterman watched as Paddy felt his way around in the darkness. From the corner of his eye a purple flash drew his attention back to Bill on the altar. The intense flash momentarily blinded Tilterman, his eyes stinging with pain and as his sight returned he saw Paddy running from the shadows. Tilterman drew back his sword and waited for Paddy to come into range.

Engel felt the pull on his reins as the sight of the opposing army came into view. Eager to do his rider proud, he shrilled and shook his black head in anticipation of the oncoming battle with the armies of Scaripdemus. Zarrif pulled back on Engel's reins.

"Steady boy, you'll feel the heat of battle soon." Patting him on the side of his neck, Zarrif turned and faced his men. Engel's black body sparkled blue in the sun as the final clinks of noise from the soldiers' armour died down and a hush fell over Zarrif's army. Standing in his saddle Zarrif spoke to his men.

"Today we fight to save that which we have held so close to us for all of our days. They can try and win this day, they can try and take our freedom but with you at my side, we will win this day and send our foes back to the depths of hell. What say ye?" A cheer blasted from his men and crossed the desert to where Scaripdemus's army stood.

Guts McCracken kicked his men into lines, his boot jingling the rusted and dirty mail of his men. Scratching his own behind as he walked out to the head of his men, he turned and looked across the desert to where a sea of banners flew high in the sky. His thought raced back to the blue seas where his men had proven their worth on more than occasion and now their biggest fight was here, in the hot and unforgiving sea of sand.

"These land lubbers are to scared to set sail and fight us on the tossing waves. So we must show them that even old sea dogs like us can fight on land and win. Splice their livers and fry their eyes men, for tomorrow we rule the world...." McCracken's men raised their cutlasses and sent up their battle cry, as he gave the order to advance and led his men across the sandy sea to meet Zarrif and his colourful army. Walking close to McCracken were five flag bearers, each one carrying a different coloured flag.

"Blue and orange flag, give the signal." A flag bearer stopped, raising his blue and orange flag high above his head, he waved it from side to side. The trundling noise of wheels slowly emerged from the rear of the ranks as several large trebuchets moved forward followed by two large wooden carts' carrying stones. As they moved to the head of the army, Guts sat watching the movements of his enemy on the other side of the field of battle.

Zarrif gave the order for his archers to move forward, a section of black and white moved to the front of the army and sank arrows into the sand in front of them. Next, Zarrif gave the order for his shield bearers to move in front of the archers and cover them should the need arise.

"My glass." McCracken held out his hand as one of his men placed a leather roll and two-glass discs into his large bent hand. McCracken formed a cylinder with the leather roll and then placed a glass disc at either end. Zarrif came within arm's length as he peered down the roll.

"His archers are moving into position, shield bearers to the front. Sound the order." A trumpet blast rang out across the men and the army divided. Large flat pieces of wood were carried to the front and placed near the troops manning the trebuchets, forming a wall of wood.

"Fire!" Zarrif gave the order to launch a volley of arrows at McCracken and his men. The arrows cut through the air as they closed in on their targets. The 'Thwack' of striking arrows on the wooden wall could be heard all the way back to Zarrifs post. McCracken's men crouched down as the arrows landed all around the trebuchets, all missing there intended targets.

"Light the stones and fiiiiire!" The trebuchets swung launching their flaming stones at Zarrif's army. The stone balls flew higher than the arrows and came crashing down on Zarrif's men, spreading them out in confusion. McCracken's men cheered loudly. He shouted the order to reload and then shouted.

"Fiiiiiiire!" Again the trebuchets creaked as they swung in their wide arch, launching their stones high into the sky. Zarrif and his men were ready for the fiery stones and the lancers had been released into the sky to deal with them. The dragons flew high and met them in mid-flight creating a wall of fire in the blue skies above Moucha. The stones cracked and broke up, crashing harmlessly to the ground. Zarrif's army cheered loudly and watched as the lancers continued their flight towards McCracken and his men.

"Ready the spears and bows. Here come those blasted lancers!!!!" Several large timber bows rolled into the centre of the battlefield and were loaded with metal spears. Flying through the air the lancers watched as the weapons that downed their comrade rolled into position.

"Form the ranks, assume the attack formation!" Captain Weldermere called out his orders to his men and watched as the lancers changed their positions in the sky. The faint sound of an order reached Weldermere's ears as they dropped on they enemies' position. The newly formed wedge shape of the lancers soared down on the bows, their wings tucked back for maximum speed. "Break." Weldermere called out his final order as the bows released their arrows at the approaching dragons. Splitting into two lines, the dragons took on separate altitudes and watched as the arrows passed between them.

McCracken called out the order to reload and fire but it came too late. Balls of fire began to pound the ground around his army, scattering his men in all directions. Their confusion soon broke into panic as the lancers released spear and flames into their ranks. Weldermere turned as the faint sound of a horn drifted across the desert floor, the sound signalled his retreat. He called out the order to his men and they broke off their attack. Zarrif saw the returning lancers and called for his Black flag to be waved.

Rolling to the front of his army came several cannons and carts of black balls with barrels of black powder. The order was given to fire at will and shortly after, the loud boom of cannon fire echoed in the sand dunes of the desert. Cannon ball after cannon ball ripped into the sand around McCracken and his men. Shouting his orders over the cannon fire, he gave the order to advance towards Zarrif and his men. Slowly, McCracken led his men forward, his orders being drowned out by the cannon fire. As they advanced, McCracken grabbed a small skinny sailor and roared in his ear. "Get back and tell them to wave the yellow flag and start firing on their cannons...!" McCracken watched as the skinny shape disappeared back through the ranks.

"Wave the yellow flag and tell them to aim at those infernal cannons!" The standard bearer holding the yellow flag waved it high over his head and watched as the cannons rolled into position. "Boom, boom, boom!" Shot after shot rang out as the cannons flashed into life, their black shots landing on the opposing cannons far across the battlefield. Zarrif gave the order to fire upon McCracken's cannons and for his men to advance and meet the enemy in battle. Engel stood on his hind legs as the order was issued and the blasting horns sounded the advance. Wave after wave of men followed Zarrif in the charge on the enemy lines advancing towards them. Battle cries filled the air matching cannon roars in their pitch.

Red and orange sparks flew from the steel blades as the two swords met in combat. Bill attacked swiftly with the enthusiasm of a young and impetuous warrior; Scaripdemus parried each of Bill's strikes with ease. Again Bill unleashed an array of high and low strikes, watching as Scaripdemus dispensed them with ease. A flash of red cloak caused Bill to drop his defence and Scaripdemus launched his counter attack on Bill. His sword flashed in Bill's eyes as two blows wounded him. As he fell to the floor, Bill watched as Scaripdemus bowed and disappeared down the stairs leading to the catacombs.

As Bill picked himself up from the ground he saw the first trickles of blood on his shirt. A scratch was all Scaripdemus managed to wound Bill with, his mail taking most of the blow. The silver mail began to turn an off brown as his blood slowly clotted on it. His side was sore but his task was greater. Standing at the top of the stairs, he watched as the last of Scaripdemus's cloak disappeared into the catacombs. Bill walked down the stairs slowly; gripping his sword firmly in his hand he prepared himself for the attack. Swinging back towards the top of the stairs Bill saw a familiar shadow approaching him. Dropping his sword to his side, he held his hand up.

"Don't come any closer shifter." The shadow stopped in front of Bill and let out a cold chilling laugh. "I've seen my uncle and know of your plot to trick me." Bill drew his sword up as the shifter began to approach him. Backing down the steps Bill checked to see if anyone was lying in wait for him. As he turned to check the shadows at the edge of the catacombs, the quick movement of the shifter came crashing down on top of him, knocking him to the ground. Bill watched as his sword slid across the floor and under an upturned coffin, its occupant spangled on the floor.

"I've got him, can I finish him?" Bill watched as the shifter talked to the shadows in the tomb. "Bill, how clever you are, for seeing that I'm not your uncle. For I am..." The shifter stood tall and proud over Bill, he announced his name at the top of his voice. "Raynor Bouche, the one, the only and by far the greatest of all shape shifters living, liquid or solid..." Holding his hands out to his side, Raynor bowed to his imaginary audience. "Listen to them Bill, do you hear their cheers, their cries of excitement at the prospect of seeing me, the great Bouche in action in these less than fitting surroundings..." Bill raised an eyebrow as he stared at the shifter and his theatrics.

Raynor drew a sword from one of the coffins and began to swing it wildly over his head, hacking at coffins and shelves where the remains of old warrior priests lay. Bill stood up just as the sword came crashing down where he had been moments before.

"You'll have to try harder than that Raynor..." Bill teased the shifter, his anger flaring at Bill's words of mockery.

Sven met the second soldiers' legs as he came running from the aisle, his metal shin guards rang out as Sven's sword laid waste to them. Cundra drew his scimitar and advanced on Sven, a smile running across his face.

"So you're the one who escaped the mines, very impressive for a little digger gnome like you. Well, we've been asked to take you back in one or several pieces but either way you're going back." Cundra struck out at Sven's head leaving him only seconds to react and duck out of the swinging swords path. Cundra swung his sword again, this time the cold steel bit into Sven's arm. Dropping his sword, Sven crumpled to the ground in pain. The dragon's head was glowing stronger its blue colour filling the cathedral with bright rays of light. Cundra saw the dragon's head opening and then saw his new kingdom in the future.

"Alas little gnome, it looks as if bigger things call to me and you have been given a reprieve from returning to the mines." Cundra turned and ran for the dragon's head, launching himself at the widening hole in the centre of its mouth. Sven forced himself to his feet and threw his sword at Cundra striking him before he could reach his escape. The hilt of Sven's sword hit Cundra in the back of the head and as he fell to the ground, Sven walked slowly towards him.

"It appears that your kingdom has yet again changed to the

present." Sven smiled as Cundra looked up from the ground. He picked up his sword and kicked Cundra's weapon into the darkness. Cundra watched as the sword disappeared. The time portal continued to grow in size.

"Gnome do not try to stop me but join us and become the strongest and mightiest of all gnomes. Think you could free your people from the mines and destroy the Goblins." Cundra slid his hand into his cloak as he spoke to Sven and slowly pulled a second smaller sword from its scabbard. "Sven, you could rule Gnomes here and travel into the future and rule there as well, think of the power and wealth you could have." Sven watched as Cundra began to rise onto one knee.

"Cundra I will never join you and no matter what wealth, freedom or power you offer, I will never betray my new friends in the order or old friends in the goblin mines." Sven took two leather straps from his belt and tossed them at Cundra. "Put them on." Cundra looked at the leather straps and began to laugh.

"Never!" Cundra shouted as he rose to his feet and struck out at Sven with a hidden sword. Sven deflected the blow and attacked with all the strength he could summon from his wounded body. The sword missed his target and Sven felt the force of Cundra's boot lift him from the floor and throw him back into the pews. Crashing into the seats, Sven lay bent, his body aching from the pain of the blows. Cundra walked towards the portal and looked back towards Sven.

"See gnome, my future kingdom awaits me and now I say farewell and never see you again..." Sven watched as Cundra stepped into the portal and in a blinding blue flash disappeared into the future.

Bill rolled and watched as the purple bolt of light flashed overhead, regaining his feet on the edge of the altar. Sword raised and poised for the attack, Bill watched as Erasmus prepared for his next move.

"Very good Bill, you are as fast as they say but now for a real test of your skills." Erasmus raised his staff and brought it back down with a loud crack. Two bolts of light flashed from the staff's end and hovered just in front of Bill. Without warning, the first bolt of light whipped forward and hit Bill on the chest knocking him off the altar and onto the hard cathedral floor. Bill watched as the second bolt followed him in flight and struck as he met the ground, again striking him in the chest.

"A mere child's game Bill and yet you are not quick enough to evade them. Here try again!" Two more bolts of light emerged from the end of Erasmus's staff and made their way to where Bill lay. This time Bill was ready, his sword firm in his hand. Slowly picking himself from the ground, he stood with only his side showing to the bolts. Easing onto his back leg, he waited for his chance to strike out. Hovering at head height, the bolts waited for their power to be released. Bill however had other plans for them. With a swift flick of his sword, he cut the two bolts from the air with one smooth movement. A look of horror fell on Erasmus as he watched them fall to the ground in small piles of purple dust. As the last one fell to the ground, Erasmus fled for the stairs leading to the roof, his cloak blocking the blue light from the orb. A blinding blue flash stopped Erasmus in his track and as he turned to see what was happening at the orb, he caught a glimpse of Tilterman jumping into the past.

Maisie watched Bill and Erasmus engage in their deadly struggle for power. She shifted slowly over to the glowing orb and stared into the depths of time. The cathedral appeared much newer and in the shadows she saw flashes of steel possibly swords locked in combat.

"Eye of Life, Eye of Time, Travel Far and Show Me Friends in

Time." A silver ball rose from a small cloud of smoke forming in her hands and travelled into the glowing orb in front of her. She focused on the images flashing in her mind. The cathedral came into view, its interior new and clean. The ball hovered in front of the portal and began to turn revealing the dragon's head to Maisie. Her suspicions were now confirmed Erasmus had succeeded in opening a gate to the past.

Flashes of sparking steel drew the ball over the cathedral floor and soon the combatants came into Maisie's view. It was Cundra and a very young Sven, their swords locked in combat. As she watched, she saw Sven stopping Cundra from escaping and as Sven fell wounded, she reached for her sword. Losing her concentration she saw Cundra jumping into the portal. Pulling back, she raised her sword waiting for him to emerge. The flash in the orb died away returning the cathedral to the now usual blue hue.

Watching as Paddy came charging out of the Shadows, Tilterman held his sword ready for attack. As Paddy came closer, Tilterman felt a surreal pain rush through his body causing him to fall to his knees. His hands trembled as he looked for the source of the pain and found only blood flowing from his side. A laugh rang out in the shadows behind Tilterman and as he turned to look he saw the bent shape of Mallard stepping into view. Paddy was now standing beside Tilterman, watching as Mallard moved into finish off his victim.

"Tilterman join us and we will save you, what is your answer?" Tilterman used his sword as a crutch to get to his feet. Mallard and Paddy held their weapons at the ready and watched as Tilterman stumbled to get his balance.

"Join you for what? A life of taking orders from a five hundred year old corpse, I think not." Tilterman stood in defiance, his wound had stopped bleeding and the pain had gone. "I have my own curse to deal with and do not want to be looking over my shoulder wondering when you are coming for me." At this he charged, watching as the Necromancer and his croney fled from the wrath of his sword.

Maisie stood in front of the orb awaiting Cundra's arrival, her sword and potion bag at the ready. Mallard shot by her closely followed by Paddy. Stumbling back to her feet she watched as they jumped into the portal and disappeared in a blue flash. Tilterman stood at her side, his wound fully healed and his firm grip was again in its rightful place.

"Can we stop the portal from opening?" Tilterman replaced his sword into its scabbard and followed Maisie as she walked around the outer edge of the orb.

"Yes, but we have to contact Bill and Sven on the other side. The amulet he wears is the answer. He must release the Dragon of Korin as I release mine. Only then can we close the gateway." Tilterman stepped in front of the orb and reached out to touch it. Its surface felt like water on the coldest winter's morning.

"No, you'll be pulled in and it's not fully open yet." Tilterman looked back at Maisie, his eyes glowing with power.

"I can feel its power flowing in my body but it does not hurt me." Pulling his hand down, Tilterman stepped back and looked up at Maisie, his eyes full of sadness. "I will go, my time here is almost ended. The Countess Kali tasted my blood." Maisie knew what was coming next. A lump formed in her throat as her friend told her of his fate. "I am becoming one of the undead, I can feel the changes happening in my body. I must travel back and try to stop what is to happen to me. I must deal with the Countess Kali and Count Endomire in the past." Maisie could see the sadness in Tilterman's eyes and explained to him what had to be done on the other side. "I will learn to control it my friend and we'll meet again. I will not forget youuuuuuuuuu." A sudden flash of light lit up the cathedral, filling every shadow with bursting rays of blue light and Tilterman's voice faded into the past. Tears welled up in Maisie's eyes as her friend disappeared from sight.

"My gate is open and now Bill, my time has come." The blue flash instilled a new confidence in Erasmus as he saw Tilterman disappear. Bill stopped as Erasmus turned and faced him, a look of triumph on his face. "Soon my generals and the dragon slayers shall arrive and all your power, skill and friends shall bow down before me." Erasmus's laugh echoed out in the cathedral, sending chills down Bill's back. Erasmus raised his staff and pointed it at Bill. "I was saving this for your end in front of my new allies but this pleasure I shall keep for myself." A flash of grey light filled Bill's eyes and then a sudden coldness stiffened his body; throwing him to the ground.

"I am now your master, your king and your saviour should I choose to spare you..." Bill lay stiff, his body held in place by the freezing cold of Erasmus's spell. "Once I destroy you and that interfering hag, Maisie, I will rule the world." Erasmus uttered some words under his breath and Bill felt himself rise into the air; drifting slowly towards the orb, leaving him to wonder about his own fate at the hands of Erasmus...

Of Fire And Ice

Bill's words infuriated Raynor, his sword swinging and crashing wildly into wooden coffins and stone sarcophagus. Bill ducked and weaved his way around the path of Raynor's sword, deflecting the occasional near blow.

"Stand still Keeper and let me end your weak little life!" Bill side stepped as Raynor's sword came crashing down towards his head, the breeze from the swinging blade rippled Bill's hair as it passed close to his face. Swinging his own sword, Bill landed a blow directly onto Raynor's shoulder, cutting deep into skin. Raynor screamed as black blood began to flood from the wound.

"Oh damn you, Keeper." Raynor swung his arms around in large circles. "You have landed a fatal wound... yes, I, I can see the light, the bright light at the end of the tunnel." Dropping onto his knees, Raynor raised his hand to his brow. "I'm dying Keeper, please grant me one last wish, will you?" Bill nodded as he watched Raynor kneel in front of him, a look of desperation on his face. "My wish is a, gurggel! Urggeeer! Simple one, for you to DIE..." A shrill laugh echoed through the catacombs as Raynor leaped to his feet.

The ground beneath his feet began to turn white as it creaked and crackled under his weight. Raynors' body began too change and morph, his shoulders bulging outwards. Bill watched as Raynor began to change and grow into a demon of ice and moved forward on him. The demon's giant ice hand reached out and grabbed him around the waist; he felt its crushing power as he was picked up from the ground. The cold breath of the demon touched his face, turning blue. Bill hacked down on the demon's ice fingers, driving his sword deep into them; striking again and again.

He was flung across the catacombs. The sudden surges of pain from crashing into wooden coffins and the wall of the catacomb came over him. As the dust settled around him, he saw the demon approach. With each step the demon took, the ground began to creak as it turned to white ice from his touch. Again Raynor picked him up in his icy hand. Bill stared at Raynor upside down, his sword just out of reach.

Stretching out, Bill felt the hilt of his sword with his fingertips, grasping in vain he tried to grip it. The blur of the catacomb walls rushed by as he was flung through the air once again, the wall stopping him in a thud of pain. A rush of air escaped from his lungs as he came to an abrupt stop. His sword was now several feet away and far out of his reach. The demon Raynor turned and slid across the frozen floor of the catacomb, stopping in front of him. Raynor reached out to grab him by the foot, his cold grip chilling Bill's entire foot.

Pushing himself off the wall, Bill slid between the demon's legs and out of reach. Looking back he saw Raynor looking through his legs staring after Bill as he traversed the floor on his backside. Grabbing his sword as it came into reach, he jumped to his feet and slid to a controlled stop beside the only remaining unbroken coffin. Reading the inscription on the coffin, he looked back at Raynor.

"The High Priest Toonarr, Great Warrior and Keeper of Secrets. Died of old age, that's how I plan to go. You'll have to forgive me if that doesn't fit into your plans." Bill shrugged his shoulders and watched as Raynor advanced slowly across the white floor. "Now I need the power of the dragon." Bill whispered to his sword and watched to see if anything was going to happen.

Bill felt the handle of his sword starting to get hot and as he gazed down upon the blade, he saw it start to glow red at the hilt. The red glow began to travel slowly at first along the blade and then as it got near the top it burst into the catacombs in blaze of red and orange flames, which circled the catacombs for a moment and then Bill saw the shape of a flying dragon, its wings spread wide as it glided on the cold air. Raynor began to move away from the burning flames surrounding the dragon. When Bill saw what was happening, he pulled his sword back and in a whip like motion flicked the flames at Raynor. As the flames found their target, Bill heard the hissing of boiling water and saw the steam coming from the melting ice demon.

"Impressive, young Bill or should I call you Keeper of Secrets?" Bill turned and saw the shape of Scaripdemus move from the shadows and stand a short distance from the steaming remains of Raynor. "You have become quiet the little warrior since I first met you. It's a shame that you won't progress any further with your skills. You shall lie here with those who preceded you, that I shall see to myself." Scaripdemus drew his sword and walked towards Bill. He prepared himself for the onslaught, his sword raised to the side of his face. Scaripdemus stopped and placed his sword at his side, a look of disbelief on his face.

"Its you!" Bill turned expecting to see someone standing behind him but there was no one. "You're the reason the gate won't open fully, your sword is the key." Bill looked at his sword and for the first time noticed how it was shaped in flames. "It's the Flame of Time, the missing key to my success." Scaripdemus rushed at Bill his sword held high above his head.

Blocking the blow delivered by Scaripdemus, Bill stumbled back and raised his sword and brought it crashing down on Scaripdemus. Dropping his sword, Scaripdemus grabbed Bill's hands and pushed him backwards across the slippery floor. Bill felt the aged knuckles of Scaripdemus landing on his chin and as he fell back towards the ground, he watched Scaripdemus pick up his sword. Scaripdemus cackled in triumph as he raised it above his head.

"My time is now, the world and the future are mine to rule... ha ha ha ahh!" Bill stumbled to gain his feet but was stopped by another kick from Scaripdemus. "Oh no boy, you'll not spoil my victory, not now!" Scaripdemus whispered some words and a small ball of black light began to glow in his hand. As it grew in size, Bill released a kick backed by all of his strength and hit the black ball back into the face of Scaripdemus. It enveloped him lifting him from the ground. As Scaripdemus screamed, Bill saw his sword drop to the ground its blade glowing bright orange.

The black ball began to expand, cracks of white light appearing in its surface. Grabbing his sword, Bill ran towards the stairs leading to the cathedral's upper levels. As he reached the stairs he saw a blinding flash of light and felt the force of a blast of warm air lift him from the ground and throw him up the stairs. Picking himself up he turned to see the catacombs covered in black slime. Scaripdemus was nowhere to be seen and Bill presumed that his own magic and greed had finished him. He turned and made his way to the top of the stairs and back to where he had left the dragon's head. Sven was bent and broken on the up turned pews. Running to where Sven lay, he picked his head up.

"Sven are you ok?" Sven opened one eye and stared at Bill, his lips moving but no words were forthcoming. "Try not to talk." Bill picked him up and placed him on a pew, using his jacket as a pillow. Sven pointed towards the dragon's head. Bill turned to see it glow blue and its surface ripple from the centre to its edges. As they watched a shape burst from it and sprawled onto the cathedral floor. Bill drew his sword and walked towards the slumped body. As he got closer, he could hear the body moan in pain and then watched as it picked itself up from the ground.

"Oh my head. Time travel is not for you Tilterman, definitely not for you." Tilterman stretched himself, bones cracking back into place as he did so. Turning, Tilterman came face to face with the shining blade of Bill's sword. "I'm a friend." Tilterman held up his hands to show he wasn't armed and meant no danger.

"Who are you and where have you come from?" Bill pointed the tip of his sword at Tilterman urging him to talk. "Quickly now, say who you are and what business you have here, talk?"

"Bill Brickton you scallywag, allow me to introduce myself. Tilterman, a friend sent by Maisie DuPont and by you five hundred years from now. Is that Sven that lies wounded?" Bill turned and nodded. As Tilterman began to move towards Sven, Bill drew his sword up to Tilterman's throat halting him from moving too close. "Allow me to tend to him and I will explain everything, I mean you no harm." Tilterman moved towards Sven and took some herbs from his pocket and began to apply them to Sven's wounds.

"Your amulet is the key to closing that gate. Maisie said to stand in front of the gate and wait till you see her. When she appears, take out your amulet and it shall react by itself." Tilterman cleaned Sven's wounds while Bill stood listening.

"But how will the amulet close the gate and what did Scaripdemus need my sword for?" Tilterman continued to explain all that Maisie had told him. "The sword is the real power behind the gate, without it the gate will only work in one direction, the direction I have travelled from. Anyone who uses the gate from this side will be trapped between times until the gate is properly activated. The amulets hold two of the Order's most powerful dragon spirits, Ason of the western skies and his brother Steinburg of the eastern skies." Tilterman finished dressing Sven's wounds and sat back on the broken pew.

"The Dragon Slayers killed their sisters, Shiryko and Rye Uki of the north and south skies. When this happened, the remaining two dragons returned to Andrukan and sent back their spirits once they had crossed over to the other side. This way the slayers were defeated and sent to Werdnad with their master Du'Ard. When they were defeated the Book of Demons was discovered in Du'Ard's lair and the Order has kept it safe ever since and right up to when I travelled back but it has gone missing again in the future. Maisie found it in the possession of Erasmus Reich, Scaripdemus's co-conspirator in the future. As we speak they are battling it out for the book and to close the gateway in their time." A surge of pain shot through Tilterman's neck causing him to collapse to the ground. Tilterman could hear strange voices in his head but could not make out their words. His change was starting and he must soon start out on his own journey to find the vampires who changed him to one of them.

Bill's body drifted slowly towards the orb of blue light, Erasmus standing on his left side muttering in a strange tongue as he moved alongside him. Pain ran through Bill's body and the cold became colder as the spell took over all of his muscles leaving him helpless. Maisie stood in front of the orb watching Tilterman emerge on the other side and saw the young Bill approach him sword drawn and ready to do battle. The smashing of a wooden pew behind her broke her concentration and as she turned she saw the helpless Bill drifting on the air.

"DuPont it's your turn to leave this world, Brickton has already taken his leave of us." Erasmus stopped in front of Maisie, a wicked smile hanging on his lips. Maisie stared across the altar at Bill's statue like body. He certainly looked dead but Maisie knew of spells that could create a Death-like appearance and she also knew how to break them.

"I'll play nicely and give you the first cast, do your worst!" Erasmus held his hands out to his sides indicating to Maisie that he was ready for her first spell. Maisie pulled a small brown bag from her pocket and poured its gold contents into her shielded hand.

"If that is what you want Erasmus I will gladly take the first cast."

Maisie raised her hands out in front of her and began to utter her silent spell. "Awaken." Maisie cast the gold dust over Bill's body and watched as he began to move. Erasmus cast a bolt of black light at Maisie and watched as it threw her back across the altar and into the shadows of the side aisles.

Bill got to his feet and as Erasmus attacked him, he jumped high into the air, spinning and hitting Erasmus in the chest with his outstretched foot. Erasmus tumbled down the steps of the altar, Bill in close pursuit. Maisie sat up and watched as Bill knocked Erasmus from the stage. Her back ached and her body filled with pains.

"Protectus totalus!" Streaks of blue light shot from Maisie's fingertips and began circling Bill. Erasmus saw the blue light protecting Bill and brushed himself down.

"So Brickton we do this the old fashion way!" He drew his sword and bowed as did Bill when he saw his opponent's courteous jester. Touching swords, Erasmus took a step back waiting for Bill to make the first move. As it came, he smashed a blue ball on the ground and white smoke filled the space between them. Erasmus took his opponent's moment of temporary blindness to flee. He ascended the stairs leading to the roof. Bill coughed and waved his hands around to clear the smoke. He caught a glimpse of Erasmus shooting up the stairs.

"Maisie are you ok? Can you close the portal?" Maisie had made her way back to the blue orb. She waved her hands and nodded to Bill, then turned her attentions back to the gateway. Bill ran after Erasmus.

As Bill reached the end of the stairs he heard fading footsteps and a distant door banging. He took the stairs three at a time until he reached the only closed door on the staircase. Slowly opening it, the fading sunlight hit him in the eyes. As he became accustomed to the brightness he saw Erasmus weaving a spell and launching it at the doorway. He rolled clear just as the door exploded into wooden fragments and small sharp missiles.

"Erasmus give it up, you've lost. Come peacefully and I'll see that the Order goes easy on you." Bill watched as Erasmus smiled and launched another spell. "So that's how you want to play it?" Bill held his sword out to his side and charged at Erasmus, the sudden burst of speed caught Erasmus unawares but he drew his sword to defend himself. The crafted blades echoed through the spires of the cathedral's rooftop as Bill and Erasmus battled it out for control.

Erasmus attacked Bill's head and as Bill raised his sword to defend the blow Erasmus changed the path of his sword dropping it to cut at his legs. Bill jumped just as the blade came slicing through the air. Rolling out to Erasmus's side, Bill launched his sword only to have it blocked by Erasmus's. Bill crouched on one knee and watched as Erasmus spun away, drawing his sword out to his side. The two combatants stood silent and motionless, watching the other as they drew deep breaths of air.

"You'll not take me so easily Bill. There are people counting on my success, very powerful people, people whom you trust as friends and members of the Order!" Erasmus smiled as he saw the look of frustration and anger creep onto Bill's face. Erasmus began to pace to and fro on the rooftop, weighing up his options of escape. Bill too had been looking for the route that Erasmus would most likely take. Perhaps the vampires would return to carry him off or had someone else been at work in the cathedral, someone not known to Bill.

"Bill, I grow tired of this. Its time to finish it..." Erasmus charged at Bill, his sword dragging on the ground sparks flying from its tip. Bill pulled his sword up and ran to meet his attacker. As they met on the roof, sparks and blades flew, meeting in loud clangs of battle and then silence. Erasmus retreated staring at his arm, the first signs of blood had begun to flow; his arm was cut. Erasmus looked at Bill his eyes wide and filled with pain.

"I may have lost this round Keeper but you'll see me again." A blinding flash of light stunned Bill, white spots flashing as he tried to focus on Erasmus. The faint sound of a gyrocopter began to break through the hustle and bustle of the city. Bill's sight slowly came back; his eyes stinging at first from the city lights and then the shadows became images. Erasmus had escaped. Slowly flying from the cathedral was Maisie's copter, piloted by Erasmus and accompanied by the Count Endomire and his faithful wife the Countess Kali. Their silhouetted shapes disappeared into the setting sun, leaving Bill to watch from the cathedral rooftop.

"The dragons control the Breaths of Flame and the Flame controls time itself. When the dragons combine and travel through time they cause the flames to slow down and collapse; closing the pathways to time." Tilterman picked himself up from the ground and continued. "Don't worry Bill, Maisie knows what she's at. Its time." Tilterman stood up and walked towards the dragon's head, Bill at his side. Maisie could be seen standing on the other side of the gateway waiting for Bill to take up his position.

Maisie took her amulet from around her neck and watched as Tilterman placed Bill opposite her in the glowing orb. Signalling to Bill she pointed to the amulet and watched as he took it from around his neck. Both amulets began to glow and spin.

"Ason all powerful, Steinburg elegant and graceful come forward and seal this crack in time..." Maisie stood frozen to the spot and waited. A wind began to blow within the cathedral; wisps of dust swirling about her; her hair blowing about her face. A blue mist began to emerge from the amulet in her hand and travelled into the orb passing through time and history. As it emerged on the other side of the gateway, Bill saw the start of a red mist flow from his amulet. The red mist intertwined with the blue and shot straight up towards the ceiling of the cathedral. As it reached the top a loud and ear splitting scream rang out causing Tilterman and Sven to cover their ears. Bill dropped the amulet and covered his ears also. As he did so he saw a powerful dragon swoop down from the ceiling. Its red body sparkled in the dim light; its wings spread the width of the altar and the cathedral itself. Fires burned in its eyes and its claws shone bright as the midday sun. Its tail whipped at the air as it weaved its way down towards the dragon's head.

Another scream rang out, shattering the windows of the great cathedral, the dragons pearl teeth glistening like gemstones in the moonlight. The new dragon circled the dragon's head and then flew into its mouth causing it to explode. Maisie dived clear as the red dragon shot from the orb and circled it, red flames burning through after it. The dragon hovered over the diminishing orb and issued forth great spouts of red flames burning the orb into nothingness. Rising into the heights of the cathedral the dragon became two, the blue dragon returned to Maisie's amulet and the red dragon twisted and weaved through the air, and disappeared in a red cloud of smoke.

A New Journey Begins

Zarrif watched as his men engaged with McCracken and his army of thugs. Slashing his sword to and fro in the fray, Zarrif issued orders from Engel's saddle. McCracken saw Zarrif and ploughed his way towards him, ending the battle for fifty soldiers on the way. Zarrif spotted his adversary crossing the sea of battling men and jumped from Engel's back, leaving him to kick and bite his way through the enemy. McCracken threw down his sword and picked up a war hammer from the ground, his knuckles skinned from the fighting.

"You'll wish you hadn't got up today Zarrif. It's going to be a bad day for you." Zarrif ducked as the war hammer swung wildly at his head. The hammer clipped the red and white plumage of his helmet on the way. Several of Zarrif's men slowed the heavy war hammer down as it clashed with their armour, allowing McCracken to swing it again as Zarrif stood to his full height. Zarrif's sword sank into the woodenhead of the hammer locking tightly into the grain. McCracken pulled the sword from Zarrif's hand and threw the sword and hammer away, choosing to fight with his hands. As the first punch landed on Zarrif's chin both men dropped onto their knees, grabbing their ears as they did so. The loud screams of a large and powerful dragon filled the desert skies, shattering weapons and armour. An old sailor from McCracken's army started to run towards Moucha shouting as he ran.

"Ason and Steinburg are back, run for your lives. We've lost..." McCracken watched as his armies deserted him and returned towards Moucha.

"Another time Zarrif, another time!!" He followed his men leaving Zarrif and his army in pursuit. The streets of Moucha were filled with the fleeing armies of the defeated Scaripdemus.

Sven peered from behind the pew where he had been lying moments before the dragon's head exploded. Bill lay on the floor, Tilterman on top of him, neither one moving. Sven crawled across the floor and shook Bill's head. Tilterman stirred and looked back at Sven and Bill.

"Is it closed?" Sven nodded and pointed to where the gateway had stood moments before. Tilterman smiled and rolled off Bill. Looking up, Bill placed his hand on his head. "Sewers, monsters, ships and dragons, I'm going home. Sven you can be the Keeper. It hurts too much, I want my soft bed..." Standing up Bill saw the sparkling of the jewels in the rubble and walked towards them picking them from the dirt.

"I've got them back, the crown jewels." He stared into the gemstones, his eyes widening in awe. "Sven look, its Cundra he's trapped in them." Sven stared into the gems and began laughing. Bill started to laugh as well but stopped as Tilterman placed a finger to his mouth. Bill listened to the sounds of men shouting in the streets outside the cathedral.

"Zarrif, quick we have to help." Bill leaped to his feet and ran into the street followed by Tilterman and a limping Sven, their swords drawn. To their amazement, McCracken and his men had started to set sail and were leaving the docks. Zarrif walked slowly up to Bill, his sword sheathed and a damp cloth in his hands.

"You did it then?" Zarrif began to wash his face as Bill nodded.

"Knew you had it in you. Now enjoy the fireworks." Zarrif nodded to-wards the ships and as Bill watched, he saw two figures jumping from the deck of the Lucipher. As they swam back towards the docks, a loud bang sounded from the ship as it flashed into an array of flames and explosions. Zarrif smiled and introduced himself to Tilterman.

"I've met you in the future, friend." Zarrif looked in puzzlement as Tilterman explained his trip through time to help Bill close the gate. "Now my friend, I have another mission and must start right away." Tilterman explained his need to find the Count Endomire and stop him from biting the Countess Kali so he could stop his own life being changed.

Bill walked through the clouds of dust that had started to settle in the cathedral, searching for Maisie.

"Maisie are you ok?" Bill called out as he searched the battle torn cathedral eventually finding her lying on the altar. Her hair stuck to her face with sweat and dirt. "We did it, we closed it and Tilterman is in the past..." Maisie began coughing her throat filled with dust.

"We can't bring him back." A tear fell from Maisie's eye as she told Bill what had happened.

"I know." Bill helped her to her feet. "Erasmus escaped with the vampires' help and your gyro. What happened to Paddy and Mallard?" Bill turned a pew over and sat down on it, wiping dust and sweat from his face.

"They jumped through the gate but they didn't emerge on the other side. I think they may be trapped between times or they came out in another time between now and where Tilterman came out. I suspect we'll cross paths again..." A shaft of light lit the pew where Bill had sat down, dust dancing in it. Silence for the first time in days filled Bill's ears. He had peace again but for how long? Maisie sat down and rubbed tears from her face, tears for the loss of her friends. It was at an end...

Things To Come...

Fredrick Time stood watching the sunset over Crintia, its orange glow disappearing steadily behind the Misty Mountains. His beard danced playfully on the light breeze blowing around the entrance to his cave. His white robe hung loosely off his aging body. Leaning against his ivory staff he thought how with each setting of the sun it seemed to grow more and more beautiful. Twelve centuries had passed since he had been appointed to his position of Father Time. Smiling he turned and walked into his home, its brown wooden door ajar, allowing the fading light to glint off his thousand time pieces.

"Ahh, another of your minutes has passed Freddy, a minute in the life of Father Time but for those in Crintia another day..." Closing the door behind his weary body Fredrick surveyed the clocks and timepieces that adorned his walls. Each one ticked while the clock next to it tocked, keeping the balance of time. His old chair sat invitingly in the corner, beside it his trusted company, George, an old and grumpy terrier. Sliding down onto his chair, Freddy watched as each timepiece chimed a new hour and the first of the next minute and day of Crintia's history.

Sitting on the arm of his chair was a small golden pocket watch, a favourite and trusted problem solver. Engraved with magical symbols of the Federation of Time Keepers of the Universe and other known and the less known places. Fredrick knew that in times of crisis or when he over slept and forgot to wind his clocks, he could reverse or pause time and solve his problem. A time travelling device and a very useful tool in time keeping, given to him by his predecessor, Harriet Chronometer.

Fredrick suddenly looked up from his watch, something had changed. An eerie silence had fallen upon the cave, as his timepieces slowed to a stop, their ticking and tocking ceasing in mid second. Rising from his chair Fredrick stopped halfway as his door swung open revealing a shadow. A long black cloak had draped itself across his floor, its dark shadows hiding the owner's pallid features.

"Who are you? What do you want? How did you find me?" A barrage of questions flowed from Father Times mouth. As he stared at the dark shadows, Fredrick saw the glint of white teeth smiling from beneath the hooded cloak.

"Why, I'm here to replace you, Freddy. I'm the new Father, no, Count Time..." Count Endomire's laugh echoed through the cave, a look of horrified amusement on Fredrick Times face as he watched Endomire slow down time and walk casually from the cave, leaving him to struggle in slow motion...

ISBN 142513311-8

9 781425 133115